Praise for *The Image of Her*

'I loved everything about this novel – its wisdom, its beautiful prose, the taut plot, and that last scene which turned me into an emotional wreck. This will most certainly be a book that I press into the hands of friends and family. A triumph'
Fiona Mitchell, author of *The Maid's Room*

'I loved it! Beautifully written and a totally original concept, two women who never meet whose lives intertwine . . . with a very clever mystery at its heart'
Elly Griffiths, author of the Dr Ruth Galloway Mysteries

'A fascinating, gripping book about a subject that was unfamiliar to me. Sonia has such a light touch in weaving so many themes together and a deep understanding of the human psyche'
Sophie van Llewyn, author of *Bottled Goods*

'A brilliant book, bringing a deft touch to more than one difficult modern issue while digging deep into questions of identity as old as time'
Fiona Erskine, author of *The Chemical Detective*

'A thoroughly original idea, beautifully written with compelling characters and a plot that just won't let you stop reading. I loved it'
Frances Quinn, author of *The Smallest Man*

'Brims with love and compassion but also the injustice that comes with relationships. A compulsive page-turner that kept me hooked well into the early hours. Emotional and thought provoking . . . a testament to an author at the height of her powers'
Awais Khan, author of *In the Company of Strangers*

THE
IMAGE
OF
HER

Also by Sonia Velton

Blackberry and Wild Rose

THE
IMAGE
OF
HER

SONIA VELTON

Quercus

First published in Great Britain in 2021 by

Quercus Editions Ltd
Carmelite House
50 Victoria Embankment
London EC4Y 0DZ

An Hachette UK company

A CIP catalogue record for this book is available
from the British Library

HB ISBN 978 1 52940 649 8
TPB ISBN 978 1 52940 652 8

10 9 8 7 6 5 4 3 2 1

Typeset by Jouve (UK), Milton Keynes

Printed and bound in Great Britain by Clays Ltd, Elcograf S.p.A.

Papers used by Quercus are from well-managed forests and other responsible sources.

For Isabelle,
and the forty other people worldwide
who have followed in her footsteps

'I am what is reborn when a world is destroyed.'

Victor Hugo, *Stella*

ONE

STELLA

Your name is Connie James.

I know this from the letter in front of me. The knowledge of you was folded neatly into a plain white envelope and addressed to me in a measured, precise hand. It looked so ordinary that anything could have been inside. Had I known it was about you, I might not have opened it. It would have been left untouched, propped up on the mantelpiece, like a wartime telegram, while I sat beside it, quietly weighing up the knowing and the not knowing.

Although I didn't know your name, there were three things I did know about you. One, that you are about the same age as me. Two, that you are a woman. Three, that almost exactly a year ago something happened to you that was every bit as devastating as what happened to me. Worse, in fact, but I don't want to think about that now. Other than those three facts, I knew nothing about you. You were just someone I'd thought about every single day for nearly a year.

Someone I built in my mind and then disassembled, as if you were a children's toy. Brown hair one day, blonde the next. I wondered how tall you are and whether you're beautiful, Connie. I know you're more beautiful than me. However I imagined you, I always knew that we're basically the same type, you and I. Of course, we are: he wouldn't have chosen us both otherwise.

But now I have your name. It's like a dressmaker's dummy just waiting to be clothed in the real you. It's too easy nowadays to find out about people. I need to think about how much I really want to know. There might be pictures of you and Mark. Do I want to see images of you kissing your husband, knowing that his mouth has been pressed against my lips too? Will seeing you on holiday – your face tilted up towards the sun, smiling at its warmth on your skin – make me think about what I have taken from you?

You begin as a flashing cursor. While the text box is empty, so is my mind. Those shifting images of you never stayed long. You were a chimera, but now I'm going to make you real. I type your name and hit return. It's not an unusual name. There are lots of Connie Jameses buffering me from the real you. I'll need to dig deeper, but before I can click my way through the layers of identities that are not your own, the doorbell goes.

I'm back now. It was just the DPD delivery guy. His name is Evgeni and he knows me better than almost anyone. That must sound odd to you, Connie, but there's something I should tell you. I've barely left the house in fifty-one weeks. Anything I need – except my groceries, which are delivered by an endless variety of drivers – Evgeni brings it for me. When I first came home, I could hardly look at him. I opened the door a crack, and he turned the parcel on its side to push it through the space. As soon as I had it, I tried to shut the door, just as he was handing me that little black box. I'm sorry to say I trapped his wrist in the door. It wasn't a good start. 'Sign!' he yelped, from behind the heavy wooden door of my mother's house, and waved the box up and down. I still didn't open the door, just took the box from him and stared at it.

'On screen,' said Evgeni, his finger jabbing through the gap.

There are two parts to my life now: the Before and the After. In the Before, I never ordered anything online. I preferred to go out to get things. That was when my life was the inverse of what it is now. I left the house for any reason. A newspaper, a pint of milk, a moment to sit on a bench and be surrounded by the reassuring sanity of a chaotic world. When was the last time you saw anyone under eighty doing that? I was just like an old person, Connie, but that's what you do when home stops being a sanctuary and becomes a prison. So, anyway, I wasn't entirely sure what to do with the device he handed to me.

'With finger.' Evgeni again, a strip of his face appearing at the gap, blinking at me with one doubtful eye. I pressed my finger against the screen. A tiny black dot bloomed in the corner. I wrote my name, *Stella*, although it came out as 'St l a', because parts of the screen didn't work. Still, good enough. I handed it back to Evgeni, who snatched it through the gap and gave me a half-face frown. That was our entire interaction on that first occasion. I can only assume he left hoping never to see my address on his delivery list again.

I took the parcel upstairs to my bedroom and laid it on the bed. It was from one of those high-end retailers, a box within a box. Brown cardboard on the outside and sleek black inside, embossed with their logo. Inside that, tissue paper with a pale candy stripe, the dress nestling inside, perfectly folded. As I pulled it out it rippled through my fingers: silk, slippery as egg white. I pulled off my tracksuit bottoms, then my favourite mustard-coloured jumper with the hole in the elbow, and put the dress over my head, letting it fall loosely over my body. Then I pulled the old army blanket off the full-length mirror, took a deep breath, and stared at the approximation of the image from the retailer's website reflected back at me. *The model is 5'10" and wears a UK size 8.* Hardly, but even so, I enjoyed that dress for quite a while, walking around in it, feeling the material swish against my legs as I turned. I looked carefully at the fit and was pleased that it tapered perfectly over my waist and hips. I just didn't look at my face, because I no longer knew the woman staring back at me. Then I took the dress off, carefully repackaged it in the candy-striped paper, and requested the return.

Evgeni was back at my house three days later.

You'll have to forgive me, Connie. Over-sharing has

always been a fault of mine. It's just that I hardly ever find someone I can talk to, so now I have, I feel I need to tell you everything. Today Evgeni has brought me an embellished wool-gabardine cape (it won't be long before the weather turns) and a pair of cutout patent-leather pumps (to go with the lace-panelled satin midi dress that arrived a few days ago). Usually I open every package straight away, but I've left it in the hall.

Right now, I'm much more interested in you.

I can rule out anyone on Wikipedia: the actresses and composers. Mark told me precious little about you, but I know you aren't well-known. Nor are you a fictional 'Connie James'. I have evidence of that, something real that I can touch and feel. Every day of my life, there is no denying your existence.

Social media, then. A trawl through fifty or more Connie James profiles. It's obvious who you aren't. I can discard most of them based on age and location. Then suddenly there aren't any left. I've run out of Connies. Not one fits the mould I've made for you. Maybe you aren't on social media. I thought I was the only person left in the world who found the thought of connecting with numerous 'friends' and 'followers' deeply intimidating and faintly pointless, but perhaps we really are two of a kind. I'm about to give up and check another site when I notice something about one of the profile pictures. It's of a woman standing on a beach, her back to the camera, a young child clasped in each hand.

She's wearing a floaty white dress with a rose print. It must have been windy that day because the hem is kicked out behind her. Arching over them in the distance is a striking rock formation. I skimmed over her before because she's listed as living in Dubai, but I'm pretty sure that picture is taken on Durdle Beach in Dorset. I click on her profile, and her face in the banner photo looms large. It takes me by surprise. I wasn't prepared for another photo so soon. I was expecting a neutral black background, giving nothing away. I almost close it down, because the sight of her terrifies me. I shut my eyes and ask myself again, How much do I want to know?

I open my eyes slowly and let her in. She rewards me with a film-star smile. Perhaps she's on a night out. Sections of other faces cluster round her, like mismatched jigsaw pieces. She has nondescript colouring: skin naturally pale, but tanned by the sun or make up. Hair, pressed against her cheek by a pouting friend, blondish, darkening towards the roots. Her complexion could fit anyone from a prim Snow White to a beachy blonde, although I'm neither of those. I stare at the image, waiting for it to give me clues. I feel like a forensic pathologist confronted with a fresh corpse. What secrets can be revealed by those who cannot talk?

Her features are anime perfect. A small mouth with full lips, neat nose fading into her face, and large, wide-spaced hazel eyes. An ideal blank canvas. Classically pretty without being striking. I assess this woman's face like a plastic surgeon, looking for the familiar and the flawed. Then something suddenly makes sense, falls into place. She has a mole just beneath her lower lip. I can see it clearly in the picture. If it were an eighteenth-century beauty mark, its placement would signal 'discretion'. Don't worry, Connie, your secrets will be safe with me.

How do I know for certain that it's you? Your last post was fifty-one weeks ago.

I don't really like stories that begin at the end, so I spool down through a life in rewind. Every so often, your past freezes as more of your memories load. I'm too curious to keep scrolling so I click randomly and halt the backwards march of your life in pictures. I don't need to know you from the beginning. I only want a taste of you. I just want to make sense of what brought us together.

The picture is of two sleeping children. They are heaped together as if they were wind-up toys that have simply toppled once the keys stopped turning. You have captioned it, *Peace at last!* I'm touched and saddened to see your children. They make my regret almost unbearable. But, still, I can hardly take my eyes off the fan of lashes on their cheeks and their softly parted lips, in silent communion with their dreams.

There is nothing in the world more adorable than a sleeping child.

CONNIE

'When are they gonna go the fuck to sleep?'

He asks her as if she's a kind of oracle, all-knowing where their children are concerned. Mark is standing in the kitchen, still grouchy from work, a glass of freshly poured wine in his hand. Connie glugs water into a plastic cup and glares at her husband. 'Don't say "fuck" when the children are still up.'

He rolls his eyes, sighs, circles his head in an exaggerated fashion, every mannerism designed to convey his exhaustion, the overwhelming pressures of his day.

Something thuds above them, rhythmic, squeaky, a trampoline bounce.

'Seriously, Con, it's nearly nine o'clock. Why haven't you got them into bed?'

Why hasn't she? She's been home all day, after all. She doesn't work, has nothing else to do with her time. Mark has already been upstairs. He has hugged his pyjama-clad children and whizzed through the briefest of stories. He has told them he loves them and backed quietly out of the door, turning off the bedroom light with a final click. The silence lasted long enough for him to get back downstairs, pull off his tie, twist open a bottle of wine and reward himself with a large glass. He has done his bit. The fact that the children still escape, like smoke, round the door is nothing to do with him. When a small voice called from the top of the stairs, 'I'm thirsty!' he pretended not to hear, burying his nose in the liquorice spice of his favourite Syrah, until finally his wife yanked open the cupboard door and pulled out a bright plastic cup. Then the banging started.

Connie picks up the water and starts to go upstairs. When she turns midway at the landing, she sees her daughter sitting at the top of the stairs, hugging her knees, a little sentinel monitoring her approach.

'Is it juice?' Alice asks. 'I want juice.'

'No,' says Connie, softly, 'it's water. You've cleaned your teeth.'

'No, I haven't.'

Connie sighs, exasperated. 'Well, you should have.' There were only three things Mark had to do. Teeth, story, get them into bed. Not rocket science for a structural engineer. It confounded her that he could ensure the world's most ambitious structures would withstand earthquakes but, seemingly, be unable to herd a six- and an eight-year-old into the bathroom.

Alice peers up at her, eyes wise and solemn, blonde hair straggling over her hunched shoulders. She reaches up to take the cup Connie offers and slurps at it, her little mouth latching onto the rim, like a sucker fish.

The thudding starts again. Connie leaves her daughter and goes into the children's bedroom. Her son lands heavily on his bed, then propels himself to Alice's, jumping repeatedly between the two, a chubby, ecstatic missile.

'Stop it!' shouts Connie. 'Stop it right now!'

Ruben allows himself one last leap, then collapses against the wall, panting and grinning.

Her first-born, the boy. The negotiated child. Everything about him had been brokered with Mark. His existence, the timing of his arrival, even his name. 'I'm not calling our son Ruben,' Mark had said, in those moments they had sat together during her pregnancy, idly discussing parenthood as if they were planning a road trip, with no idea how gruelling and arduous it would be. Then the baby was born and the names he had hoped for had fallen away in the face of his wife's screaming sacrifice. 'Okay,' he told her, 'we can name him Ruben, but day-to-day we'll call him Ben.'

'It's not bedtime yet,' announces Ruben-but-we'll-call-him-Ben.

'It *is*,' insists Connie, through the fug of her own tiredness. How was it possible for a grown-up to struggle to get through a day while a child was still bouncing around at 9 p.m?

From the doorway comes a wail, fragile and wavering. 'That's *myyyyyyyy* bed.' Alice runs across the room and launches herself at her brother, landing futile punches on his arms and chest. Connie is often astonished by her daughter's bravery, her complete disregard of her own youth and toothpick limbs, a plucky David to her brother's Goliath. Ben swats his sister away. She finds the casual violence her children inflict on each other rather chilling.

'Right, in bed.' She has a child's arm in each hand, is trying not to squeeze too hard, but her own hunger, fatigue and the utter tedious repetition of this bedtime pantomime make her hands clench round their little wrists. She leaves Alice on her bed and takes Ben to the other. 'In!' she orders, and he does as she says, pulling the covers up to his chin and wriggling into the softness of the bed, relieved, almost. It will be better, she tells herself, when we move to a bigger place, where the children can each have their own bedroom. Divide and rule.

Their relocation to Dubai was sudden, a blur of frantic searches for school places for the children and a villa near by. A year on, they're still in the same rather shabby villa in Jumeirah, constrained now not by time or money but inertia. The irresistible pull of the familiar. Every so often, Mark talks vaguely about moving to a better villa, as if that would cement their connection to this dusty city with its ever-changing landscapes.

As she leaves the room and turns out the light, she remembers their teeth. She should go back, she thinks, get them up again and make them brush them, but the calm darkness of their room is too precious to disturb, her own fatigue too overwhelming.

Later, when she goes back in to check on them, she sees that Alice has climbed into Ben's bed and that the old adversaries are piled over each other, like kittens. She is so taken by their peaceful unity, the silent companionship of their sleep, that she takes the phone from her pocket and photographs them where they lie.

TWO

STELLA

Breathe. Smile. Swallow. Blink.

I'm standing in front of the bathroom mirror, holding a lollipop stick between my lips. Press, release. Press, release. Five repetitions. This is what my life is now. It centres on the smallest of movements, and what should be the simplest of tasks. The face in the mirror is blank and expressionless. Facial sensorimotor re-education. I have been told to imagine the desired facial expressions occurring when I think of the emotion: joy, surprise, anger. The anger's easy. Joy, less so. But the face stays the same regardless. It's as if my personality has been erased, like I've been rebooted and returned to factory settings.

Can you be happy if you cannot smile? Have you ever thought about that, Connie? It's called facial feedback theory. Our smile reinforces the happiness we feel. Without that expression, our joy has nowhere to go. Pleasure just dissipates out of us, like an exhaled breath.

Press, release.

I must try to think happy thoughts: the smile won't come without them. I enjoyed seeing your children, Connie. I don't have any of my own. Perhaps that's a blessing, given what happened, but I can't help feeling regret when I see children playing in the park or clutching their mothers' hands in the street. Maybe it's all tied up with approaching forty and the realisation that the chances of having a child are slowly dwindling.

When I was a child I thought I was made of glass. That I might shatter if anyone touched me. That's how I grew up, a fragile icicle of a child. Women who are made of glass can't have children, can they? Children would splinter us, break us into a million pieces, so that the fragments of ourselves could never be put back together. Or, at least, that's what I always imagined.

Press, release.

I do know I'm not made of glass, Connie. I do know that. Most of the time.

Bad thoughts again. I can't help it. Still, if I'm going to get to know you, I suppose you'll want to know all about me too. The thing is, no one knows what really happened. No one at all. Not Mark, not the doctors, no one. Well, *she* knew, but she's dead, and the dead always keep their secrets. Don't they, Connie?

I shouldn't call her 'she': it's rude. It's just that it wasn't easy at the end. My mother had semantic dementia, which means she couldn't remember familiar words, got them all mixed up. Horses became dogs and sofas became pillows. You get the idea. Sometimes, when things got really bad, the irony would almost make me laugh. My mother was a novelist, you see, and quite a successful one. Sixty-six romance novels over a twenty-five-year career. Hardly Barbara Cartland, but still. Can you imagine? A writer losing her words. It's hard to beat, really, like a perfumer losing his sense of smell.

The lollipop stick is hanging from my lip, stuck to the moist inside that turns slightly outwards nowadays. I'm trying to do my final press and release but I can't get the stick back between my lips. They feel numb and swollen, as if they belong to someone else. I look like a grouper with its thick-lipped gape, opening and closing its mouth, gasping to survive.

Do you enjoy romance novels? I have to say I've never cared for them, especially the ones written years ago. The endlessly repeating plots, the dark and dominant hero pulling the vulnerable heroine into his manly arms. That's just not a world I can relate to.

The lollipop stick finally peels away from my lip and clatters down onto the vanity unit, becoming wedged in a cityscape of pill bottles of varying shapes and sizes; tacrolimus, prednisone, mycophenolate mofetil.

That's what I hate most about romances, Connie. The inevitability of the happy fucking ending.

I've tried to stay away from you, I don't know why. It's been a few days since I saw the picture of your children, but I do want to know more about you. I started to look yesterday, but I got no further than the profile picture of you with your friends. There's something uncomfortable about the way you're looking at the camera. It feels as if you know, as if you're staring right into my soul.

I'm going to try again. I whizz down the page with my eyes shut. When I open them, you're gone. I'm on safer territory now. The occasional cake you've baked, inspirational quotes, marginally funny jokes. It takes a while to get back to that picture of your children. I suppose a lot must have happened after that. I see pictures of just you skim past, but I don't stop to look closely at them. I need to avoid, just for now, the ones where I can clearly see your face. Then there's a picture of a table full of people. You're sitting next to a jovial-looking older man, but only half of you is in the shot. It looks like a family gathering, nothing very exciting, except that I'm drawn by your enigmatic expression. Unusual, amid all the perfect smiles you usually post, and somewhat at odds with your caption: *So lovely to see Mark's mum and dad for two whole weeks.*

CONNIE

Connie is standing in the kitchen, pale, sticky chunks of chicken dropping from her fingers into yoghurt laced with spices, crushed and pummelled over the previous hours. She squishes the chicken into the mixture, inhaling the scent of cloves and cumin, garlic and ginger. She enjoys the methodical precision of measuring out the spices, dry-roasting and grinding them down to release their pungent aroma. The jars line the worktop, like silent little soldiers, neat and orderly, giving up their contents on request. So unlike the chaotic, endlessly brokered existence she has with her children.

The kitchen is quiet. The children are distracted by the novelty of their grandparents' arrival last night. In the living room, they take one grandparent each, perching on their knees and enjoying the tight pull of familiar arms round them as they rip open presents and take out bright plastic toys, which are too young for them but still make them squeal with joy.

Julia and Frank settle back in the sofa and watch their grandchildren play. They feel tired, but satisfied. They're glad they made the trip all the way out to Dubai, and take a moment to enjoy what that says about them as grandparents. They are 'hands on'. No one could accuse them of not being part of their grandchildren's lives, even after the family's move to a place they find a little strange and hard to understand. They didn't really approve of the move, found it unnecessary and disruptive to the children's schooling.

'But *why* do you want to go to Dubai?' Julia had pleaded with Mark. 'You worked so hard to get Ben and Alice into that lovely little primary school. You'll never get them back in when you come home.' She was careful to frame everything by reference to the children, suppressing the selfish thoughts of her own loss, which threatened to sour her words.

'It's a great opportunity, Mum,' Mark had responded. 'The architecture there, it's incredible. When you and Dad come to visit I'll show it to you, and there's more going up all the time. I can get involved in building some world-class structures.'

Julia had nodded but remained tight-lipped. Not speaking, just withholding her approval. Just like when Mark was a child.

'Come on, Mum,' he chided. 'Connie reckons the move will be great for the kids. Think of all the different children from all over the world they'll meet.'

Julia could well imagine Connie saying something like that. Her daughter-in-law prickles with liberal values. It doesn't surprise her that a perfectly good primary school in a nice London suburb wasn't good enough for Connie's children. No, they'd had to come here, to be educated in culturally enriching subjects, like Arabic, among a class of globally representative children.

'Anything I can do to help?'

Julia has wandered into the kitchen. She eyes Connie slightly warily, taking in her obvious industry, the bowls of salads accumulating on the kitchen counter, the cake with its careful arrangement of sliced fruit.

'Goodness, no,' says Connie, wiping her hands on a kitchen towel. 'You've only just arrived!'

Julia nods, unconvinced. 'Well, if you change your mind?'

'Really, it's fine. Everything's under control.' Connie's voice is singsong happy. They're treading carefully, these two. Perpetually engaged in a respectful dance around each other, with Mark in the middle. The offers of help not always matching the need for assistance. The desire to be involved sometimes rebuffed. 'Just relax and make the most of your time with Alice and Ben,' she says.

Connie steps outside into the little courtyard patio, fretting that she hasn't swept the floor. The desert gets everywhere in this place, settling over the cars like snow and creeping under doors. She feels the dust in her lungs and her eyes, almost tastes the sand in the arid air. The overhanging branches of an ancient frangipani have deposited browning yellow and white blooms all over the table. It's been a while since they've eaten outside. Until this month, the heat had rolled in like fog every time she opened the door. She decides it will be comfortable enough to eat outside a bit later. She wipes the table, then the lid of the huge gas barbecue. She brushes the layer of fine sand off the concrete patio slabs and tidies up discarded buckets and spades. The bright plastic has faded and cracked in the relentless sun, red turning an anaemic pink and bright blue becoming grey. A flaccid inflatable water ring tears in her hand as she picks it up. Only the ocean and the desert are resilient under the Dubai sun. Sooner or later, everything else disintegrates.

'I'm hungry.' Ben's voice is whiny as he leans out into the patio, clinging one-handed to the doorframe. Connie takes him to the kitchen and offers him a range of snacks, starting with a raw carrot to munch, and escalating through a glass of juice, before she finally thrusts a biscuit into his hand. She feels annoyed with herself as he turns away, triumphant, but she doesn't want a healthy-eating confrontation with her son in front of Julia. Besides, she has too much to do. The marinated chicken needs to be skewered, and she still has to pound the coriander seeds, cloves and cardamom for the pilau rice. As she breaks fragrant cinnamon bark into chunks and drops it into the water with the rice, she remembers she hasn't taken the lamb for tomorrow out of the freezer.

'Any chance of a drink round here?' Frank is in the kitchen opening all the cupboard doors, looking for a glass.

'Of course,' mumbles Connie, grabbing one before Frank starts on the wall units. 'What would you like?'

'Oh, just a Jack and Coke, thanks.'

Frank grins at her while she unscrews the whiskey specially purchased before his arrival. He is a solid man, with the big, hairy hands of a bare-knuckle boxer. The children adore him, flinging themselves at him and begging to be swung from his sturdy arms or lifted onto his broad shoulders. Connie hands him his drink.

'And a G-and-T for Julia, if you don't mind. Ice and a slice, if you have it. We're on holiday, after all!'

There's a hiss from the stove as the rice water boils over. Connie lurches over to pull it off the gas. Frank starts telling her about their flight, about the screaming baby they had to sit next to, about how he bets she's glad to be past all that. She looks behind Frank, with his whiskey and Coke grasped firmly in his thick fingers, and wonders where on earth Mark is. She turns the heat down under the pan and grabs half a lemon left over from the skewers and hacks off a slice. Once Frank has his drinks she manages to shepherd him back towards the living room.

It's 6 p.m. when they sit down to eat. The October sun still lurks behind the spiky leaves of the date palms, and the night-scent of the frangipani has begun to build, alongside the timbal song of the cicadas. Connie has laid the table with the salads and rice, and Frank and Julia are sitting at it, asking the children what they would like to do the next day. Connie lifts the tray of kebabs off the kitchen worktop, ready to take them out to the barbecue. This is the bit she enjoys, the bit that makes all the hours of preparation worthwhile.

As she reaches the patio doors, Mark appears. He glances at the tray in her hands, laid out with colourful skewers of alternating wedges of chicken, lemon and peppers.

'Here,' he says, reaching for the tray, 'let me help you.'

'Help me?' Connie finds herself repeating his words, as if she can't quite understand them.

'Yes,' says Mark, lifting it out of her hands. He walks out onto the patio and over to the barbecue and begins to lay the kebabs on the hot grill rack. Julia gets up and joins him, resting her arm on his shoulders and exclaiming, 'Oh, don't they look lovely!' Frank opens a beer and hands it to his son as he turns the kebabs.

Connie stands at the patio doors for a moment, watching them as if they are a little tableau in which she has no place. She wonders when they will even notice she's not there. Somehow, Julia and Frank manage to make her feel like an outsider in her own home. She joins the children at the table, preparing them to eat, asking if they've washed their hands and depositing slices of cucumber and carrot on their plates, ignoring Ben's look of disgust.

Julia finishes her gin and tonic with a flourish. 'Right then,' she says, 'time for a photo.' Everyone returns to the table. Frank settles himself into the chair next to Connie's and pulls one of the children onto his knee. Mark leans in behind them. All of Julia's nearest and dearest crammed round one table. Then she takes the picture and Connie wonders whether she's even in it.

THREE

STELLA

'Please don't contact me again.' That was the last thing Mark put in his letter. Just before that, he told me he doesn't understand my fascination with you, that he can't deal with being in touch with me. I'm rereading his letter now. I've read it so many times it's beginning to curl at the edges. I see his personality in it, in the clipped sentences, frank to the point of being abrupt. He doesn't pull any punches – this man who connects us – does he, Connie? He likes to be in control. Even his vowels and consonants are neat and ordered, each perfectly spaced, one from another. Not like the jumbled letter I sent him, with my breathless words skidding across the page. In my defence, I was confused and anxious when I wrote it. We had a history by then, Mark and I. There was so much between us, yet the distance seemed more than could be bridged by just a letter. Am I glad I wrote it? I'm still not sure, but I do know that I'll respect what he has asked of me. All I will ever have now is what I'm holding in my hands: his letter and another, smaller, sealed, envelope. On the front, Mark has written, *Open if you want to know more.*

I put the letter, and the sealed envelope, on the kitchen table, splay my hands over the knotted wood, close my eyes. It's as if I need to be anchored, connected through touch to my past, not my uncertain future where I don't even know who I am any more.

Do you think it's strange that I still live in the house where I grew up? It might be unusual, but life doesn't always turn out the way you think it will. We both know that, don't we, Connie? I didn't always live here. I moved out once, laden with bags and guilt, to a pretty little terrace only a few streets away, with shutters on the windows and terracotta pots full of flowers by the porch. I came back every Sunday and sat at this table, warming my hands round a cup of tea, while my mother served up tales of loneliness and isolation with her perfectly crusted Bakewell tarts. My mother incubated grudges, like they were eggs, and her friends had come, then gone, over the years. I used to encourage her to get out more, hoping that if she socialized with real people, rather than the characters in her head, she would be less lonely. But she preferred to spend time with those she could control completely. In the end, it wasn't her complaints, or even her sadness, that brought me back to her. It was a Victoria sponge.

The kitchen table was laden with bowls, jugs and ingredients. My mother bustled round it, a set of measuring spoons jangling at her fingers, like a jailer's keys, laying out caster sugar and flour. I had my nose in a cupboard retrieving the strawberry jam.

'Where is it?' asked my mother.

I turned round with the jar in my hand. She was standing by the table looking agitated, plucking at her apron and searching the kitchen table with her eyes.

'Where's what?'

'The thingie,' she insisted.

'What thingie?' I was almost laughing now, as if this was some kind of childish guessing-game.

My mother's face was serious. 'The thing for jumbling up eggs.'

'You mean the whisk?' I picked it up and offered it to her.

'What is whisk?' she asked simply.

'Come on, Mum,' I said, wondering if she was teasing me. But her face was blank as if she was so busy searching inside her own mind that she had nothing left to show on the outside. She brushed wisps of greying hair away from her face, brusque, as if she had no patience with herself.

'Give whisk,' she said, holding out her hand. I gave it to her and watched while she beat the eggs with a concentrated fury, as if they had humiliated her deliberately.

It was just the whisk that day. The bowls and spoons and the Old Country Roses chinaware all behaved themselves. But, in time, more and more objects seemed to flummox her. One minute she would be fine, the next baffled by a toothbrush, quite unable to name it. I should have seen it coming sooner. There are other signs that are harbingers of this kind of dementia. It was just that lack of empathy, insensitivity and rudeness weren't easy to spot as symptoms in my mother.

My finger slides over the flap of the envelope, tentative, like I'm stroking it across the skin of a first love, unsure how far to go, whether I should even be doing it, but doing it anyway. *Open if you want to know more.* It has lifted at the edge, almost as if Mark wants me to see what's inside. I hold it up to the light, just for a clue, no more. It looks like a folded document, stubbornly opaque, revealing nothing. I go to slip it back into the bigger envelope, but I see that I've missed something. I tip the envelope upside down and a photograph falls out, face up now on the table, unavoidable. I *have* to look at you, and when I do, you seem to flush through me, like a drug injected straight into my vein. For a long time I just stare at you, taking in the curve of your lips and the smooth landscape of your face. Your hair falling in waves almost over one eye, smoky with makeup. You look lovely, Connie. I know that's why Mark has chosen this photo to show me. And he is standing next to you, his arm round your shoulders, pulling you towards him. You're both dressed up as if you're going out somewhere.

I want you to be glaring at me. I want you to be confronting me with a fierce expression, demanding that I face up to the role I've played in all of this, insisting that I see you stand next to your husband and know that there never

should have been three of us. But you're not, and that is
what I cannot cope with. It's your vulnerability, the look of
complete trust on your face, that sends my hand sweeping
across the table and your photo spinning onto the floor.

CONNIE

'Stand over there,' directs Julia, 'in front of the frangipani.'

She pronounces it *frangeepangee,* and Alice, already in her favourite ballerina pyjamas, giggles. 'It's not frangeepangee, it's fran-jip-arrnie,' she says, picking up the ends of her tutu between her fingers and pirouetting on a freshly bathed foot in the middle of the dusty patio.

'Goodness, what a clever girl you're becoming,' says Julia, a little tersely. Alice smiles, then perches on the edge of the patio table to watch her parents shuffle sideways so that they stand under the branches of the magnificent shrub. She loves to see her mother dressed up, enjoys watching her in the bathroom mirror as she lines her eyes with kohl and coats her lashes with mascara. When Connie puts on lipstick, Alice mimics her, pressing her lips together and rubbing them against each other, instinctively, almost without realizing she's doing it.

Connie is wearing a new dress, a pale blue vintage-style tea dress with a pattern of tiny swallows. The material is flimsy and the skirt floats round her knees in the hot breath of the Dubai night. Mark glances at his wife, almost taken aback by the hair loose round her shoulders and the unexpected redness of her lips. Since the children were born, she has seemed almost to fade away, becoming a paler, tenser version of herself, often makeup-less, with her hair pulled back into a severe ponytail. He puts his arm round Connie and draws her closer to him. Once Julia has taken the photo, he asks his mother, 'Will you send it to me, please?'

It's Friday. The weekend in the Middle East – like Saturday in England, or maybe Sunday, Connie could never quite decide – and almost the end of Julia and Frank's holiday.

'Do go out, just the two of you,' Julia had implored. 'We'll babysit!'

So a taxi ride later, they're face to face in a hotel restaurant by the turquoise waters of its subtly lit swimming pool, sitting under a terrace of cascading bougainvillaea. Connie shifts in her seat, peeling her dress from where it has already begun to stick to the backs of her legs, wishing they had sat inside, while Mark fields a final email on his phone as they wait for their drinks.

Date night. She wishes he would put his phone away, idly wonders what happened to those nights before they were married, when dinners out were fuelled by cocktails and lust, and the conversation never stalled.

'Almost done,' he says, glancing up at her, his fingers hovering over the screen. He sees the expression on her face and smiles, wanting to appease her. 'Here, look at this,' he says, tapping on the screen, then twisting it round to face her. It's the picture of them Julia took before they left. 'Lovely, eh?' She nods, looking more at Mark and the boyish way he's grinning at her than the picture.

The waiter brings wine and fancy breadsticks pressed with rosemary and olive fragments. The outside of her glass is already damp with condensation from the humid air and she traces a line in it, waiting for Mark to finish what he's doing.

'Right,' he says finally, slipping the phone into his trouser pocket. 'Cheers! Here's to us, Con.'

They clink glasses and Mark leans back, hanging his arm over the back of his chair. 'Nice place.'

She looks round, taking in the couples sitting at the elegant tables and the waiters bustling round them, busy serving alcohol to Westerners in the middle of this dry Islamic state. She takes a sip of her Chablis and tries not to think of the children at home, but an image comes to mind anyway. It's of Julia leaning over the back of the sofa, attempting to grab the iPad out of Ben's hands while he hides, wedged against the wall. Julia stands up, pushing her glasses up her nose, and exclaims to Frank, 'Are there no rules in this house?' Then she imagines Alice, eyes brimming with tears, twisting the threadbare ear of her rabbit round her finger, refusing to sleep until Mummy tucks her in.

'We should do this more often,' says Mark. 'You know, make it a regular Friday-night thing.'

She knows what's coming. His forehead has begun to wrinkle in the way it does when he's going to say something he knows she won't like. He turns the stem of his glass in his fingers. 'It would be so much easier if we had a housemaid.'

Connie bristles, taking another large mouthful of wine. How many times have they had this conversation? 'It's not right,' she says. 'It's taking advantage of someone because of their nationality and socio-economic status. Who would *choose* to live in a box while spending every day cleaning someone else's house?'

'That's not true,' says Mark. 'By employing them we're helping support their families back home. They earn more here than they ever would in Sri Lanka or the Philippines or wherever.'

'So I'm meant to have a woman I don't know living with me, helping to look after *my* children while she's separated from her *own* children back home. I can't do that. It's just awful!'

The heat, or exasperation, makes Mark blow air up towards his forehead, lifting the hair sticking to the skin. 'Everybody does it, Con. Everybody. We are the *only* people I know who don't have a housemaid. You know what the children are like. It would help them to be looked after consistently by the same person. Someone who has authority with Ben, and who Alice can feel comfortable with. I'm going to have to travel a lot, sometimes for days at a time. You need some help while I'm away. It's not like we have family here to help out.'

'I don't want our children brought up by a stranger.'

'Jesus, Connie, you need to let go a bit. No wonder we don't—' He stops, shuffles back, as if he's come up against the sheer drop of a cliff.

'No wonder we don't . . . what?' Her voice is slow, deliberate.

'I don't know . . . Spend time together any more. Do stuff as a couple. Maybe it would be good for you to have some help with the house and the kids. We could have more of a social life. We've been here a year already and, seriously, who are our friends?'

Connie hears his words as accusation, as if their social life was now her domain, something to be arranged and organized while he's busy at work. Something he could step into, ready-made, at the weekend, along with a beautifully kept home populated by neatly turned-out children. Had she relocated, or stepped into the 1950s? Sometimes she wasn't quite sure. But it was true that she had found it hard to settle, sometimes overheard the other mothers at school talking about parties she and Mark hadn't been invited to. In England she had always worked. This world of playdates and pedicures was something new to be navigated.

Mark reaches across the table and takes her hand, squeezes it. 'Having that kind of help is one of the perks of being here.'

'Isn't it enough that I'm here at all? Or do I have to abandon my principles as well?'

He drops her hand, leans back, rakes his hands through his hair and inhales deeply. Suddenly it's the draping bougainvillaea that holds his interest and he studies it, looking for answers among its curved spines and papery flowers. 'You agreed to come,' he says, still staring at it.

It's like they're sitting on a cart, rumbling along the same dirt track. She tries not to go over old ground, but somehow the wheels keep getting stuck in the same muddy grooves, locking her into the same conversations.

'I agreed because I didn't have any choice. We had to come because of your job.'

'Right,' he says, drawing out the word. 'I thought you

said you were looking forward to spending more time with the kids. In fact, I'm sure you also said it would be a good experience for all of us, especially the kids, to live in a different country.'

'I do think all those things, but I'm used to working and I miss my job.'

'I understand,' he says, although she suspects that he doesn't. Not really.

'We're here now,' he's looking at her again, head slightly tilted, 'and it's only for three years, so we have to make the best of it. If we had some help at home maybe you could look for a job in Dubai.'

'Maybe,' she says, 'but jobs in my field aren't easy to come by.' Especially not here, she wants to add, but doesn't.

'You could try something different – do voluntary work even. Something to keep you fulfilled and your skills current ready for when we go back.' He pauses for a moment, takes a measured breath. 'I know you loved your job, Connie, and you were bloody good at it, but you could see this as an opportunity. Whatever you want to do, I'm totally behind you, okay?'

'I know you are,' she says, and she means it. In England, when they had both worked, there had been a better balance to their relationship. It had been more of a partnership. It was only now, with her not working, that he had stopped helping so much with the children and around the house. It made sense – was fair, even. There was just a lingering feeling that she hadn't quite signed up to this, a tiny bit of resentment that when Mark had been given this great opportunity her own job had seemed to count for so little.

Mark grabs the neck of the bottle of Chablis and pulls it from the ice bucket. 'If you're serious about getting some kind of work, we really are going to need a housemaid.'

She tilts her head back and laughs. 'All right, you win.'

'Don't feel bad,' he says, topping up her glass. 'We need the help and they need the work, and I promise you, somewhere in the Philippines some kid will be getting a great education, just because you don't do your own laundry.' He stares at her straight-faced for a moment, then laughs.

'That's not even funny,' she says, snapping the end off her artisan breadstick and throwing it at him.

They're home by 10 p.m. Julia is on the sofa doing a sudoku and Frank is beside her, open-mouthed and snoring. Connie scans the quiet of the house for distant sounds of banging, or wailing, or bickering.

'I hope the kids weren't too much trouble, Julia,' she says. 'It's just that they're not really used to being left with other people in the evenings.'

Julia fills in the final square of her sudoku with a flourish. 'I don't know what you mean,' she says, looking up. 'They've been as good as gold with us!'

Liar, thinks Connie.

FOUR

STELLA

I can tell you what it's like to die.

This is the path the bullet took. It entered the underside of my chin and travelled up through my lower jaw, then the point where the hard and soft palates meet, until it exited just underneath the frontal sinus. *Ballistic trauma*: the wake of a bullet as it ploughs through flesh and bone. Like dominos falling, first my mandible disappeared, then my teeth, the maxilla, and finally my nose. Penetration, cavitation, fragmentation. The relentless progress of nine millimetres of metal.

There aren't many things that fill you with wonder when you're a grown-up, are there, Connie? No waking up to see a stocking full of presents at the end of the bed, no hands searching under pillows for the Tooth Fairy's coin. The magic just seems to go out of the world. In fact, there's only one thing that still makes me gasp with joy, and that's opening the curtains in the morning to see everything covered with snow. It's as if all that was dirty and flawed and ordinary is suddenly made perfect.

That's what dying was like. Pure, brilliant, white.

I left this chattering world, with its frustrations, annoyances and petty slights. I reached up towards that incredible brightness, as if it was life I was drowning in and the light that would save me. I can't even describe the relief, the complete absence of pain and worry, as it surrounded me. I simply peeled off this existence, like shedding a skin. There were billions of stars, and they were all shining for me. It was the unconditional love that I've sought all my life, and never found.

The people who come back are brought back by something. The thumped intrusion of a defibrillator, the rush of pure oxygen through flaccid lungs. Or someone. The thought of someone still needing you. A young child lost without your care. An elderly relative. Even then my mother wasn't prepared to allow me to find love and happiness without her.

I could see her beneath me, wearing her pink bed jacket over a crumpled cotton-rich nightie. She was staring at me as I lay on the floor. Not calling an ambulance, she lacked the reasoning by then even to think of doing that. Instead, she looked as if she was chewing something, moving her lips around like she had gristle in her mouth.

I didn't need her to call an ambulance because Mrs Wilson, our new neighbour from across the road, raised the alarm. I would see her sometimes, when I went out for my paper or that pint of milk, deadheading flowers in her front garden or pulling little weeds from the cracks between her block paving. She would call to me, 'How's your mother, dear? I must pop over to see how you're managing.' Or perhaps, 'I'd ask you in for a cup of tea, but I'm just off out when I've finished in the garden.' I should tell you that I've never actually had a cup of tea at Mrs Wilson's. Ever. But at the sound of the gun going off she popped up like a meerkat. I could see her, because I could see everything, even myself, bloody and broken on the carpet. It was bin day the next day, and she was struggling up her drive wearing big gardening gloves, a clutch of cut blooms in one hand, a wheelie-bin almost as big as she is in the other. For a moment she stood perfectly still, then ran inside, white roses scattering over the drive.

Minutes later, as the street swelled with the sound of a siren, my mother found the piece of gristle she was searching for and spat it out.

'Selfish bitch,' she said.

Then it was over.

My mother had barely spoken more than the same few words in months, but in that moment she managed to destroy my brilliant white world, like she had stuck a pin in a balloon. And all I could think was, I didn't even put the rubbish out.

You're a good person, Connie. I know that already. I can see it in the smiles of your children and the way Mark is holding you in that picture. You care about people, don't you? I'm a people-pleaser. I cannot bear the thought of anyone being angry with me. Especially not her. I even came back when I knew she was annoyed about me dying. But I wish I could make people happy in the way that you seem to, instinctively, as if just being you is enough.

I've been reading about your career. According to LinkedIn, you have a master's in international development and are co-director of the Strategic Philanthropy Bureau. Your CV says you have an interest in 'systems change' and 'policy influencing'. I don't think I know what either of those really means. I was a teaching assistant for the reception year. I'm not sure what Biff, Chip and Kipper would make of systems change. I never intended to be a TA. I wanted to be a primary-school teacher, but just before I was due to go to university, my mother had a bad fall and fractured her leg in three places. Or, at least, I'm pretty sure it was fractured. Anyway, it certainly took an age to heal. There was no one else to help her, so I agreed to defer my bachelor of education degree and take a gap year working as a TA in a local school instead. My mother told me it would help me learn some valuable skills, and it did seem to make sense at the time. Then, somehow, it never happened the next year either, or the next. I never decided *not* to do my BEd, but I didn't quite get round to starting it either.

I had to give up work when Mum got bad. The school was very good about it. They let me work part-time, but that only lasted a few months. It got to the point that Mum couldn't be left, even for a few hours, so I had to give it up completely. At least I was able to. That's the good thing about sixty-six ripped bodices and breathless heroines, I suppose.

I couldn't go back to teaching after she died, of course. I knew they wouldn't have me: they'd think I'd frighten the children. I'm not even sure I would have, though. Small children are just curious. They don't judge, just accept. We teach them fear and disgust.

Philanthropy. I love the sound of that word. It means the love of humanity, doesn't it, Connie?

CONNIE

'*Maganda!*' says Rosamie, crouching in front of Alice and clasping her little hands. 'And you, *gwapo*,' she says, looking at Ben. He eyes her warily, as if a smile might mean agreeing with her, and he doesn't know what he's agreeing to.

Rosamie stands up and turns to Connie. 'Your children are beautiful.'

Alice beams, and Ben looks relieved that a *gwapo* isn't a strange Pinoy vegetable he's being offered.

'And you have a lovely home,' she continues, looking around her, pronouncing each word carefully, as if they're lines she's been taught.

'Oh, thank you,' says Connie, a little awkwardly, unsure what to do with the compliments Rosamie doles out, like sweets. 'We're so glad to have you here.'

Alice studies this new person intently. 'What did you say your name was?'

My name's Rosamie.'

'Ros-me,' says Alice.

'Rosamie.'

'Rosme.'

Rosamie smiles. 'Yes, Rosme.' Then she offers one hand to Alice and the other to Ben. Alice slips hers into Rosamie's like they're old friends, but Ben gives his reluctantly. Rosamie doesn't seem to notice as she leads them to the kitchen, asking if they want some milk and a biscuit. Connie had been worried about introducing Rosamie to the children – a new person come to live with them, an added dimension to their little family – but this girl is already chattering to Alice about cutting out some paper dolls after their snack. Not girl, Connie corrects herself, *woman*. Rosamie is over thirty, but there is something so girlish about her smooth oval face and glossy poker-straight hair, the easy smiles that dimple her cheeks.

Connie finds herself standing alone in the living area, something about the open plan and tiled floor making it seem suddenly cavernous and empty. She feels as if the children have been expertly lifted from her, the way a visiting royal is swiftly relieved of a gifted bouquet.

She follows them into the kitchen. The children are sitting at the table, both swinging their legs under their chairs. Rosamie has already poured milk and is looking for the biscuits. 'They don't usually have biscuits so close to dinner,' ventures Connie, ignoring Ben's reproachful stare.

'Oh, sorry, madam,' she says, carefully closing the kitchen cupboard.

'No, don't worry, it's fine. Maybe just this once.' Connie takes the biscuit tin from the shelf, opens it and hands the packet to Rosamie.

'Thank you, madam.'

Connie watches Rosamie open the digestives and slide them out onto a plate. Their hands almost touch as they both reach for the plate to take them to the children. 'Sorry, madam,' says Rosamie again.

Connie feels herself blush. 'You really don't have to call me *madam*. Connie is fine.'

Rosamie looks unconvinced. 'Okay, madam,' she says, picking up the plate and taking it to the children.

Connie hovers while the children eat. Rosamie chatters about the children showing her the park after dinner, when it's cooler. She reaches up to Alice's face and brushes crumbs from her cheeks. Connie half expects Alice to shrink from the touch of this virtual stranger, throw wary glances at her mother for reassurance. But she doesn't.

'Have you settled into your room?' asks Connie. She feels the need to remind Rosamie she is still there. Something about the three of them feels too cosy.

'Yes, madam,' says Rosamie. 'It is very nice room, thank you.'

'I want to see your room!' exclaims Alice, putting down her half-eaten biscuit.

The room. Why did she mention The Room?

Rosamie had arrived when Ben and Alice had been at school. Connie had helped her with her bags, giving a cheery 'Right, here we are!' as she had shuffled down the little corridor connecting the garage to the kitchen. Midway a door opened onto a tiny utility area, with a washing machine, dryer and miscellaneous buckets, mops and brushes propped against the wall.

When they had first viewed the house, before taking the lease, she had been a little shocked by what lay beyond the utility area. A box room with a single bed and small chest of drawers, taking up almost all of the floor space. A dilapidated air-conditioning unit was mounted on the wall; the tiny en-suite had mouldy corners and a broken sink. 'Maid's room,' the agent had said, as matter-of-fact as if he had been pointing out the car port.

When they had offered Rosamie the job, Connie had told Mark she wanted her to have the spare room, but Mark had pointed out that they didn't even have the space for the kids to have a bedroom each. And where would Frank and Julia sleep when they came to stay? So Connie had scrubbed and tidied that little room, and had someone come in to fix the sink and look at the air-conditioning. By the time she had bought new bedding and a bright rug for the floor, it looked quite respectable. Certainly, it was bigger and better than the windowless cupboards she had heard about in the apartments of Hong Kong and Singapore. Most importantly, it had its own external door, so Rosamie could have some privacy and come and go as she pleased.

Still, she had been nervous when she opened the door for Rosamie to step inside, bracing herself for the look of disappointment, even disgust, at the sight of such modest surroundings. But Rosamie had just smiled and put her belongings on the bed. It was that – the complete absence of expectation for anything better – that had broken Connie's heart.

'You can see it later,' says Connie to Alice. 'It's not too hot now, why don't you show Rosamie where the park is?'

'Can I have the iPad?' says Ben, hopefully.

'No, you can go to the park too.'

'Park' was a grand name for the dust bowl with a

climbing frame and a couple of swings on their compound. Connie had spent hours sitting on the little bench while Ben kicked a football unenthusiastically over the sand, and Alice swung upside down from the monkey bars, hair a blonde sheet almost touching the sand. Connie had looked out for someone to talk to but had seen only tight groups of house-maids chatting to each other in Tagalog, Hindi or Sinhala. Where are the mums? she had wondered. Where are all the mums?

'Okay, madam,' says Rosamie. 'I'll get the children ready.'

'Don't worry, I'll do it,' replies Connie. She plonks sun-hats on her children's heads, then kneels in front of Alice to hook the thong of a flip-flop between the toes of each foot. When she's finished, she sits back on her heels. 'There, you're good to go.'

Alice regards her solemnly. 'Thank you, madam,' she says.

FIVE

STELLA

Bonnie and Clyde was my father's favourite film. You must have seen it, Connie, everybody has. I loved it all, but it's the final scene that really stuck in my mind.

They are in their stolen V8 Ford driving along a lane on a sunny day. Bonnie reaches behind her for a pear. Oh, that juicy, ripe pear! They take turns biting into it, their enjoyment of this simple pleasure, and each other, so striking. Faye Dunaway is exquisite as she rests her head on Warren Beatty's shoulder. Then they see someone on the side of the road having trouble with their truck, so they pull over to help. Clyde gets out.

Only the sudden flight of a flock of birds foreshadows what's about to happen.

It's a trap, you see. An ambush. The cops are waiting in the bushes. In the moments before they open fire, there's a stillness to the world. All you can hear are the birds, and thrumming cicadas, as Bonnie and Clyde look at each other.

They know they're done for, so they can only stare at each other with desperate love and longing. Then Clyde begins to dance under the hail of bullets, a gruesome puppet, jerked this way and that until he falls to the ground and rolls over, leaving that glorious half-eaten pear lying in the dirt. Bonnie takes fifty-three bullets and ends up slumped half out of the car, her hair trailing in the Louisiana dust.

That's my kind of love story, Connie, not the mawkish shit my mother wrote. Theirs was real love, messy and futile. Something almost unbearably sweet to be savoured for the briefest of moments before it's taken away from you. Just like that pear.

Do you know what they found strapped to Bonnie Parker's leg after she was shot all those times? The real Bonnie, I mean, not gorgeous Faye with the pear juice dribbling down her lip.

It was a .38-calibre Colt Detective Special.

My father showed it to me once, told me he had been presented with it as a gift by an admiring fan. 'Look at this,' he said, taking it out of its special case. 'See these marks?' He rubbed his thumb over the chequering on the wooden grip panels. 'They were left by the medical tape Bonnie used to strap the gun to her thigh. If only she'd got it out sooner, eh? This little beauty could have saved her.'

It was only later that I understood what he meant.

That I began to think how a gun could free me.

Evgeni is coming today. I saw him yesterday, when he came to collect the wool-gabardine cape and cut-out pumps.

'You don't like?' he asked me, frowning at the parcel, puckered into an odd lopsided shape by the thick brown tape I'd wound round one end.

I shook my head from behind the almost-closed door. 'No.'

'You never like!'

He's right about that. They all go back. The glossed croc-effect leather shoulder bag, the floral poplin shorts, even the ruched metallic bandeau bikini (I admit I was having a bit of fun with that one). I simply order online the life I don't have. Then I live it a little bit at a time, alone in a room in my mother's house. I could never afford to keep any of those things, and even if I could, what use do I have for them?

Today, Evgeni is bringing me an Hermès picnic blanket. What a treat! Pure wool, in Prussian blue. I will lie down on it later and imagine I'm in a meadow in the middle of July, with Cabbage White butterflies fluttering above me against a perfect periwinkle sky. When I close my eyes, I will hear bees hovering over the flowers that surround my blanket and I will feel the fragrant heat of the summer envelop me, like a bath. There's just nothing better than the warmth of the sun on your face, is there, Connie?

The police came with the ambulance and took away the gun. A few months later they came to the hospital to ask me about it. A young lad, trying not to look at me, and an older guy. A bit more worldly-wise that one. You could imagine he'd seen some things in his time. He sat right on the edge of the chair next to my bed, straight-backed and professional, as if determined to resist its squishy leatherette charms. He was Detective Constable Bains, he told me, and he just wanted to ask me some questions. Then he spread his knees wide, rested his elbows on them, and leaned forward.

'Where'd you get the gun from, Stella?'

I was still writing down my answers at that point.

It was my father's, I wrote, with my blue pen, on the A4-sized whiteboard on my lap.

'Did he have a licence for it?'

Wipe clean, then, *I don't know. He left.*

Not long after he showed me that gun, Connie. I had just turned seven.

'Oh, I see.'

Anyway, no licence. It's antique. Made in 1927.

DC Bains laughed then, put his head back and chuckled, as if I'd managed a great joke with my blue pen and dry-erase whiteboard.

'That gun ain't no antique.'

Bonnie Parker used to own it! My letters stretched up a little taller, like eyebrows rising.

'Bonnie Parker?' He swivelled round to look at his colleague. The boy shrugged and shook his head.

And Clyde?

'Bonnie and Clyde? Are you serious? Look, we've traced the gun and it's . . .' he stared at his notes, shuffling them round a bit so he could read directly from them '. . . a third issue Colt Detective Special revolver, with nickel finish, made in 1973.'

But the medical tape, on the handle? Okay, that's what I wanted to write, but I didn't. There are some conversations you just can't have on a whiteboard.

'Listen, love,' he said, more kindly, 'we don't want to upset you, not with everything you're going through. It's just that people aren't allowed to have guns at home without a licence, let alone fire them, even—'

At themselves?

I start scribbling. *It was at my mother's house.*

'Your mother? She . . .' He glanced at his trainee again, the one whose job it was to know the facts, not do the talking. The boy gave a slight nod.

Passed away? Yes. Eventually. No need to write that down.

'Did you know the gun was there?' he asked.

A shake of my head, no. DC Bains took a deep breath and shifted on the edge of his chair.

'But you must have found it at some point?'

I gripped the whiteboard, touched the pen to it, then took it away. DC Bains stared at the blue dot left behind. Then he looked up, right at me. Not like he was forcing himself, only to flick his eyes away a moment later. Looked at *me*, not the strange craggy contours of my shattered face, patched back together with skin from my thighs, my new features doughy, as if a child rolled them out of pastry and stuck them on.

'What do you want to tell us, Stella?'

The pen started writing.

Mother did it.

Bains sat up, leaned forward again. 'Did what? Found the gun?'

No. Pulled the trigger.

When Evgeni comes later today, I will open the door just enough for him to slide the blanket through. Then I will stand behind it so that he cannot see me while he logs the delivery in his little black box and hands it to me to sign. Then he will call, 'Goodbye, lady,' like he always does, and I will only nod with the door almost closed, because there's just nothing worse than the sun on my face.

CONNIE

Life with Rosamie takes on a different shape. She moves quietly in the background, deftly tidying and sorting, putting away all the things that used to cause tension. Connie begins to look out for the mugs left on top of the dishwasher, never inside it, the clothes scattered on the bedroom floor, the disposable contact lenses Mark has flicked towards the bathroom bin that miss, then stare up, filmy and sightless, from the tiled floor. She feels almost disappointed when she no longer finds them, the marital instinct to find fault oddly thwarted.

Mornings become quite relaxed. Alice eats her cereal without complaint because Rosamie has bought her a new bowl from Carrefour. She spoons at the brown sludge with fresh enthusiasm, eager to reveal the Disney princess, with her pink, plastic smile. The lunchboxes are waiting on the kitchen counter when Connie gets up, lids flipped open in readiness, yawning mouths that she has only to fill with a selection of the things that start to colonize the fridge in little containers.

She is faintly nostalgic for the fraught school runs that characterized their life in England. There was something real about the breathless rush to get out of the door, always ten minutes late, stuffing hands into mittens, and following the children, winding scarves round necks while they searched for a lost school shoe among the umbrellas and trainers piled in the hallway of their Victorian semi. Now the children wait for her by the kitchen door – faces scrubbed, shoes shiny – and there is something alien about their von Trapp wholesomeness.

Life returns to normal as soon as they are out on the Sheikh Zayed Road. Sunday morning, back to school. Ben finds a sweet in the car – sticky and sandy, from some long-forgotten party bag – and flicks it at Alice. In the rear-view mirror, Connie sees the trajectory of Alice's hand as she lunges at her brother.

'*Muuuum!*'

She doesn't care which one it is. Whose fault it is. Who started it. She has to focus on the road, the constant swipe of gas-guzzling 4x4s cutting in front of her, undertaking her, whooshing past at terrifying speeds. Billboard ads loom over them, Gucci and Bvlgari, expensive watches alongside images of smiling Emirati families strolling through computer-generated new developments.

At school, the children tip out of the car and kick through the stretch of sand that serves as a car park, book bags banging round their knees, hair blond with sun and youth. Even after a year, Connie doesn't feel part of this Stepford existence, still braces herself for the bamboo forest of Lycra-clad legs that stalk towards her each day, still prickles under the gaze of oversized sunglasses, both blank and judgemental.

When she gets to Ben's classroom all the other mothers seem to be in groups already, chatting and laughing. She stands beside a couple of mums of boys Ben is friends with, but neither turns round, so she is kept on the periphery, an outsider looking in. Just *say something*, she tells herself, but they are in the middle of discussing whether it's better to have a private swimming tutor for their boys or for them to join group lessons. She can't think of anything to say, or even find a suitable pause in which to say it, so she gives up and busies herself reading a faded PTA newsletter stuck to a board to pass the time before the doors open at 7:15 a.m. and not a minute earlier.

'Hello, Connie.'

'Oh, hi, Ruby,' she says, hoping her voice doesn't sound too relieved, too grateful.

'Yucky weather, isn't it?' Ruby plucks at her T-shirt and flaps it against her skin. 'Going to be a sandstorm later.'

'Really? I was planning to take the kids to the beach after school.' There's always an 'after school' to think about when the school day ends at 1:30 p.m.

'Why don't you come over to ours? Would be good to get the kids together.'

'Oh, that would be lovely,' says Connie, trying not to gush.

'Got to keep them occupied, haven't we? Seb! STOP DOING THAT.' Ruby glares at her son, standing on top of a brightly coloured mound on the astroturf, pushing his sister, Emily, backwards every time she tries to climb onto it.

Emily and Seb are in the same school years as Alice and Ben. Both the boys and the girls are friends. Ruby sought Connie out – *You're Alice's mum!* – arranged playdates and chatted at the school gates. Connie immediately warmed to Ruby, with her eye-rolling irreverence about the worthy members of the PTA, and her ability to hold a conversation about something other than her own children. There was a fit between them, a synchronicity. Ben and Seb, Alice and Emily, Connie and Ruby.

Now that she's talking to Ruby, other mums wander over to join them as they stand under the mean slices of shade offered by the wooden pergola over the classroom doors. The women seem to cluster round Ruby like iron filings without her even having to try. Ruby is makeup-free in the early morning, blue eyes, mid-brown hair. No logos or flashy brands, just a loose white T-shirt and denim shorts. Flip-flops and her hair in the kind of messy ponytail that Connie could never quite master; effortless, as if tied up on her way out of the door with one of her daughter's Frozen scrunchies, grabbed from the kitchen worktop. An Anna, not an Elsa.

'I'm looking forward to our girls' brunch on Friday,' says one of the mums to Ruby.

Connie suddenly feels awkward. She doesn't know anything about a girls' brunch. She glances around, looking for Alice, thinking she can slip away on the pretext of soothing a scraped knee, but Ruby just turns to her and smiles. 'I'm organizing a Friday brunch for Chloë's birthday,' she says. 'I'd have asked you to join us, but I know childcare can be tricky for you.'

It's a bit of a lame excuse, but she has to give Ruby credit for her fluid and graceful gesture.

'No problem,' says Connie, equally graciously. Then, 'We've got a new housemaid actually.'

'Have you?' says Ruby, lifting her sunglasses up onto her hair and grinning at Connie. 'You can come, then!'

'No, really, it's fine, but thank you.'

'Don't be silly,' says Ruby. 'It'll be fun. I guess you must be enjoying your new-found freedom.'

'Well . . . it's nice to have the help, and she does seem very sweet.'

'That's it now, you know,' Ruby declares. 'You're never going to leave!'

'What d'you mean?'

'Everyone comes here thinking they'll just stay a few years, but they never do. Why? Because the men can't bear to be parted from their tax-free salaries, and the women can't bear to leave their housemaids.'

Connie hears Mark's voice in her head: *It's just for three years, Con. Then we'll be back*, he had promised her. Is Rosamie part of some plan he has to keep them there? It worries her that she might slowly adjust to a life of privilege that will prove impossible to give up, but she just laughs and says, 'Is that what happened to you and Adrian, then?'

'Too right it is!' Ruby grabs Seb as he rushes past, simultaneously planting his bag in his hand and a kiss on his head.

The patio doors of the classroom glide open and airconditioning barrels out. Ben's teacher, Mrs Lane, greets the waiting mothers with an equally frigid smile.

'I might have to invite Liz and her three lovely boys along this afternoon, if you can bear it,' says Ruby, as they walk the girls round to their classroom. 'She's desperate to talk to me about *arrangements* for the school fair.' Ruby stifles a pretend yawn.

'No problem,' says Connie, grinning.

'And I'm going to call the Westin and add another place for brunch on Friday, okay?'

Connie nods. 'Thanks, Ruby. That would be lovely.'

Connie squats down in front of Alice and smooths her hair away from her face, bracing for tears, little hands clutching at her top. But this morning there are none.

'Mummy,' says Alice, 'can Rosme bring me to school tomorrow? Please! Please! Can she?'

SIX

STELLA

DC Bains was right. Bonnie's .38-calibre Colt Detective Special was sold in 1978 to someone called Raymond Brown, in Texas. Medical tape indeed! Must have been the remains of a sticker. A two for one special on personal firearms.

Men can be very selective about what they tell you, Connie. Even Mark. Especially Mark. He never told me about your job, for example. I wonder whether it was because he didn't want me to know that you're the kind of person who would devote your working life to making other people's lives better. Maybe he didn't want me to feel guilty about you. Or guiltier than I already do, as if it would make what happened even more awful. It's not my fault, though, Connie. I didn't know you then. We have to compartmentalize all the time, isolate conflicting thoughts and emotions. That's how people manage to have affairs. The partners and children, their domestic responsibilities, they're just sitting in a completely different box from the great sex they're having with their new lover. Still, it doesn't matter about Mark now, does it? We're getting to know each other just fine without him.

I'm catching up with you today. I feel a little more resilient, more able to cope with seeing you. I wouldn't say this to anyone but you, but I wonder whether Evgeni might have something to do with my better mood.

When he delivered the Hermès blanket (gorgeous, by the way) I stood behind the front door, holding it slightly open, as usual. I'm sure Evgeni's quite used to this – think of all the people not opening their door properly because they're still in their pyjamas. The problem was that the box was bulky and as he was passing it to me it slipped. Instinctively, I let go of the night latch and grabbed the parcel with both hands to stop it falling. There was a breeze and the door just slowly swung open. I didn't know what to do. I could hardly slam it in his face, or hide behind the box, so I just stood there in front of him, feeling more exposed than I ever have in my life.

Evgeni seemed a little surprised at first and looked past me into the arts-and-crafts gloom of my mother's hall. No, not my mother's hall, *my* hall. It's mine now. It was almost as if he was expecting someone else to appear. I was momentarily *overlooked*. For the first time in two years, my face was not the thing that was stared at. Then, he did look at me, searched my features with his dark brown eyes, his gaze raking over me, as if he was dragging his fingers over my skin (okay, I got that from one of my mother's novels but, actually, it really was a bit like that). I think I stopped breathing for a moment as I looked at his face just as intently as he was looking at mine. I wish I could have asked him what he saw. I wish I could have seen myself reflected in his gaze and known who I now was, but he just lowered his eyes to find the little device I always have to sign.

He didn't seem shocked, though, and he certainly didn't seem horrified. Curious, perhaps. When I was signing I could sense him looking at me again, studying the scar that runs under each eye and over the bridge of my nose, like a red seam joining the two halves of my face.

Anyway, I think Evgeni appreciated the new openness between us, because when he left, instead of saying, 'Good-bye, lady,' like he usually does, he actually smiled and said, 'Have a great day, lady.'

I tried to smile back, Connie, I promise you. I really, really tried.

You have 378 friends on social media. When you post a picture you usually get around eighty likes and there are always a few comments. You have one friend, Ruby Davey, who likes almost everything you post. I'm guessing she's one of your best friends. I had a quick look at her page too. She seems to have 826 friends. I have to say I find it hard to believe that someone has 826 actual friends. I know this poking around people's social media is a bit stalker-ish, a touch creepy even, but it's all public information, so I don't feel it's wrong to look. It makes me feel a bit sad, though, like I'm an outsider looking in on the world – the Little Match Girl staring into the flame of her struck match, seeing visions of the warm and comforting life she never had.

I'm not on any social media. I guess I never thought my life would be that interesting to anyone else, and now I'm thinking that maybe it would be a little bit *too* interesting. Either way, it feels like putting myself out there to be judged. I already went through life worrying that I didn't have enough 'friends' or that people didn't 'like' me. I don't need to have that quantified in absolute terms.

I doubt you have ever had to worry about anything like that, Connie. Your feed is full of pictures of you and your family at the beach, on playdates, going to parties and at restaurants. You obviously have a very busy life full of social engagements. I'm looking at your November posts and there's a picture of you at someone's 'Bubbalicious Birthday Brunch'! You and at least fifteen of your friends are sitting at a long table outside, shaded by huge white parasols. You're all wearing colourful summer dresses and holding up slim glasses of Prosecco in a silent, smiling toast. One of your friends from England has posted 'Missing you!' in response to the picture, and asks when you'll make it back to the UK. You replied, 'Booked up now till June. Crazy, isn't it?!!'

It's not crazy for me, Connie. My diary is empty save for hospital appointments that pop up like mushrooms in its dark and musty pages. But even before that I would say I've never been one for eating out. For a start my mother never enjoyed it. Why, she would say, would you go out to eat what you can very well make at home? Why would you put up with the inconvenience of other people around you? Their chatter and their smells, the constant flap of the door to the kitchens or the toilet opening and closing right next to you. Suffering a draught, or the oppressive heat at a table right next to the radiator. So expensive! And the noise! It was all just too much.

The closest I have come to eating out since my injury was at the hospital canteen. It was during the months I spent in a specialist centre. The first thing the doctors did was to try to reconstruct my face the best they could, over multiple surgeries. They took bone and skin from my hip and thigh and pinned them to my face with titanium bolts and plates. Then, alongside my general reconstruction and healing, I began extensive physical and speech therapy to try to regain the muscle control lost in the concussive trauma caused by the bullet. I was there for almost a year. One day, they sent me down to a little café on the ground floor. It was part of my recovery, learning to socialize again, as if I was any good at that to begin with. At least it was early in the morning, so not too many visitors. I sat at a little table in the corner, next to a window looking out onto a patch of lawn, with a wooden bench placed in front of a square brick pond. No curves or natural lines, just trapped carp swimming in futile right angles. The weather was dreary, and rain smashed silver daggers against the glass. I was trying to summon the courage to go to the counter when a girl came over. Only young, maybe eighteen.

'What would you like?' she said.

She was studying her little notebook, her pen poised. I was thinking what to have, so I paused a while. As the silence went on, she lifted her eyes up to my face, then immediately lowered her gaze again. I felt sorry for the girl because she obviously felt uncomfortable so I just scribbled, *Cup of tea, please.*

Have you ever heard of the Tin Noses Shop? After the First World War, when so many men had had their faces blown off by bullets and shrapnel, there was a place just outside London where they made them new ones. They took casts of the strange, cratered moonscapes their faces had become and made masks to fit over them, out of copper, painted in enamels. They copied the features from photographs of the men as they once were. Moustaches were popular, great big ones curling at the ends, worthy of an officer of the British Raj, made out of real hair. The torn flesh was covered with galvanized noses and chins, secured by spectacles, or ribbons, round their ears. Then those soldiers could contemplate the world again with a new unblinking eye, framed by eyelashes made of slivers of tin foil, tinted, curled and soldered into place.

That's what I had, Connie. A tin nose.

The girl nodded, then returned a few minutes later with a mug of tea made from one of those industrial water heaters that always seem to make scalding tea.

Sorry, could I have a napkin too, please? Always necessary, these days.

She went off again and I leaned over the tea. It was an odd sensation, being able to feel the steam cluster wetly on only parts of my face. These days, tin noses are held on with special glue, but what they didn't tell me is that steam melts that glue. My prosthetic nose started to feel loose and began coming away from my face. It's hard enough drinking hot tea through a straw as it is. After a minute or two, I got fed up with it slipping around, so I pulled that tin nose right off, and put it on the table next to me. The tea felt better then. I liked feeling the steam all over my face, breathing it in. I was wondering what the point of the tin nose really was when the girl came back with the napkins, a whole bunch of them grasped in her hand. The moment she caught sight of me her hands flew up to her face, and the napkins fluttered down around her, shapeless paper birds falling from the sky.

I'll tell you something else interesting, Connie. The park benches nearest to the Tin Noses Shop were painted blue. It was a warning, you see. A heads-up to the townsfolk to sit somewhere else so they wouldn't have to look at those poor men and their obliterated faces.

CONNIE

Connie returns from the school run to a house that only seems empty. Rosamie's presence can be detected in the clear kitchen surfaces, and the table free of the globs of smeared and congealed Weetabix that used to welcome her home. For a moment, she wonders what to do. All the tasks that she would usually rattle through have already been done. She decides to go for a run on the treadmill in the little room next to the compound's pool that serves as a gym.

On her way out via the garage she passes Rosamie's door. It's unusual for her to be in her room, so she taps with a knuckle, calling, 'Are you okay?' to the white-painted MDF. From inside the room comes the ping of an arriving text message.

'Sorry, madam.' Her voice is small, muffled. It's followed by a scuffling and the door opening. 'I'm coming right now.'

Rosamie appears holding her phone and starts looking for her house shoes, foamy flip-flops with a garish pattern on the inside sole, bearing the indent of her feet over many steps. They slide away from her over the tiled floor as she tries to push her feet into them. She lets go of the door to lean her hand on the wall and it swings open.

Connie feels almost embarrassed to be staring into Rosamie's room. It is a window into an existence she's not sure she wants to confront. There's the small bed with a flowery duvet crumpled on top. The chest of drawers is scattered with a bright string of rosary beads, twisting round a framed picture of Rosamie's five-year-old son, Gabriel. Clothes are creeping out of the open drawers, dangling arms of garments reaching over the edge as if trying to climb out. Every inch of space has been used. A single electric hotplate sits alongside a rice cooker. Arranged next to them are table salt, a cluster of plastic pots containing spices in various shades of brown, and a huge bag of rice, its size out of all proportion to the room itself. On the wall, a maudlin image of the Madonna and Child oversees everything from underneath the struggling air-conditioning unit.

Connie's house is now so clean and well ordered that she expected Rosamie's room to be the same, as if Rosamie's existence were just an extension of her own, rather than a chaotic bolt-hole in which to eat, wash and sleep.

'So sorry, madam,' says Rosamie, again, coming out of her room. 'I didn't know you were back already.' She grabs the handle of a bucket piled high with cleaning products, sponges and cloths from the utility area and waddles towards the kitchen with it banging against her legs.

'No, I didn't mean . . .' says Connie, following her. Rosamie puts her phone on the kitchen worktop as she passes, to free an extra hand for the bucket. 'Really, Rosamie,' insists Connie. 'I wasn't checking up on you. I just wanted to know if you were all right.'

Rosamie glances over her shoulder at Connie. There is something sad, poignant even, about the smile she gives her. 'I'm fine, thank you, madam,' she says. Then she disappears through the door with her bucket, her flip-flops slapping up the marble-tiled stairs.

Connie turns back towards the door to head out for her run. As she does, Rosamie's phone gives another ping and lights up. It's instinctive to glance at it, and Connie does so before she even remembers it's not her phone. It's from someone called Marijo: *Help me rosie pls. i'm scared.*

Ruby lives on the Palm Jumeirah. Even Ben and Alice are momentarily quiet as their car sweeps onto the trunk of the Palm. When they stop at the security point for entry to Ruby's frond, Connie secretly enjoys telling the security guard Ruby's name and villa number and watching the barrier lift to allow her through.

When she arrives Liz is already there. She's sitting at the table with her hands round a mug of tea when Ruby brings Connie through to the open-plan living room, its floor-to-ceiling windows overlooking the private pool and the beach, although today the view is hazy and peppered with dust.

'Where are the kids?' asks Connie, looking around for evidence of Liz's three boys.

'They're all in the playroom with Jasmine,' says Ruby. 'Why don't you take Alice and Ben through while I get you some tea?'

Connie leads the kids towards the playroom, Ben rushing on ahead, Alice suddenly shy, dragging on Connie's hand. The playroom is at the front of the house, with an old sofa and a huge storage unit against one wall, made up of row upon row of shelves holding coloured boxes full of toys. Two boys are lounging on bright red bean-bags in front of an Xbox while Seb hovers behind them, his hands twitching towards the controls as he shouts instructions to shoot, *shoooot*! Ben runs over to join them, launching himself onto the nearest bean-bag.

Ruby's housemaid, Jasmine, sits on the sofa with a Filipina Connie doesn't know who has a small boy on her knee. She is bouncing him up and down and waving a plastic vehicle in front of him, while she talks to Jasmine in fast, animated Tagalog.

'Hi, ma'am,' chorus both maids, looking up. They extend the syllables so it comes out 'Hi, *maaaaam*'.

'Hello, ladies,' replies Connie. Then, 'Alice, there's Emily.' She encourages her daughter towards Emily sitting at a little table and chairs in bright primary colours. The table looks as if a chest of pirate's treasure has been emptied over it – glitter, sequins, plastic jewels in the shape of flowers and hearts – which Emily is enthusiastically gluing to a flat cardboard cutout of a crown.

'Look,' says Emily to Alice, picking up the crown and wrapping it round her head, 'we can be princesses.'

Connie goes back to join her friends. Liz has brought a laptop with her and is showing Ruby her spreadsheet of the rota for the school fair. Their class is doing the coconut shy and, lest that be too straightforward, Liz is suggesting all the class mums get together to paint a desert-island-themed, life-sized cardboard backdrop for the stall.

'I think we could get it done in a week if we spend every morning doing it. We can meet at my villa – I've got a huge patio out the back, which will be just perfect!'

Ruby catches Connie's eye and grins. 'Here's your tea,' she says, sliding the mug towards Connie.

'Right then,' says Liz, angling her laptop towards Connie, as if it were a cannon. 'What slots can I put you down for?'

'Umm, ten thirty a.m.?' suggests Connie. Liz taps on her keyboard, then looks up at Connie again, her fingers hovering. 'And?'

'And?'

'Everybody is doing *at least* two slots, Connie.'

'Oh, okay. Eleven a.m. then?'

'Hmm,' says Liz, leaning in towards the screen. 'I'll see if I can work it. It might mean me swapping my slots on Freddie's class's bouncy castle with Ruby's on the refreshments stall. Anyway, leave it with me. Now, cakes?'

'Cakes?' asks Connie.

'What cake will you be baking for the cake stall? I'm heavy on the chocolate cupcake, rocky-road side of things at the moment, so maybe something a little more wholesome. Flapjacks? Carrot cake?'

'Er, can I let you know?' says Connie. This is what happens when a woman who used to be a project manager for a large multinational joins the PTA, she thinks.

'How's everything with Rosamie?' asks Ruby, changing the subject.

'Great. The children adore her already, especially Alice . . .' Connie's voice tails off.

'Sounds like there's a but,' says Ruby, taking a biscuit from the plate on the table and biting into it.

'Not really. It's just that this morning, I saw a text come up on her phone. It was an accident, I wasn't looking, but it was from a friend of hers asking Rosamie to help her. It said she was scared.'

Liz slaps down the screen of her laptop. 'Do *not* get involved in their problems. Seriously, just don't do it.'

'But what if this girl – Marijo – is in trouble?'

'They're always in trouble! If it's not them, it's their friend. If it's not their friend, it's their mother back home.'

Connie looks at Liz. It's interesting, she thinks, who you end up spending time with just because your kids are in the same class at school.

'Why don't you just ask her if everything's okay?' says Ruby, ignoring Liz. 'You don't need to say you saw the text.'

Liz rolls her eyes. 'You were *meant* to see the text, silly. I bet she just happened to leave her phone right where you could see it, didn't she? The second you mention it, she'll ask for money. I promise you, just wait and see.'

'It wasn't like that,' says Connie. 'Rosamie seemed genuinely worried this morning, even before I saw the text.'

Liz gives a dismissive little snort and picks up her tea, leaning back in Ruby's plush sofa. 'Why was the text in English, then?'

Connie starts to say something, but the words come out as an exasperated sigh. She takes another deliberate breath. 'I don't know, Liz. Maybe they just get used to speaking English all the time.'

'Rubbish.' Liz takes a sip of her tea, continuing to eye Connie over the rim. 'You're being set up. Listen,' she puts her mug on the table and leans forward towards Connie and Ruby on the sofa opposite, 'the other day my housemaid asked me to give her a pay rise to three hundred dirhams a month *above* the set wage just because her husband had lost *his* job!'

'You pay her the minimum wage?' says Connie, incredulous.

'Of course. That's what the law says.'

'No,' says Connie, trying not to raise her voice. 'That's the minimum required by law. But it isn't a fair and decent wage.'

'So what do you pay yours?'

'Twice that!'

Liz just laughs. 'No wonder she thinks you're a soft touch!'

'Come on, Liz,' intervenes Ruby. 'That's not fair.'

'I honestly don't mean to be rude,' says Liz. 'I just think that even if there *is* something going on, it's still better to stay well out of it.'

'Really, why?' Connie starts to feel her heart accelerating in her chest. She should let it go, get back to planning the scenery for the coconut shy, but she can't. 'Why wouldn't you help someone if they're in trouble?'

'I would,' says Liz, 'if they came and asked me. But that's not the same as going looking for a cause. You say you want to help her, but I wonder who you're really doing it for. Her or you?'

'What does that mean?'

'I understand you want to help, but maybe you also want to be needed, to be useful. Seriously, Connie, if you're feeling a bit bored at home there are other ways to keep busy and fulfilled. What about being next year's class rep? I've done it three times now – Harry's year, Ollie's year, and now Freddie's year.'

'I'm not bored, Liz! I just thought I might be able to help.'

'Maybe they don't *need* your help. Have you ever thought about that?'

Connie is silent for a moment. The playroom door opens and she hears the children chattering and laughing.

'Maybe they don't,' says Connie, shrugging, 'but the sad reality is that migrant domestic workers are taken advantage of all the time.'

'And you're going to be her white saviour, are you?'

Five boys and two girls pile into the room, pulling off their T-shirts and wriggling out of their shorts. Liz's housemaid shuffles behind them, picking up their Hansel and Gretel trail of discarded clothes.

'We're going swimming,' announces one of Liz's boys.

'There's a sandstorm!' protests Liz, but they're already flinging the door open and running, shrieking, into the gritty smog.

'So,' says Liz, turning back to Connie, 'shall I put you down for class rep next year then?'

SEVEN

STELLA

This is where I found the gun.

It was in an old suitcase, wedged into the wardrobe in the spare room. I hadn't known it was there as it was covered with my mother's old clothes. She didn't like to get rid of anything. There were Crimplene A-line dresses, hanging alongside a wide-legged jumpsuit in a geometric brown and orange pattern, and a mothy fur coat from some unidentifiable animal. I can't even remember what I was looking for. Perhaps I was just seeing what was there, making some kind of mental inventory of items collected over a lifetime. Carefully accumulated by one generation, only to be casually dispersed by the next, destined for house clearance and charity shops.

I parted the clothes, like I was stepping into Narnia, and there it was. My father's suitcase. Brown and battered, with reinforced corners and tarnished bronze latches. I dragged it out because I was surprised to see it there. I'd thought all traces of him had gone after he left, as if my mother had wiped the house clean of him, just like I could erase an ill-judged remark from my whiteboard.

His suitcase was stuck all over with peeling travel stickers. *The Peninsula Hotel, Hong Kong, Mexico City via Pan American*, and a rigid-looking policeman bringing *Greetings from Nassau*. I flipped the latches and lifted the top to reveal a faded checked pattern inside. Not much, a few items of clothing – pyjamas, a cardigan – and a few papers, their marriage certificate from 1982 being the most interesting. I lifted the cardigan and smelt it. It was sharp, like mothballs and old sweat. Not the comfortable scent of fatherhood I'd been hoping for – all print newspapers, sandalwood and Sunday dinners. I was about to drop the cardigan back into the suitcase, when I noticed there was a box underneath it, tan leather with a carrying handle. Inside was the Bonnie Parker .38-calibre Colt Detective Special that turned out to be every bit as genuine as my father.

I carefully lifted out that beautiful honey-coloured case and opened it. Inside, the gun lay flat in a moulded black suede interior, alongside a cleaning rod and a cartridge block with a single two-inch round-nosed piece of metal slotted into one of the holes. The world was closing in on me by that stage, Connie. My existence was narrowing to just me and my mother, her diminishing capabilities and increasing needs, with nothing to break it up, save the occasional, *We really must have that cup of tea*, from Mrs Wilson. I'm not saying I intended to use it, but it did make me feel better to have it there. Just like you don't feel so afraid of the dark when you know you have a torch in your pocket. I know it's wrong to lie, especially to the police, but I couldn't tell DC Bains that I found that gun, that I kept hold of it without a licence. He went away after he visited me in hospital. He was able to tick off his enquiries as 'completed'. There wasn't much further he could take them. It wasn't as if he could bring my mother into the station and start questioning her.

I don't know why she kept those things of my father's and got rid of all the rest. She was beyond the ability to explain by the time I found them. Maybe she prepared that suitcase in the hope that he would come back one day. Perhaps she imagined his delight that she had kept his favourite possessions. Perhaps she thought she would let him get comfortable in his old pyjamas and much-loved cardigan, then shoot him for what he had done to her.

That was when she started writing. She never seemed to meet anyone else, or at least no one very suitable, or permanent. Instead, she filled the void with characters. People whose thwarted desires always triumphed in the end. People who made love with a passion that intensified with every book.

You know how the saying goes, Connie. Those who can, do. Those who can't . . . write about it.

Do you have certain friends you tell certain things to? We all just want someone to understand us, don't we? I want to tell someone how I felt before the gun went off, about the isolation and frustration, the feeling of being trapped in my own life, suffocated by it, helpless. And the anger, the toe-curling rage, mixed with indescribable guilt and profound grief. I want to tell you, Connie, but when I look at your life I worry that you won't understand. It's like your life is full of sunshine. That's the only way I can describe it. It's not just the beaches and the cloudless skies, not just the rippling hexagons of light trapped in the turquoise swimming pools you stand beside: it's the smile on your face and the way you're always touching someone – your children, your husband, your friends. Your arms are always round each other, your faces pressed close. It's as if there are no dark corners in your world.

Then I noticed something just after a post about a 'Playdate on the Palm!' and a slightly hazy photo of a tiny pool churning with seven laughing children (43 likes, 10 comments). You have shared a link to a report by Human Rights Watch entitled, *Abuse and Exploitation of Female Migrant Domestic Workers in the United Arab Emirates*. I've lost almost the entire day to this report, and all the other stuff I found after I read it. I had no idea this kind of thing still happened.

There was one thing I wish I hadn't seen, though. Grainy, jolting mobile-phone footage of a woman, flowery headscarf and loose clothing flapping in the wind that buffets a high-rise apartment block. She is dangling over the balcony, clinging to the edge of the glass balustrade. 'Crazy! Come back!' says the woman holding the mobile phone.

But surely there is no coming back from the white-knuckled grip this woman has on life. 'Hold me!' she begs, but the other woman just stands there and films, and keeps on filming as the woman falls, spinning down towards an unconcerned landscape of rooftops, dusty cars and endless desert. What was life like in that unremarkable-looking apartment, with its laundry drying on the balcony, and tinted windows resisting the curious gaze of the outside world? Why was there only one way out?

Maybe I was wrong to think you wouldn't understand, Connie.

CONNIE

Rosamie is in the children's room making their beds. She shakes out Alice's duvet and smooths it over the bed. Connie is pulling out one of Ben's drawers and emptying the contents onto his bed. She sits down next to the jumble of clothes and begins to sort through them. 'Would you like any of these for Gabriel?' she asks.

Rosamie looks up from where she is plumping Alice's pillow into shape. She nods. 'Yes, thank you, madam.'

'They grow so fast, don't they?' she says, holding up a pair of Ben's trousers that now seem comically small. Rosamie doesn't respond, just smiles politely and turns back to Alice's bed, carefully arranging Little Rabbit's floppy, threadbare limbs over the pillow.

'I'm sorry, Rosamie,' says Connie, folding the trousers onto her lap. 'You must miss Gabriel.'

Rosamie shrugs. 'He is okay. My mother take good care of him.'

'Of course,' says Connie. 'Still, it must be hard for you not to see him every day.'

'Yes, but I am working to pay for his education. He will go to college, not like me. With the money I send home we build house in Philippines. Nice house for our family. When I go back we will have good life.'

Even though Connie and Mark pay Rosamie twice what many other domestic workers in Dubai earn, the wages are still modest. It humbles Connie to think that what they pay

Rosamie could pay for a child's education and a family home.

'What about Gabriel's dad?'

'His father gone. That man no good, not like sir Mark.'

For a moment, all the uncharitable thoughts Connie has ever had about her husband prickle her mind like pins. She knows she has been short-tempered with him recently, snapping at small things that shouldn't matter, feeling resentful when he comes back from work too late to eat dinner with her, or too tired to help put the kids to bed. She can't complain about the lack of help because of Rosamie, but it isn't about who's doing the ironing or emptying the dishwasher. She has all the 'help' she could ever need, yet she still feels unsupported. It's as if they are not a partnership any more, as if their connection is unravelling. There had been a solidarity of sorts in the way Connie had gone to work early, and Mark had given the kids breakfast and dropped them off at school. In the way that Connie had left work at four on the dot and had time with the kids until Mark came home. They always used to cook dinner together and chat about their day. Had they stopped talking, or was it that she now struggled to find anything interesting to say? But Rosamie's comment makes her see things differently. Their dynamic has changed, that's all. Mark is just working hard for their family, trying to earn some money so they can go home and have a good life. It's what everyone in Dubai is doing.

Connie turns back to the pile of clothes and picks out a

new T-shirt, smoothing it over the bed, and folding it ready to be put back into the drawer. Rosamie comes over and perches on the edge of the bed. 'I help you, madam,' she says, in a bright voice, taking the T-shirt from Connie and placing it in the drawer.

They sit in silence for a while, Connie sorting through the clothes, inspecting them, then handing the ones Ben still wears to Rosamie to fold and put back in the drawer.

'You nice family,' says Rosamie, after a minute or two. 'I'm happy here.'

Before Connie can answer, tell Rosamie that she's happy too, there is a ping from somewhere deep in Rosamie's pocket. Rosamie's hands still as she matches up the two stripy legs of Ben's pyjama bottoms.

Connie looks away and busies herself balling socks while Rosamie delves into her pocket and brings out her phone. From the corner of her eye, she sees Rosamie's face pucker in concern.

'Is everything okay?'

'Yes, madam.' The knee-jerk response. *Yes, madam, no, madam, okay, madam.*

'You can tell me, you know.' Connie gathers the last few stranded garments from the bed and drops them into the drawer, clearing the space between them, then shifts round to face Rosamie, who is staring at her phone as if awaiting instructions on how to proceed.

'Is it Marijo?'

Rosamie startles and looks up.

'I saw a text she sent you. I'm sorry, I didn't mean to.'

Rosamie shakes her head. 'Marijo in trouble,' she says.

'What kind of trouble?'

'The family she works for is not kind. No off day, not enough food, too much working. Madam shouting all the time.'

Then why doesn't she leave?'

'What can she do?' Rosamie lifts her arms, palms facing upwards, phone still in one hand. 'They take her passport.'

'They can't do that!' Connie leans forward, her voice urgent. 'Tell Marijo her employers are not allowed to do that.'

But Rosamie just looks sad. 'What can she do?' she repeats quietly.

There must be something she can do, thinks Connie, as she scrolls through her search results. The position of migrant domestic workers in Gulf countries makes for grim reading. She reads horrifying articles about physical and sexual abuse, even murder and suicide. Yet the Middle East is full of migrants. The spectacular buildings rise from the toil of swarms of construction workers clad in blue boiler suits and yellow plastic hats, scarves wrapped round their faces as protection against the punishing sun. The homes run on the labour of women, caring for the children and the elderly, cooking and cleaning. They come in search of a better life. Not for themselves, but for the families they support back home. They are working to find a way out, but instead they become trapped.

She is shocked and saddened by what she reads, but then a creeping thought plays at the back of her mind. Is she like an eighteenth-century abolitionist, decrying slavery at the same time as adding sugar to her tea? She almost wants to send Rosamie home, but she has seen photos of the house that Rosamie's family is building in Quirino Province with the money she earns. If she is treated and paid well, what is the difference between Rosamie and an au pair in England?

Kafala is a word that Connie didn't know before. It refers to the sponsorship system in Arab countries whereby the migrant worker must have a local sponsor to obtain a visa. If your right to live in a country is tied to the individual you work for, no wonder domestic workers can't complain when they're treated badly, she thinks. But the *kafala* system is being reformed in the UAE. There are new laws in place that protect migrant domestic workers and establish rights in relation to salary and time off. This is good news for Marijo, although Connie wonders why she hasn't tried to enforce these rights already. Perhaps Marijo doesn't know about them because the law is new, or perhaps she thinks it would just be too hard or cost too much money. She makes a few notes of the key points, thinking she'll pass them on to Rosamie to give to Marijo.

She's about to shut down the computer when something occurs to her. Her mind feels totally engaged for the first time in more than a year. She hasn't felt so energized since she left her job.

She types, *jobs strategic philanthropy Dubai*, into the search box and presses return.

EIGHT

STELLA

This is my last memory of my father, and if I hadn't made that *almighty mess* it would never have happened.

He used to call me Twinkle. ' "Stella" means star,' he told me, 'and nothing shines as bright in my life as you, Twinkle.' He was an entertainer on a cruise line. He had a sixty-minute routine of slapstick comedy and cheeky songs, king of the burlesque and the double entendre. He met my mother aboard the *Ocean Ambassador* in 1981, when she was twenty-two and working as a show dancer, a slender, ostrich-plumed thing in opera gloves and sparkly shoes. She was playing shuffleboard with the guests on the promenade deck one morning, and he was pointing out King's Wharf, Bermuda, in the distance to a group of ladies from the Mothers' Union. Apparently – and he loved this bit of the story – she was so busy staring at him from under her floppy, wide-brimmed sun hat, that she shot her disc straight at the thickset ankles of the president of the Totnes WI. Fortunately, he stopped it just in time with his canvas deck shoes, which I imagine were the same brilliant white as his smile. She must have been grateful, as they were stealing kisses on the balcony by Aruba, and in love by Acapulco.

My mother wasn't meant to be a show dancer on a cruise ship. She was *destined for better things*. I'm not entirely sure what those things were. The stage or screen, perhaps. She was always a bit vague when I asked her, but she was clear that she had been *much admired*. Principally by her doting parents, it seemed, but also by any number of instructors of music, drama and the performing arts, all of whom seemed to have taken significant amounts of her parents' money in return for limited instruction but endless flattery. Nevertheless, she insisted she was only doing cruise-ship cabaret for a year, to get some experience of performing, before her career took off in the way that she was certain it would.

I put paid to all that though, Connie.

They married as soon as their contracts ended, and three months later I was born. My mother mourned what might have been – as if I had grown fat inside her on a diet of her hopes and dreams – but my father genuinely missed his life at sea, adrift on the adoration of his audience, buoyed by their laughter and applause. He became a used-car salesman instead, while doing odd gigs in pubs and working men's clubs, but it wasn't the same without the captive audiences, the glittering chandeliers and the endless promise of a huge expanse of ocean.

I think that was why he cherished that Colt Detective

Special. He told me it had been a gift from a Texan oil baron who had been a regular on his cruises. A token of his appreciation for all the nights of entertainment my father had given him. Knowing what I know now about the gun, I wonder whether even that was true, but it made a nice story and that was all that mattered to my father. I'm not sure how Bonnie Parker came into it, but I suspect that it was my father, not the Texan oil baron, who spun that particular tale. He was obsessed with Bonnie and Clyde. He romanticized their disdain for small-town life, their love-on-the-run existence and devil-may-care attitude. I think he saw them as people who lived life the way *they* wanted to, no matter the consequences. No matter who got hurt.

And my mother? She became what is left when unrealistic dreams, fed by excessive praise, are stripped away. A rather bitter little thing, slowly revealed from behind the colourful feathers, glittering sequins and stage makeup already turning tacky under reality's glare.

Anyway, back to the memory.

It was my birthday, and I was turning seven. My father was taking pictures of me with his Kodak Pocket Instamatic. My mother was sitting on the sofa, face pinched with disapproval, asking him why he was *wasting all that film*. I still have one of the photos. I'm kneeling on the carpet in a mustard-coloured corduroy pinafore dress with a box in front of me, wrapped in Holly Hobbie wrapping paper. I think I remember all those little details, but I'm not sure whether they're recorded in my mind, or in that photo.

When I think about that day, it's that image of me kneeling on the carpet that comes to mind, as if the photo has over-written the memory in my brain. It's become a peg on which to hang all my other recollections of that day. I find that a lot. My key memories are based on photos, and I can just scroll through them, like an Instagram feed.

'Because my girl's so pretty,' my father replied.

I glanced at my mother and couldn't make sense of the expression on her face. It made me feel guilty, like I'd done something wrong. I'm trying to picture her in my mind, but I can't wind back the years like that. If I want to remember what she looked like when she was younger, I have to think of a photograph of her, like the one where she's standing in front of the California Lighthouse in Aruba, her hair long and feathery in the wind, her pupils pinpoints in eyes as cerulean as the distant ocean. But that photo doesn't fit with this memory because in it she's smiling so much her young face has creased, making ripples of the freckles on her skin. She's not smiling at me from the sofa. Instead, her face is set, as perfectly expressionless as a porcelain doll's. It made me want to tell my father to stop taking pictures of me, stop telling me that I was so pretty, and pay more atten-tion to my mother so that she would smile again and I could go back to enjoying my birthday.

'One more, Twinkle,' said my father, and I had to drag my gaze away from her, look at the camera and smile.

Inside the box, wrapped in the Holly Hobbie paper, was a set of Russian tea dolls, nesting together. They were carved from wood and left unfinished, so you could paint the design on yourself with the paints that came with them. It was quite late in the day, but I wanted to paint them straight away, so my father took me to the dining-room table, brought me water for my brushes and sat there painting with me. I was so *happy*. I can't picture the dolls, or remember how I painted them, but I remember my father's attention like the warmth of a bath.

Some time later, my mother came in. Whether it was minutes or hours, I can't remember. 'Haven't you finished yet?'

'Sorry, Mummy,' I said. 'I'll tidy up now.'

Then I moved the paints and there were marks everywhere, all over the table. Little circles the paints had made on the wood, and smears of shocking colour where drops of paint had dripped from my brush and I had leaned on them with my arm.

The happiness ran cold in my veins. What had I done?

I couldn't look at her, just stared at the table. The table stared back at me with round eyes of red, yellow and blue.

I heard her gasp and tut. 'What an almighty mess you've made, you thoughtless girl!'

My father stood up very suddenly. 'It's nothing, Linda, I'll clear it up.'

The memory fragments after that, like a single strand of spider silk catching, then breaking, in the breeze. But I remember them shouting at each other, the words buzzing like angry bees round me. I didn't know what to do. I wanted to slip away, go and hide in my room, but I couldn't leave the *almighty mess*.

I went into the kitchen and got a damp cloth. The irony was that I could wipe the paint away easily, but I couldn't do the same to all the upset I'd caused. They were still arguing even after I'd put myself to bed. I lay awake listening to them. The tone had changed, the high-pitched rage muted to low growls and snaps.

Then my father came into my room, which was odd because it was late.

'You awake?'

I nodded.

He sat on my bed and gazed at me. It was dark, but I can recall what he looked like then in sepia shades, from the whites of his eyes, to the pitch black of his hair, slightly wavy and swept to one side.

'I just want to tell you that I have to go away for a bit. For work.'

'You mean the ships you worked on?'

He nodded, and gently gripped the tops of my arms. 'I'll write to you, Twinkle, I promise. Send you some postcards of places you wouldn't believe existed. Would you like that?'

Then he hugged me, a ferocious embrace that crushed me with regret.

When I got up the next morning he had already gone.

My mother sat at the kitchen table with her forehead resting on the heel of her hand, a lit cigarette between the fingers. She looked exposed, as if grief had peeled a layer from her and left her raw underneath, her eyes red, her skin crumpled

86

and damp. Not much left now of the showgirl's red-lipped smile.

I hadn't even spoken to her since the *almighty mess*.

'I wiped up the table, Mummy,' I said.

She looked up at me and laughed, a hollow choke from the back of her throat. Then she took a drag of her cigarette and let the smoke out slowly, studying me from behind its pluming veil.

'It doesn't matter any more,' she said. 'Nothing matters any more.'

CONNIE

When they arrive Liz is tying bunting to a sign:

Green Apple English School Dubai
Founded 2014.

She catches sight of their car and secures the multi-coloured flags round the metal pole, before clambering down from her stepladder.

'Nice and early, well done,' she chimes at them, once they have parked and walked up to the school entrance. 'Come and see the stall.'

Liz leads the way to the playing field. On two acres of sandy turf, some approximation of an English village fête has been recreated.

'We've been here since seven a.m.!' she announces, indicating the tombola, the bouncy castle and the many opportunities to Splat a Rat, or Hook a Duck. Victoria sponges slump under an awning on the playground, oozing their fillings, while Rice Krispie cakes turn sticky in the heat.

GAES had not been their first choice of primary school for Ben and Alice, but the established English-speaking schools in Dubai had waiting lists years long. As with their villa, when they arrived they'd had to make the best of it. The children had ended up at one of the many new schools that had sprung up to absorb the offspring of desperate expats, with little to recommend them save an appealing name and impressive termly fees.

'Here you go.' Liz thrusts a book of numbered tickets and an empty Tupperware box into Connie's hands when they get to the coconut shy. 'It's five dirhams a go. Maybe you could do it together,' she says, beaming at Mark.

Five coconuts, like hairy Easter eggs, perch on stalks tied with forlorn bits of coloured ribbon. An old sheet is spread-eagled behind them, pinned taut, braced for the haphazard onslaught of wooden balls thrown by the under-tens. No enthusiasm for the life-sized desert-island fresco, then.

Mark, who is hung-over from a work do the night before, appears to be in physical pain. He mumbles something about keeping an eye on the kids and stumbles off in the direction of the refreshments stall, while Alice and Ben shoot off to join their friends.

Connie sits on a foldaway chair to await the rush. After ten minutes, all five coconuts remain resolutely on their stands, the bag of plastic tat serving as prizes untouched. A handful of coins scatter the bottom of the plastic tub.

'God, this is bloody awful,' says Mark, handing her a coffee and unfolding another chair next to hers. 'When can we go? I'm literally dying.'

'We've only just got here!'

'What's the point, though? Don't we pay enough in fees?'

'The children are having fun,' she says, watching Ben and Alice fling themselves round the bouncy castle.

'I'm not.' Mark rakes his hand through his hair and takes a swig from his can of Coke.

'Hey,' says Connie, hoping to distract him, 'I had a look for Dubai-based strategic philanthropy jobs the other day.'

'Any luck?'

Connie wrinkles her nose. 'Not a lot, to be honest. There's a few jobs around but they all need fluent Arabic.'

Mark nods slowly, rotating the Coke can in his fingers. 'My company's always talking about doing more for the community. I didn't say anything to you because it's not definite yet, but they're thinking of appointing a corporate social responsibility manager. I know it's not quite the same, but it's a UK company so the Arabic might not be such an issue. I really think you'd be great at it, Connie.' He turns his head to look at her, smiling and squinting in the light.

'Thanks, Mark,' she says, grinning back at him. 'D'you think it would be a good idea, though? You know, husband and wife working at the same place.'

'It would be a great idea,' he says, putting a warm hand on her leg and rubbing it. 'Just don't go on any of their bloody nights out. I feel like I'm going to be sick.'

'No takers, eh?' Ruby is walking across the field towards them. She's wearing a navy blue maxi dress and a straw trilby. Once she gets under the canopy of the stall, she takes off the hat and fans herself with it.

'It is a little slow,' admits Connie.

'Hi, Mark,' says Ruby.

The sugar and caffeine must have got to him, because he's

brightened suddenly, springing up from his chair and air-kissing Ruby.

They chat about the children for a few minutes, until Connie spots Liz marching towards them with a clipboard in her hand.

'Yikes, better go,' says Ruby. 'Don't want to get roped into another slot. Listen, though, do you guys want to come over for supper later? Nothing fancy, just a takeaway and a few drinks after the kids go to bed?'

'Umm,' begins Connie, 'I dunno, Mark had a big night last—'

'That would be great, thanks, Ruby,' says Mark.

NINE

STELLA

I. Like. Peach. Pie.

This is what I tell the woman looking back at me from the mirror. I try to enunciate each word clearly, forming the words in the way that my speech therapist told me to. Six months ago the words would have come out as *I ike each ie*, indistinct noises echoing in the back of my throat. But now I'm speaking them rather than just releasing them, barely more than breath over my vocal cords.

I take my makeup bag out from the vanity unit. Not much inside, just a sticky mascara and a stumpy grey eyeliner. Circles of powder in shades of taupe and beige, foundation that has oozed into the bag. It's been two years since I last wore makeup – the year that has passed following my final operation and the year I spent in the specialist unit. I take the foundation and squeeze some onto my fingers, dot it round my face. The skin below my eyes is slightly paler than it is on my forehead, as if I've blanched at the sight of myself. I blend in the foundation and wonder what I'm trying to cover. Who I'm trying to cover. It's not me. It's not the face I judged in this mirror a thousand times over three decades, despising the shape of my nose, spindly eyebrows or blemishes on my skin. It is Stella 2.0, a different version entirely.

When I've finished, the skin tone is even, the eyes darkened and defined. Even the scar under my eyes is somewhat camouflaged. I try to look at myself as a stranger would, wondering if they'd be able to see past the layer of tinted paste to the fractured person beneath. Would they see what I see – someone still alien – or would they see a woman who is almost ordinary? A little swollen, a little scarred, but otherwise just another face in the crowd.

I should stop focusing on my face. My recovery requires a *holistic approach*, and to that end I ordered a new exercise bike. They delivered it yesterday. Not Evgeni, he doesn't do that kind of thing. It was two men – my mother might have called them 'burly' or 'strapping', perhaps. They staggered in with their grunts and puffs and 'Where d'ya want it, love?' then even set it up for me in the back room, looking out over the garden. I have to exercise. Physical therapy is part of my rehabilitation and I need to build up my stamina. I cycled a few kilometres just now. Not bad for someone who only leaves the house for hospital appointments, and even then it's in an Uber, door to door.

It's the small things I miss. Getting that paper, or a pint of milk. I know I did it just to get out of the house, but I quite enjoyed it. It made me feel connected to the world, as if I were a small part of it, not someone locked away in an ivory tower, a strange-looking Rapunzel, without all the hair. Everything just comes to me now.

I particularly miss going to the library. It's not just about the books, is it? It's a place to go, for the sake of going. Mums with toddlers, the elderly, all kinds of people sitting at a table spread with the day's newspapers. A blind man used to come to my local library. He was there almost every time I went, and he navigated it expertly, the ball of his cane rolling over the polypropylene carpet tiles leading the way to the desk, where the staff knew him by name. It seemed as though the landscape of that library was as familiar to him as his home.

I used to read a lot when Mum was bad. You might think it was escapism, but I didn't even try to escape. I confronted it head on. Know thy enemy, Connie. That's what I thought. I read every book about memory and dementia that I could find. I wish I'd stopped there, but that's not all of Sun Tzu's advice, is it? It's *Know your enemy, and know yourself.* It was when I tried to know myself that I really got into trouble.

I used to think of memory as something that either worked or didn't. In the same way that the heart beats or is still. I thought there was nothing between remembering and not remembering. I didn't know how flawed memory can be. How it misleads us, tricks us, so that even we don't know what's real any more. One of the books I read was called *The Seven Sins of Memory* by Daniel Schacter. It's all about how memory lapses in all of us. Not just the misplaced spectacles, and the words on the tip of your tongue, but how we distort our own past, remember things that never happened, mistake fantasy for reality. I so desperately want to know what happened to you, Connie, and I feel so frustrated that all I can glean about you is what I piece together from what I can see and read. But even if we could sit down together and talk for hours, I would still see only a version of you. Your life according to you. The narrative you have recorded because it fits your perception of yourself and the people around you.

Trips to the supermarket. That's another thing I oddly miss. Not trips with my mother, though. They were hard. In fact, the next thing I remember happening after the Victoria-sponge incident, when she couldn't recall the word for a whisk, was in a supermarket. I didn't think much of it at the time, but it's only with hindsight that we see these things for the harbingers they are.

We were in the frozen-foods section, nearing the end of our shop. I always helped her with her shopping, even after I'd moved out. It wasn't an easy job. I would tread every aisle with trepidation because I just couldn't seem to get it right. If I put too much in the trolley, she would tell me I was wasting money and that it would all be spoiled by the time she got round to using it, but I also had to make sure I didn't forget anything. If I did, she might put the kettle on when we got home, then open the jar of teabags and give a conspicuous sigh. 'What a shame', she would say, 'that you didn't get me any more teabags.' Once I asked her just to write me a list, but she said she didn't know what she might like until she got there.

She hadn't made a cake since the Victoria sponge, so I suggested we get some ingredients for a Bakewell tart. She was a little reluctant, claiming it was too much for her these days, but we had already got as far as the ground almonds and raspberry jam, and she seemed happy enough. When I reached down into the freezer for a bag of petit pois, I noticed some pre-rolled shortcrust pastry so I grabbed some, thinking it might make things easier for her. When I put them in the trolley, the peas landed flatly over a cylinder of Goldfish and Coldwater Flake Food.

'What's this?' I asked, pulling the tub from under the peas' icy embrace.

She studied it for a moment. 'Fish food.'

'Yes, but you don't have any fish.'

She looked cross, as if annoyed that I'd questioned her, or at my stupidity. Then the annoyance faded and she just looked lost, like a child flummoxed by a riddle.

I put the fish flakes back on the shelf as we made our way to the checkout. I was a little annoyed, if I'm honest. I thought she was just trying to wind me up, so I put it out of my mind. Then I found something else. Another bizarre item, apropos of nothing, that I excavated from under the mountain of our shopping as I loaded it onto the conveyor-belt. I'm trying to remember what it was now, so I can tell you, but I can't because at that moment my mother spotted the shortcrust and a look of fury appeared on her face. 'Do you think I can't make my own pastry?' she said

That's the first of the seven sins of memory, you see, Connie: *absentmindedness*. I can't remember what that item was because I wasn't paying enough attention.

I thought a lot about you and your life in Dubai while I was exercising on my new bike, so when I finished, I allowed myself another look at your social media posts.

I've just found a lovely picture of you and Mark. Just the two of you. A selfie, all toothy grins and crinkly eyes. Not the most flattering picture I've seen of you, but definitely one of the happiest. You're on holiday somewhere. Not Dubai, somewhere lush and green, with mountains behind you and an impossibly blue sky. 102 likes for this one.

I've read all 43 of the comments. You have some nice friends, Connie. They have all put some variation of '*Hope you're having a wonderful time*' and/or '*Gorgeous pic!*' Some university friends have even been kind enough to point out that you and Mark have barely aged at all. Everyone seems in agreement that you thoroughly deserve a romantic week-end away, just the two of you, and that Julia and Frank are heroes for holding the fort with the children.

She's pretty, that Ruby Davey, isn't she? Her profile picture crops up everywhere on your page, and she's quite eye-catching in that elegant yoga pose on the beach, with her strappy little top and colourful leggings. I keep finding myself slowing down when I see her picture. There's a post of hers that she's tagged you in. It's a picture of a long beach and a line of houses on the other side of a narrow stretch of water. They're huge, these houses, in various shades of cream, brown and terracotta, with arching tinted windows, balconies and pillars. The kind of house you might find perched on a hilltop in Andalucía, but all squashed together in a row, with gardens falling away towards the beach, in terraces like paddy-fields. Ruby is standing in the shallow water grinning, arm outstretched towards the houses across the water, wearing a neon-pink bikini. *The Jameses dared me to do it!* she announces in her update. But does she really have to be wearing a bikini to tell us that, Connie? What does it mean anyway? I can see it's prompted quite a discussion in the comments, which I suppose I'll have to read to find out. I'm scrolling down to see what you have to say, but you haven't posted any reply at all, even though she tagged you. Strange. Mark has, though. He says, 'That's not how I remember it!' with a rolling-on-the-floor-laughing emoji. Ruby's left him a string of emojis in return, which are hard to decipher, but I think mean that she finds the whole thing extremely funny.

I suppose she thinks she's being cute, but it all seems a little attention-seeking to me.

CONNIE

Connie steps out of the sliding doors onto a patio suffused with golden light. November has brought warm, balmy evenings, a perfect few weeks that mark the tipping point between the ferocious summer and chill winter nights. It's almost seven o'clock, and Connie has a glass of wine in her hand, which she places carefully on the table while she brushes the dust off the cushion of the outdoor chair before she sits down.

This is a delicate time of day, made for sipping aperitifs that make your head spin on an empty stomach, and chasing the last of the sun round the garden as it slowly sinks in the sky, leaving behind an evening luminous with anticipation. How long is it since she's done this? Her children swallowed this hour whole when they were babies, and they show no sign of relinquishing it. For eight years, she has spent this precious moment of transformation kneeling on a bathmat, filling the tub with water and making up amusing voices for bobbing plastic ducks, wrapping damp bodies, stuck all over with tufts of bubbles, in towels. Getting milk and a biscuit, then reading stories with a child in the crook of each arm, warm and fragrant in their clean pyjamas.

She takes a sip of her wine, its gooseberry freshness an almost guilty thrill. When she had called a slightly weary 'Bath time!' to the children earlier, Rosamie had appeared and said, 'You are going out tonight, madam. I will do it.' At first she had resisted, but Rosamie was already shepherding

Ben towards the bathroom, Alice skipping along beside her, singing, 'Rosmee, Rosmee, Rose-ah-meee!' Four hours of the school fair that morning had left her with little enthusiasm for a chaotic bath time, and it wasn't as if Mark – who was taking a shower – was going to do it.

It takes her a few moments to relax, eight years of relentless routine present in every layer of her, like the writing in a stick of rock. She turns her face towards the setting sun, letting it warm her skin.

I hope everything's okay, she thinks. Perhaps she should pop up and check. It's strangely silent up there. Alice always sings in the bath and Ben usually complains. Then an awful thought surges into her mind on a little wave of guilt and blame. Wasn't there some horrific case of two children killed in the bath by the nanny? In New York, wasn't it? She tries to contain the thought, but it's already fogging her brain, smothering the glimmer of her earlier enjoyment. Why was Rosamie so keen to bath them, anyway?

Then she hears Alice scream. Not her usual attention-seeking wail, but a piercing cry of real alarm. Connie scrambles up from the chair and runs back inside.

'*Mummeeeee!*'

Alice's cry makes her take the stairs two at a time. With each leap she berates herself. How could she have left her children with someone she barely knows? She's already imagining Julia's face, so sad and sympathetic, but at the same time judging her. *Qualifications, Connie! And did this girl even have any references?*

When she reaches the door of the children's bathroom, her hand is trembling as she pushes it wide open, her heart thudding in her chest to the same relentless rhythm, *how could you, how could you, how could you?*

Alice is sitting on top of the closed loo seat, hugging her knees with her eyes screwed shut. Rosamie is bending over the bathtub with her flip-flop in her hand, slapping it repeatedly over the plughole. 'Wah!' she exclaims, straightening. 'That *ipis* fast!'

'Is it gone, Mummy? Please tell me it's gone!' Alice has opened her eyes but is still balled like a woodlouse.

'He dead, nasty little *ipis*,' says Rosamie, beaming.

Connie struggles to contain her own revulsion as she peers at the cockroach lying upturned in the bath, long antennae still forlornly waving, hairy legs twitching. Connie spools reams of loo paper round her hand.

'I'll, um, just get rid of it, shall I?' she says, reaching out with her toilet paper glove towards the insect.

'Crush him good,' advises Rosamie. 'Otherwise he coming back tomorrow.'

Adrian, who is a good ten years older than Ruby, is wearing loafers with tassels, and chino-style pink shorts. He has popped the collar of his polo shirt. The meal is finished and she is sitting opposite him, wondering what to talk about next. Before tonight, she had barely exchanged more than a few words with Ruby's husband. They have covered his work (something to do with private equity, or maybe hedge funds, he definitely mentioned those) and the kids (he was a bit vague, been very busy at work these past few weeks). He seems an odd fit, this rather monosyllabic man, with her charismatic friend.

Connie tunes into Mark and Ruby's conversation, hoping she and Adrian can join in. Mark is telling Ruby that his favourite movie of all time is *The Shawshank Redemption*, when Connie knows it's actually *Animal House*.

Ruby gasps. 'I love *Shawshank*! It's such an incredible study of male friendship.'

Before Mark can come up with a response, Ruby notices Connie looking over. 'One last bottle?' she says, pulling Adrian's nice little Chablis out of the ice bucket.

'Umm . . .' Connie hesitates.

'Why not?' says Ruby. 'It's not as if you have to get back for the babysitter. And it's Saturday tomorrow! You don't even need to get up with the kids. Rosamie can do it.'

Ruby is right. Rosamie has solved all their problems. They have live-in twenty-four-hour babysitting and could spend Saturday morning nursing a hangover for as long as they wanted, just like before they had kids. There wasn't a single reason not to drink a bottle of wine each and stay up chatting until 5 a.m. Except . . . Connie wasn't sure she *wanted* to. She'd rather skip the next bottle and go swimming with Ben and Alice tomorrow morning instead.

But Mark has already taken the wine from Ruby and is busy twisting the corkscrew. 'You're right about *Shawshank*,' he's saying to her. 'It's just so refreshing to watch a film with strong male leads that doesn't involve car chases or robots.'

'Or boobs!' Ruby laughs and holds out her glass for Mark to fill.

Only Ruby and Mark drink the Chablis. Adrian has poured himself a whisky and, suddenly, he's like a different man, animatedly telling Connie why he only ever drinks Macallan. Somehow, at some point, Connie has stopped enjoying herself.

Then Ruby gets up.

'Let's go for a swim!' she says.

TEN

STELLA

I've been sitting here so long my computer has gone into sleep mode, but I'm still staring at it. There's a face reflected back at me in shades of black and grey. Behind this silhouette the kitchen window is vaulted squares of bluish light, appearing cathedral-like in this little image of my life.

There are no lollipop sticks, no forced expressions, no trying to paint a smile on this mouth as if it were lipstick. Just features in repose. I imagine that this is what mothers might do when they first gaze on the face of their newborn, looking at every crease and fold, travelling the unique landscape of cheek and brow with a fingertip touch. Except there is no love here, no wonder, no promise of future beauty unfurling from the crumpled skin. Nevertheless, like a mother, I'm looking for an identity. I want to find a feature and claim ownership of it. A father's nose, perhaps, or a grandmother's chin. Or even just the blend of my ancestors that I used to be. Uniquely myself.

It is a face, but it isn't *my* face.

One of the eyelids droops a little more than the other, giving me a near-permanent wink. I am almost an emoji: *winking face*. I stick my tongue out, *winking face with tongue*. It's almost funny, but this face never smiles.

Do you know what one of my first memories was in the hospital after I came out of the ICU? It was the smell of toast, before I even opened my eyes. It must have been breakfast time as I could hear the squeak of the trolley wheels over the polished floor, the clank of trays and the gurgle of tea filling cups. But it wasn't the sounds that struck me, it was the smells. Not just the toast, but the astringent burn of medical lotions cutting through the earthy smells of cloistered humanity, all suddenly as potent to me as smelling salts. And then there was the shocking intimacy of it, the inside of my cheeks now slippery smooth against my probing tongue. You think your face is about the way you look, but that's just the surface. It's about every smell you've ever smelt, every word you've ever spoken and every kiss you've ever had.

On this face, there is a tiny scar, just beneath the lower lip. I didn't notice it at first, but as the swelling subsided and the wounds healed, it began to strike me as odd to have a scar there, so I asked them what it was. I am *immunosuppressed* now, Connie. They wouldn't risk leaving a mole on this face, not when they could just take it off.

In the hospital there was a little library and no prizes for guessing which book I chose: *Frankenstein*. It was meant to be ironic, some of the doctors even laughed, but that was how I felt lying there. I was not myself, but something created. I existed only because of the very limits of someone else's vision of what might, one day, be possible.

I reach for the mouse, then hesitate. If I touch it, this face will disappear. For once it is not my computer screen that will give me the answers.

It's time. It's finally time to know.

Mark's letter is in the kitchen drawer. It looks so ordinary lying there, jumbled together with carefully folded plastic bags, scissors, odd buttons and tangles of string. My mother's collection of Things That Might Come In Handy. I bring the letter to the kitchen table and open it again. You and Mark observe me from your photograph, pinned to the fridge door with my mother's Princess Di fridge magnet. I don't read Mark's letter – I know it by heart already. It's the other envelope I'm looking for.

Open if you want to know more.

I don't know why I didn't open it immediately, why I couldn't face the knowledge that must be inside. I think it was because there are some things that, deep down, we know to be true, but don't want confirmed. Like a husband's affair, perhaps. Or my mother's illness. For months I lived in a limbo of my own creation. I knew there was something profoundly wrong, but I didn't take her to the doctor, as if it was the diagnosis, not the symptoms, that would make it real. There is something about writing things down, isn't there? We can deny what our intuition is telling us, but there is no ignoring something when it's written down in front of you, in black and white.

I open the envelope. I was right, there is a document inside: a poor-quality photocopy, slightly blotchy but legible. Only too legible.

A death certificate is like a story: it has a beginning, a middle and an end. We become defined by the moment we enter the world, and the very minute we leave it. In between there is only 'occupation'. I am a little saddened to see that someone has put 'homemaker'. It doesn't seem right, given what I know of your career. In terms of the beginning, I can see that you're one year older than me. When you died you had just turned thirty-nine, the age I am now. We have almost the same birthday, both Geminis. Celestial twins.

Lower down there is a box. I don't want to look, but there it is:

1(a) Disease or condition directly leading to death: Diffuse Axonal Injury.

This means nothing to me so I have to look up what diffuse axonal injury is.

It's a blunt trauma to the brain.

Three likely causes.

A fall.

A car accident.

Or an assault.

I saw an article once about the concept of twin flames. I can't remember what I was reading, some magazine in the dentist's waiting room most likely. I don't usually go in for that kind of thing, but I was quite taken by the idea that a soul could split into two and land in different bodies. Everyone is meant to have a twin flame. They are the other half of your soul, someone who will completely alter the course of your life and help you become the highest possible version of yourself. You just need to find them first, but when you do, your opposing energies are supposed to unite. Perhaps we're not twins, but opposites. I am yin to your yang. You were perfect on the outside, left untarnished by what happened to you, but on the inside, you had gone. Inside me there was the same warm rush of blood there is inside anyone, but the surface was damaged, smashed, like I really was made of glass. But we are not conflicting forces, we are complementary. In ancient philosophy there can never be light without darkness. That's the tragedy of you and me.

I finished *Frankenstein* before I left the hospital. A single line has stayed with me ever since: *It is true, we shall be monsters, cut off from all the world; but on that account we shall be more attached to one another.*

Mary Shelley could have written that about us, Connie. It's almost like I don't need the rest of the world.

I have you.

CONNIE

Now she thinks about it, she can't actually remember when they last had sex. She racks her brain, going back over the last weekend, then the one before. Not that long ago, surely. Out of the corner of her eye she glances at her husband, lying on the sun-lounger next to hers. He used to run when they lived in London, pounding canal towpaths and tracks through sprawling parks for hours. In Dubai, it's 'too hot' to run. Too hot for everything. Too hot to pump your own petrol, too hot to wash your own car, clean your own house, walk anywhere. There are maids to clean for you, gardeners to garden, and drivers to drive you to your Friday brunch. All you can eat, all you can drink. This lifestyle has written itself into the subtle changes to their bodies. Mark's belly has started to look . . . not fat exactly but *inflated*. As if he has been pumped up with a bicycle pump. Sometimes, when they make love, she has the sensation of rolling round on top of a barrel.

She laughs at the thought, then turns it into a cough. Mark looks round and smiles eagerly at her, misinterpreting her wry humour for a thaw in the icy relations that have existed between them since last night.

'Ben's swimming has really come on,' he says, with the forced brightness of a waiter in an American diner.

Their son has just surfaced from retrieving a dive stick with a shark's head. Alice is gripping the sides of a huge inflatable ring in the shape of a pink flamingo and spinning round and round. It hurts Connie's eyes just to watch her, and she didn't even drink that much last night.

Ben swims to the edge of the pool, bug-eyed in his goggles, and tosses the dive stick at Mark, sprinkling them both with pungently chlorinated water. 'Throw it again, Daddy!' he gasps, getting his breath back.

And Mark does, sitting up on the lounger and drawing his arm back for his best throw. See? Who says he has a hangover?

Ben inhales, grabs his nose, then sinks under the water, while Alice kicks over to another little girl playing on the wide pool steps with a plastic watering can. Mark flops back onto his lounger.

'How long are you going to keep this up, Connie?

She doesn't answer, just stares ahead at a myna bird stabbing with its bright yellow beak at the remains of a grasshopper.

The night before, Ruby and Mark had decided to swim across the narrow stretch of sea that separates the Frond Ruby's villa is on from the next.

'I dare you!' Ruby had said, already changed, holding out a pair of Adrian's swimming trunks to Mark. Her cheeks were flushed with excitement, or maybe wine.

'You're too bloody drunk, you fools,' Adrian had grumbled from behind the whisky bottle. He was checking the label so he could tell Connie exactly which distillery it had come from.

'Okay, you're on,' Mark had replied, grabbing the trunks from Ruby. A moment later, they were both off down the beach, laughing as they stepped into the water. 'It's so cold!' Ruby had exclaimed, as she breast-stroked into an ocean black as treacle.

'Is what they're doing dangerous?' Connie asked Adrian.

'Probably.'

'Maybe we should—'

'Stop them? I've given up trying to stop my wife doing anything.'

There was something about the way his words fell flat onto the table between them that made Connie search his face to interpret them. But Adrian's expression was dead-pan, muted by whisky and resignation.

In a few minutes, Mark and Ruby had reached the other side and were sitting next to each other at the edge of the water where it laps the beach. Connie could hear them talking but couldn't make out what they were saying. Then Ruby laughed, and the laugh bounced across the water, silvery and delicate as moonlight. They're not actually doing anything wrong, Connie tried to tell herself, but something about the scene felt threatening.

'You know what really bothers me?'

Mark sighs, and visibly sags on his lounger.

'You didn't even ask me if I wanted to do it with you.'

'What?' splutters Mark. 'First you're angry I did it, now you wish I'd asked you to do it?'

'No, I didn't *want* to do it. I wanted to be *asked* to do it.'

Mark leans forward and presses his fingertips against his forehead. His eyes are closed. '*Okaaay,*' he says slowly.

'It was like I didn't even exist. You barely spoke to me all night, and neither did Ruby. You were too busy chatting about books and films and blah, blah, blah, leaving me to talk to Adrian – who's the dullest man alive, in case you didn't know, having never actually spoken to him yourself – then suddenly, you're both half naked and skipping off down the beach together!'

'Half naked? Oh, come on!'

'Well, why didn't you ask if I wanted to swim?'

He is silent for a moment, then, 'Honestly, Con?'

She doesn't stop him, so he carries on.

'I knew you'd never do anything like that.'

'What d'you mean?'

'Well, you never . . .'

'Never what?'

Mark takes a deep breath and pauses. Connie can almost see the words being carefully lined up in his mind before he releases them. 'You don't really like doing . . . anything risky, do you? I don't mean stupid stuff, just things that are a little bit . . . daring.'

Connie doesn't respond, silently adding this to her collection of objectionable things her husband has said to her.

'I mean,' Mark starts to flounder, 'if I'd tried to get you to come, you would have started to go on about jellyfish, or stomach cramps or, I dunno, maybe a stingray. I thought it would be better for the two of us to go. Sometimes I just want to do something and not think about it too much.'

The two of them? That has a nice ring to it.

'Mummy, watch me!' Alice has scrambled out of the pool, and scampered with flat wet feet over to where her parents are sitting. She leaps back into the water clutching her flamingo and spins round, grinning as her mother gives her a clap.

'Well,' says Connie, quietly to Mark, 'sorry I'm so dull. Guess I'm just too busy being a mum to do all these *daring* things.'

Mark shakes his head, staring out into the middle distance. 'I'm going in the pool,' he says, climbing off the sun-lounger.

Connie watches as the myna bird squawks and dives round a hollow in a tree. That's what those birds do, she thinks. They find a nest that another bird has made, then drive away the mother bird.

ELEVEN

STELLA

I tried writing a romance once. It was set in Regency London, and the male protagonist was called Rafe. I thought Rafe was an excellent choice of name because it sounds a bit like 'rake' and all the best heroes in historical romances are rakes, aren't they? The heroine was called Scarlett because she was a beautiful, feisty redhead. It had carriages and parasols and dashing officers fresh from the Napoleonic Wars. I must have been about seventeen when I wrote it, which was probably the right age. I needed a certain naivety to write a romance. I had to believe in that happy ending. Either that, or be like my mother, and create the happy ending you never had in the closing pages of sixty-six books.

I wanted to show my novel to my mother. I had spent seventeen years trying to make her proud of me and nothing had seemed to work. I knew I wasn't as pretty or popular as she had been at school, and I couldn't dance or perform like her either. I saw my own mediocrity reflected back at me every day in my mother's resigned sighs and little comments. It became increasingly obvious that I was not someone *destined for better things*. I remember trying on a dress in a shop when I was about fifteen. There was some dance, or disco, at school and she was actually letting me go. It was such a lovely dress, one-shouldered in dark teal with a fitted bodice and full skirt. I couldn't believe how grown-up I looked. Not a gauche girl, folding in on herself all the time, but someone else entirely, as if I were *revealed* by that dress, instead of covered by it. I undid my ponytail and the hair fell out over my shoulders and softened my face. I was so busy looking at the person I had become that it took me a moment to notice my mother had come into the changing room and was standing beside me, looking at our reflections.

'What d'you think, Mum?' I asked her, a little breathless.

'We'll keep it in mind.'

'Don't you like it?'

'It's lovely,' she said. 'I'm just not sure it's quite right . . . on you.'

'Why not? I think I look nice.' My voice was fading then, becoming quieter with every word, as if I were beginning to doubt what I saw right in front of me.

'I do admire the way you don't care what people think,' she said, 'but I couldn't let you go to the party like that. It wouldn't be fair. Pop that off and I'll find you something else.'

She left me then to slip that beautiful dress off my shoulder and step out of it. I felt like I was letting go of something, a would-be Cinderella divested of her beautiful gown. I was standing in my underwear when she stepped back round the curtain with a long dress on a hanger that she held up in front of me, right under my chin. It was a peachy colour in shiny material, with huge puff sleeves.

I wanted to cry.

'Oh, Stella,' she said, 'you'd be pretty if you just smiled.'

In the end I didn't go to the dance. Instead, I stayed at home with my mother. She baked a two-layer carrot cake, with pecans and cream-cheese frosting. 'There you go,' she said, as we settled down in front of the telly. 'Here's an extra slice.'

I ran out of ways to be the daughter I thought she wanted me to be. Then it occurred to me that the way to impress a writer might be to write. You cannot talk to the nightingale, Connie, you have to sing. So sing I did. One hundred and twenty-three handwritten pages of Regency romance.

I didn't show it to her first. I told myself I shouldn't waste my mother's time with nonsense, but, really, I was desperately afraid that she might not think it was any good. So the first person to read it was my English teacher, Mrs McCarthy. Everything about Mrs McCarthy was soft and curved, from her round glasses and her little suede pumps to the way she pronounced *homophone* with an Irish lilt. She took me to one side after the lesson and handed the bundle of papers back to me. 'You've done us proud with this, Stella,' she told me, putting her hand on my arm and giving it a little squeeze. 'Keep going with it, won't you?' That made me think she was telling the truth, that she really did like it.

People don't usually touch you when they lie to you, do they?

I skipped home from school that day. My mother was in the kitchen when I got back. I told her all about my book and what Mrs McCarthy had said. All the while I was telling her, she just kept peeling potatoes in long, deliberate strokes. Then she stopped and wiped her hands on a tea-towel.

'She's probably not even read it,' she said, turning round. 'Most teachers barely read homework, let alone novels written by pupils. She'd have said anything to stop you pestering her.'

That whole evening, she barely spoke to me. She went to bed early, and when I popped my head round her door to say goodnight, she didn't look up from her book.

'Is everything okay, Mum?' There was always a sick, twisty feeling in my stomach when I had to ask her this, because it was always something I'd done.

Then she told me. It was very hurtful, she said, that I had preferred Mrs McCarthy to her. She was humiliated that Mrs McCarthy's opinion was more important to me than hers, even when (by then) she'd written nineteen books of her own.

She was right, of course. It *was* disrespectful of me not to have shown it to her first. The next day I picked some sweet peas from the garden and put them in a vase on her desk, alongside my Regency romance, with *Sorry Mum* written at the top of the first page.

She never said a word to me about that book to the day she died.

I don't know why I'm even telling you all this, Connie. I think it's because I saw a picture of your son performing in a school concert. You'd written, *Move over, Louis Armstrong!* I agree, it's quite something to be playing the trumpet at such a young age. I'm sure you'll have told him how talented he is, and how proud of him you are.

There's one more thing I want to tell you. Something a little bit odd. After years of writing contemporary novels, my mother suddenly announced that she was going to try her hand at historical romance. I think this one turned out to be novel number twenty-four. It was called *The Lieutenant's Scandal* and it was about a young soldier, just returned from the Battle of Waterloo, who thinks he can never love again after all the terrible things he's seen in the war. That is, until he meets Scarlett, the admiral's wayward but captivating daughter . . .

He was called Rafe, that handsome lieutenant.

It wasn't actually my mother's fault, though, Connie. It was *cryptomnesia*. That's another of the Seven Sins of Memory. We have an idea that we genuinely believe is our own when actually it's something we've already read or heard about, perhaps years before. My mother didn't deliberately steal my idea. Rafe and Scarlett must have been lurking somewhere in her brain, and when she needed to think of a new storyline for her next novel, her mind offered up this stored memory as if it were completely original. It's part of the sin of *misattribution*. The memory is correct, it's just that the source is wrong.

That must be the explanation for what my mother did, because the alternative is that Mrs McCarthy was right.

My book *was* good.

Thou shalt not succeed. Or, at least, thou shalt not be better at anything than I am. That's the holy grail of the narcissistic mother.

God forbid I would ever have tried to bake a cake.

CONNIE

To the left of her mobile phone, which she is holding up in front of her, Connie can see Mrs Lane glaring at her. Ben's form teacher is marshalling a group of jittery eight-year-olds up onto the stage. Connie lowers her phone, having followed Mrs Lane's pointed stare to the school's *No pictures during school performances* sign. Still, she managed just one before she buckled under Mrs Lane's disapproval. She has a quick look at it before the morning's recital starts.

It was important, Mark and Connie had decided, for their children to learn a musical instrument so they had taken Ben and Alice to a music shop. Instead of thumping the keys of a piano, or grabbing an electric guitar, Ben had taken a brassy yellow trumpet off the stand and held it aloft, the curved bell rising, like a sun, to eclipse his face. *Maybe something easier to learn?* Connie had suggested, steering him towards the recorders, but Ben had been adamant: it was the trumpet or nothing. Now there he was, captured on her phone, waiting at the back of the stage, hair sticking up, eyes bright with excitement, clutching his new trumpet in front of him like a Yeoman Guard. Connie uploads the photo and quickly types, 'Move over . . .' Move over who? What *was* the name of that famous trumpet player?

'It's starting,' hisses Liz, sitting next to her, as Freddie walks to the front of the stage and begins to bash out 'All Things Bright and Beautiful' on the glockenspiel. Connie mutes her phone and slips it into her bag, feeling a little smug.

Liz's boys are on the A team for every sport, but from the opening bars it looks like their musical ability might not match their sporting prowess.

There follows a rendition of 'Amazing Grace' on the violin from a little girl in Ben's class, and a grade-one piano performance from a boy she recognizes as one of the few winners on the coconut shy. How did they get so good, so young? wonders Connie. She glances at Ben, who is beginning to look nervous, clutching his music sheet so tightly it has crumpled. When the school had emailed the parents and asked if they wanted their child to perform in the year-four music recital during morning assembly, Connie hadn't hesitated. *Of course* she wanted to watch Ben show off his new talent. Admittedly, she didn't often hear him practise, and her negotiations to exchange playing the trumpet for screen time were often unsuccessful, but the lessons had been going well.

Hadn't they?

Ben comes to the centre of the stage. The air-conditioning cannot compete with the crush of doting parents and fidgety children. Under the stage lights Ben's skin takes on an amphibian gleam. Mrs Lane tiptoes across the stage and places the music stand in front of him, giving it a quick push down to its lowest height. Connie feels suddenly protective of her firstborn, as he puts his music on the stand and sticks a slightly chubby finger into the slide ring.

'I will be playing "Happy Birthday",' announces Ben, in a small voice swallowed by the rustling of restless parents, only really interested in hearing their own child play.

Ben raises the trumpet and places his fingers on the valves. Connie finds that she's holding her breath, that her heart is beating its own skittish rhythm of apprehension for her son at his first musical performance, in front of his year group and their parents.

Seconds tick by, measured out by a clock on the wall with Arabic numerals. Ben lowers the trumpet, swaps his fingers onto different valves, then raises it again. If the school gym, with its makeshift stage and foldaway chairs, hadn't been silent before, it certainly is now. It's the kind of silence that people pay attention to, a cavernous silence that grows with every second that isn't filled with the simple melody of 'Happy Birthday'.

G, says Connie, in her head, it starts with G. She wants to mouth it to Ben, but then it would look like she didn't believe in him, that she was sitting there expecting him to fail. So she finds her most confident smile and sticks it on her face, while inside she screams at herself, *Why did you think he could do this?*

Ben inhales and blows into the trumpet, pressing down hard on the valves. It emits a surprised squeak. Even the least musically inclined in the hall know that this squeak is not the first note of 'Happy Birthday'.

Mr Silva, the music teacher (and giver of expensive trumpet lessons), decides to intervene. He arranges Ben's fingers on the correct valves, then purses his lips together and pulls back the muscles of his face into an odd rictus. Ben nods miserably at him.

Then 'Happy Birthday' begins to emerge as a reluctant, shrill flatulence, which Ben forces out with hamster cheeks and eyes screwed tight shut against the indignity of it all. In her head, Connie sings along to the halting notes with the familiar refrain of eight years of birthdays. Eight cakes made, eight presents given, eight parties organized for her adorable, perfect little boy.

When it's finished, Liz leans in towards Connie, who is clapping furiously. 'Gosh,' she says, 'I'm glad Freddie didn't choose the trumpet.'

Connie makes a quick exit from the sports hall, not wanting to stand around in a group of parents hearing all about how their talented child has been invited to audition for the Juilliard School or, worse, enduring their sympathy. She is almost at her car when she sees that Ruby has parked alongside her. Apart from a thank-you-for-having-us text, she hasn't been in touch with Ruby since the night they went over to dinner. Ruby had replied to the text suggesting a coffee, but Connie hadn't got round to responding. At the recital, she had turned right as she walked down the aisle of chairs and taken a seat next to Liz, rather than seek out Ruby.

Connie gets into her car and digs about in her bag, looking for her mobile. As she retrieves it, Ruby's face appears, framed by the car window. Ruby grins and makes the motion of winding down an old-fashioned car window. Connie swings open the car door and swivels round to face her.

'I absolutely *loved* Ben's individual interpretation of such a classic,' Ruby says, and her smile is so genuine that Connie cannot help laughing.

'Well, he has only just started learning . . .'

'Exactly. Even Louis Armstrong had to start somewhere.'

Of course! Louis Armstrong, that's who she was trying to think of.

'Listen,' continues Ruby, suddenly more serious, 'is everything okay? It's just I haven't seen much of you since the other night.'

Connie shifts in her seat. The morning sun is climbing higher, and her legs are sticking to the leather. Even wearing sunglasses, Ruby shields her eyes with her hand as she leans on Connie's car door. In the face of the uncompromising glare, and Ruby's frank question, Connie's reaction to what happened begins to seem a bit petty. She tries to think of an excuse for why she's been too busy for that coffee, but Ruby saves her.

'I'm really sorry, Connie. Adrian told me after you left how *inappropriate* I'd been. I blame the wine. And Adrian, actually.'

'Adrian?'

Ruby sighs and rakes her raised hand through her hair, scrunching it on top of her head. 'He's just so straight about everything. Sometimes I think I do these things just to get a reaction out of him. D'you know what I mean?'

'Hmm,' says Connie. 'I did think he was quite different from you. But opposites attract and all that.'

Ruby shakes her head. 'He didn't used to be. I don't know

how he got so middle-aged so soon. He really wasn't like that before the kids . . . and the responsibilities . . . and the all-important hedge funds . . .'

'And the whisky?' asks Connie.

'Oh, God, he wasn't banging on about whisky, was he?'

'Only for an hour or so.'

They giggle like schoolgirls. Then Ruby straightens and lets go of Connie's car door. 'I've got to run, but maybe we can meet up for a coffee soon, just us this time.'

'That would be lovely,' says Connie.

She shuts the car door and starts the engine. She ought to call Mark to let him know how the recital went. She unlocks her phone and it opens to the picture of Ben and her half composed post. Her first impulse is to delete it, as if Ben's performance wasn't good enough to share, but actually she'd never felt more proud of her son than when she'd watched him persevere and finish the piece, in the face of a shaky start and a hundred judging parents. She types in the rest of the caption and posts the picture.

Ruby is the first to like it. She replies, 'Go, Ben!' with a row of clappy hands.

TWELVE

STELLA

Mrs Wilson from across the road, who has perfected the art of Meaning Well, is coming over for a cup of tea today. I'm not sure why we're finally having it. Perhaps it takes a catastrophe to make us all wonder what we could have done differently. I've been avoiding it for months, but then she popped a card through my door, signed by all the neighbours, and it felt churlish to refuse after that. She'll be here in a few minutes, so I ought to take off the 'diaphanous tulle' gown I have on. The editor's notes on Net-a-Porter promised a 'voluminous silhouette', and they weren't wrong. It's glorious. A lace bodice with a full skirt – reams of black tulle. When I walk, the different layers lift and separate round me, almost as if I'm swimming through the deepest depths of the ocean.

I'd love to wear it for my cup of tea with Mrs Wilson, but if I open the door in this, she might not come again, so I undo the zip and let it drop from my shoulders. It settles on the floor, like an enormous puffy soufflé, and suddenly I'm a peacock transformed into a peahen, stripped of my plumage. There is nothing to distract the eye from exactly what I am, and what I look like. Not a single flash of diamanté, or sequin sparkle, so I pick up the grey army blanket crumpled on the carpet and drape it back over the full-length mirror, where it belongs.

I bought a lemon drizzle cake to have today and Mrs Wilson is nudging a slice onto her plate. 'What about you, dear?' she asks, but I shake my head. First, I don't eat in front of anybody. Second, I have not eaten a single mouthful of cake since I first moved out of my mother's house. This seems to put her off eating her own slice, and she rests my mother's bone-handled pastry fork on her plate and puts it down.

We're sitting in the living room, perched on the edge of opposing sofas, either side of the fireplace. I know everyone entertains in their kitchens, these days, but my mother simply would not have allowed it. The shop-bought cake was indignity enough.

Mrs Wilson's sofa faces the large window looking out onto the south-west-facing garden; mine faces the door. It's polite to give a guest the nice view, and I always sit with the light behind me. It's late October and each afternoon pulls the sun lower in the sky.

'The tea's ready,' I say, picking up the pot and giving it a swirl.

'Lovely,' says Mrs Wilson, sliding her cup and saucer towards me over the coffee-table. She's trying to have a good look at me, I know she is, but as she leans forward the autumn sun catches her eyes and makes her squint.

I pour the tea, trying to think what to say next. The things we *aren't* talking about are so huge, so significant, that trying to talk round them is like skirting a boulder at the top of a cliff face.

Mrs Wilson leans back so the sun isn't in her eyes and looks past me towards the garden, taking a tentative sip of tea. That's another reason I wanted her to sit there: it gives her something else to focus on.

'Your asters are still doing well, aren't they?' she remarks. 'So lovely to have some autumn colour in the garden.' She uses the word 'lovely' a lot. Everything is 'lovely' and, often 'super' as well.

'My mother loved the autumn asters,' I say.

Actually, she didn't particularly, but someone had to mention her. Mrs Wilson gives a little startle, as if she bumped right into that boulder. She places the teacup carefully back on the table.

'I'm so sorry,' she says finally.

'What about?' I'm not going to make this easy for her.

I don't think she actually means my mother dying. They only met once, after all. As soon as that single gunshot blew our world apart, they took my mother straight into a nursing home, to be looked after by professional carers. The same professionals who should have been looking after her in the first place. It wasn't long before she caught pneumonia. When she died I was in my specialist centre so, in the absence of any other close relatives or friends, all the grim *arrangements* fell to death administration. I had nothing to do with it.

'I feel I could have done more, Stella.'

Probably.

'What d'you mean, Mrs Wilson?'

'Pamela, please. I mean, I could have offered you more support. Honestly, though, I had no idea how hard it was for you . . . in here.' She glances around her, as if the problem lay in the swirls and flowers of the William Morris-style wallpaper or was reflected in the polished green tiles under the surround of the dark wood mantelpiece. 'That morning I came over after I first moved in,' she says, lifting her eyes to mine and waiting for a sign I remember (of course I do – how could I forget?), 'I saw how . . .' she pauses then, searching for a suitable word, '. . . *challenging* her behaviour was. It's just that you always looked like you were coping so well.'

I wasn't, though, Pamela. I wasn't coping at all.

Then she looks straight at me. It's an involuntary thing. She's asking me to absolve her, like we're the priest and the penitent. But when she does, she can see the result of her neglect staring back at her. I see her visibly swallow, and her face begins to crumple.

If in doubt, cry. We learn that as children, don't we? Honestly, looking at Mrs Wilson is like being back at my job as a reception-class teaching assistant.

'Please, don't worry,' I say.

Why is *she* the one crying?

She hasn't stopped, so I clearly haven't offered her enough reassurance. She wants to be fully absolved of her modest sins. 'There's nothing you could have done,' I add.

Her chin firms up again and she dabs under her eyes with her fingertips, although they seem pretty dry to me.

She has what she came for, so I wonder if she'll go now.

'That may be so, but I still feel I should have spotted the signs. I mean, it didn't all just come out of the blue.' She takes her lemon drizzle and settles back more comfortably into the sofa. 'Or did it?'

Ah, that's why she hasn't gone yet.

Mrs Wilson is the street's special emissary, a Trojan Horse of sympathy and concern sent to my door. Now I've let her in, their real purpose has spilled out. Simple neighbourly curiosity. They want details, Connie. Titbits to trade over fences and discuss at coffee mornings.

'I don't really remember now.'

She looks a little disappointed, but there's nothing she can say. It's the most fundamental sin of memory, after all. *Transience*, the way our recollections are not our own to keep. Memories aren't trinkets, to be collected and stored indefinitely: they're delicate as cobwebs, prone to disintegrating over time and just floating away.

Mrs Wilson nods. 'Of course you don't. No one could be expected to remember much about such a traumatic incident.' She finishes her cake, pressing at the last crumbs with the back of her fork.

'Would you like some more?' I ask her.

She eyes the cake warily, as if it harbours evil designs on her waistline. 'Maybe a smidgen,' she says, offering up her plate. I should have known that Mrs Wilson would use a word like 'smidgen'.

After a few minutes spent complaining about her next-door neighbour's planning application for a ghastly conservatory, she tells me she has to go.

'Ooh, it's getting chilly,' she says, pulling the sides of her jacket together as I open the front door. She pauses before she leaves, suddenly looking at me closely, standing in the light coming from the open door. I can see the subtle movements of her eyes as her gaze shifts from mine to the periphery of my face, tracking round the edge of it, resting momentarily on the swollen area above my cheekbones underneath the scar. Then she looks away, fiddling with the zip of her jacket, even though she is only walking across the road.

'If there's anything I can do . . .' she says, pulling the zip up to her chin and looking at me again.

Then I'm the one looking carefully at her, trying to read her expression for distress, shock or revulsion – all the things I'm used to bracing myself for – but, like Evgeni, there's nothing save a trace of something that looks like sadness or regret, but could even be sympathy.

'No, thank you, Mrs Wilson.'

Then she smiles a final goodbye. I know why she's smiling. Her trip hasn't been wasted: she's had a good look at me, after all. That alone will give them all plenty to talk about.

★

I do remember what happened, Connie.

I remember so clearly it's as if every second were a photograph, and if I flip through them fast enough, the whole scene is replayed in perfect clarity. You see, *transience* is only half the story. It's like there's a coin with heads on one side and tails on the other. For every memory we lose to transience, another sticks in our brain, like grit in a wound, and there's no getting rid of it. They call that *permanence*. These are the memories that never leave us, the ones that come back to us in the middle of the night and haunt our dreams. The petty slights and injustices of years ago, which we've never been able to let go, jostle for space in our crowded minds with the true horrors. The flashbacks, the PTSD, the memories our brains refuse to relinquish. I'll never tell the likes of Pamela Wilson what happened the day that gun went off. There's only one person I'm going to tell what really happened, and that person is you.

I collect the tea things and carry them through to the kitchen. Then I take my antibacterial spray and a cloth, and I squirt everything in the house that Mrs Wilson touched. The door handles and the table top, the little Coalport porcelain flower arrangement in the hall that she picked up and declared *quite lovely* just before she left. Then I go back into the kitchen and fill the kettle so I can wash everything in scalding water. As I'm waiting for the kettle to boil, you catch my eye from your picture on the fridge, the one with your smudgy makeup and floaty tea dress. It makes me wonder what happened to your memory of that night with Mark. Did it dissipate like smoke, or become a stain in your head that you could never scrub out, no matter how hot the water?

CONNIE

Mark looks blank. 'I don't remember.'

'You know,' prompts Connie, 'the one I wore when we went out to dinner while your parents were here.'

'What – with them?'

'No! Just us. It was date night!'

'Oh, yeah,' says Mark, but he still looks vague. 'Wear that one.'

Mark's work is holding a 'Brunch and Polo' family event at the Polo Resort and Club, and Connie is trying to decide what to wear. It's no use asking Mark, she decides. He seems not to care any more. There was a time when he would have been pleased if she'd asked him what dress she should wear. 'Wear the white one,' he might have said, 'I love that dress on you,' then grinned at her in an almost comically roguish way. But now he's sitting on the edge of the bath with a towel round his waist, cutting his toenails. Some are missing the bin.

She turns to the mirror, rewrapping her bathrobe round her and knotting the belt. 'I look old,' she says, to her reflection.

'No, you don't,' says Mark, to his toenails.

'Old*er*, then,' she murmurs, not loud enough for Mark, who's not really listening anyway, to hear.

She peers at herself more closely. With her face in complete repose she looks much as she always did. She smiles, then frowns. The little lines on her face are like tributaries:

she can alter their course with different expressions. Behind her, reflected in the mirror, Mark pads out of the en-suite to their bedroom. She puts her fingertips on her cheeks and lifts everything upwards. Almost thirty-nine. Then, after that, forty. Shit. Maybe she needs to overhaul her beauty regime, buy some new creams or something. What does Ruby use? Probably just raw organic coconut oil.

Oh, God, Ruby.

Thirty-five-year-old Ruby.

Ever since that night with Ruby and Adrian, Connie has tried to make more *effort*. It wasn't Ruby's fault that Mark gave her so much attention. Their marriage had just become a little . . . What was the word? Mechanical. As if she and her family were all just little cogs, grinding each other forward every day.

'Hey, Connie!'

It's Mark's voice from the bedroom. What is it now? Can't find his underpants?

She comes out of the en-suite and Mark is standing by the wardrobe, holding up one of her dresses on a hanger. Pale blue, with little grey swallows on it.

'You looked incredible that night,' he says, handing her the dress.

When they all get home at around 5 p.m., Ben is dressed as a pirate and Alice has a glittery butterfly wing painted round each eye. Mark flops down on the sofa and lifts his feet onto the pouffe. The kids cluster cross-legged in front of the TV screen, like little devotees. Connie picks up the remote and switches it on for them, then sits down next to Mark.

'That was fun,' Mark says, leaning his head back and closing his eyes. 'Exhausting, though. D'you think Rosamie would help with the kids? They've had so much sugar, it'll be a nightmare getting them to bed.'

'It's her day off!'

'Yeah, but it depends what you mean by "day", doesn't it? I know plenty of people who give their maids "a day" off.' He makes little quotation marks in the air with his fingers. 'Like, Thursday five p.m. to Friday five p.m. That's "a day", isn't it?'

'No, it isn't!'

Mark grins at her and puts his arm across her shoulders, draws her onto his chest. 'Christ,' he says, into her hair, 'how did I end up with someone with a social conscience, eh? I should've married a banker. Then Rosamie would be bringing me a martini, right about now.'

He chuckles and she feels his laughter rumble against her ear. He smells of the aftershave she bought him two Christmases ago, which he still saves for special occasions. There have been sticky fingerprints on his smart shirt since Alice came back from the chocolate fountain and climbed on him, and in his breast pocket is the bumpy outline of Ben's plastic eye-patch, which Mark promised to keep safe.

She pushes herself up from his chest. 'I'll make you a martini,' she says.

★

In the kitchen, Connie finds herself humming along to 'The Circle of Life' when Mark puts *The Lion King* on for the kids.

' "*Naaaaants ingonyamaaaa*," ' she sings, as she looks for the vermouth she's pretty certain they don't have.

Then she stops. There's the sound of a woman crying from the little corridor leading to the utility area. Not gentle weeping, but great gulps of distress, punctuated by urgent snatches of Tagalog. Then another voice, Rosamie's, speaking calmly, shushing her, like she would a child.

Connie walks out into the corridor, unsure what to do. From inside Rosamie's room she hears running water, followed by a high-pitched shriek. Connie knocks on Rosamie's door, and waits a moment, but there's no response. Perhaps they didn't hear her over the girl's sobs.

If someone's hurt in her house, Connie reasons, she needs to help. She knocks again, then opens the door a little and pops her head round it. 'Rosamie, what's going—'

Rosamie is standing by her sink, holding the wrist of another Filipina. She looks younger than Rosamie. Her face is blotchy and tear-stained. Strands of hair have come loose from her ponytail and hang over her eyes. She looks terrified when she sees Connie.

'Sorry for noise, madam,' says Rosamie, bleakly, shutting off the tap.

'Don't be silly, Rosamie,' says Connie, stepping round the door. 'What on earth's happened?'

Rosamie lets go of the woman's wrist. They stand there without answering, looking at the floor, like schoolgirls maintaining a conspiracy of silence. Rosamie's friend reaches up to tuck her hair behind her ear with trembling wet fingers.

'My goodness, what have you done to your hand?' Connie steps towards the girl, but she snatches her hand away. Rosamie pulls a towel from the rail and clasps her friend's hand again. The skin over the back and down towards the thumb is an angry red.

'Very bad thing happen to Marijo, madam,' she says, carefully pressing Marijo's hand dry round the damaged skin.

'Can you tell me what happened?' Connie asks, but the girl just stares at her with eyes as velvety dark as moleskin.

'Rosamie?' she tries.

Rosamie looks at her friend for permission. When Marijo gives a small nod, Rosamie tucks the towel back on the rail and takes a deep breath.

'Marijo's madam doing this,' she says, her voice quiet, almost apologetic.

'Her madam? But why? Was it an accident?'

'No accident!' exclaims Marijo. 'I ask for off day, then Madam getting angry.'

'But Friday is always an off day,' says Connie, slipping into the same idiom.

'My madam not giving rest days,' says Marijo, matter-of-factly. 'But this day I *have* to go out. My daughter is sick in Philippines, and I have to send money. Just a few hours, I tell her, but Madam shouting. Then she grab my wrist and hold it over the sink.' Marijo's face puckers at the memory, but she doesn't cry again. Instead she sniffs and sets her shoulders defiantly. 'Then pouring kettle water over me.'

At first Connie is incredulous, then sickened, as if her horror at what has happened comes from somewhere deep within her and is mixing with the lavish brunch she's just had. The Prosecco and the steak, flame grilled while you wait. The fan-tailed shrimp and a hundred pretty desserts, all berries, mirror glazes and white chocolate curls, scattered like jewels over the tables.

'You have to go to the police,' says Connie, trying to keep her voice level.

'No police. Madam kill me for sure then!'

'But your hand,' insists Connie. 'Do you need a doctor?'

Marijo holds up her hand and clasps and unclasps it. 'It's okay,' she says, giving a little shrug. 'Madam waiting too long for her tea already. Water not so hot any more.'

Then Marijo grins. A brave, wobbly smile that breaks Connie's heart.

Connie hands Mark a beer.

'Everything okay?' he asks her. 'You were gone a while.'

She's about to tell him, but he has already turned away from her, and is watching Simba explore the forbidden elephants' graveyard with the same rapt attention as the children. Something is stopping her saying the words. She knows her husband and, for all Mark's jokes, if she told him, he would leap up, demand that Rosamie tell him where

Marijo works, go over there to confront them and insist on calling the police, no matter what Marijo says.

Maybe that's exactly what they *should* do.

'Con?' He's looking at her again, half an eye on Simba and Nala.

But what if they do interfere? What can the police do if Marijo's employer just says it was an accident? And what if Marijo is right, and they punish her even more?

It's Marijo's decision as to what to do, not theirs.

'I was just looking for vermouth,' she says.

'Oh, babe.' Mark lifts his arm, inviting her to sit next to him. 'The martini was just a joke.'

'I know,' she says, curling against him. His arm tightens round her and she inhales the scent of security and home caught in the folds of his linen shirt.

THIRTEEN

STELLA

Evgeni is currently making *delivery number 15*. I am *delivery number 16*. He is approximately *15 minutes away* from me and should be with me between *10:39 a.m. and 11:39 a.m.* *Evgeni is currently running a little behind*, but it doesn't matter *because he should be with you shortly.*

I am live-tracking his progress because I enjoy watching his red van icon get closer and closer to my blue house icon. I particularly like the little circular picture of him in the top left corner of the screen. I still avoid eye contact when he knocks on the door, so this way I can have a really good look at him. I'm guessing he's Romanian. He has a widow's peak of curling dark hair falling onto his forehead, and eyebrows like pointy circumflexes above an *o*. In the picture, he is clean-shaven, but when he delivered the gown I ordered, I noticed his jaw was darkening into the beginnings of a beard. It suits him. He's smiling on my screen, but I doubt he will be when he arrives at my house. That diaphanous tulle creation he's coming to collect came in a *very* big box.

I'm not very good at waiting. Waiting creates a vacuum with nothing to fill it except pacing and drumming fingers. That's why I talk to you so often, Connie, because when my mind is empty, there's only one thing that comes to fill the space: the day it happened.

It was 20 June. Late afternoon tipping into early evening. Cool enough by then for Mrs Wilson to decide to pick up her secateurs and pop outside to cut some of the flowers from the Madame Alfred Carrière rose that arcs so prettily over her kitchen window – they smell so *lovely*, you see. It was the moment she spotted the bin and decided to put the rubbish out while she had on her nice thick gardening gloves. It was the exact second she took hold of the wheelie-bin and started dragging it up the sloping drive.

There's something I want you to think about, Connie. Would you give a liver transplant to an alcoholic? They will die without it, but if they continue to drink they will destroy the donor liver just like they destroyed their own. Maybe someone else could have had that liver. Someone with autoimmune cirrhosis, perhaps, their body suddenly gone maverick through no fault of their own. When they hand you a lifeline like that, Connie, they need to be sure you're going to make the most of it.

Dr Isabelle Clove introduced herself to me as a clinical psychologist. We met while I was at the specialist centre, just after my initial reconstruction, in one of those hospital rooms that tries very hard not to look like it's in a hospital. Comfy sofas replaced the waiting-room-style chairs, and there was a shelving unit against the wall with all the things you might find at home. Knick-knacks and a vase of flowers. Fat airport paperbacks and a little lava lamp, its globular bubbles endlessly rising and falling.

The only thing that gave it all away was the ubiquitous box of tissues on the table between us. Competent psychology professionals always have a box of tissues to hand.

Dr Clove, in her smart trousers and shiny patent brogues, did a great job of putting me at my ease. We even shared a joke or two, dashed out on my whiteboard. Then she leaned back in the sofa opposite mine and crossed her legs, resting her notebook on her lap.

'Do you really need the whiteboard?' she asked.

Yes, I scrawled.

'Would you like to try talking?'

No.

'Why not?'

Silly question, Dr Clove. My pen hovered over the board. How to begin explaining that one?

Embarrassing.

'There's no reason to feel embarrassed.' Then she leaned over and reached out, her hand closing on the edge of the board. 'Can I take it?' I felt the board beginning to slide away. I clung to it and she stopped. It was almost a cartoon moment, a Tom and Jerry push-pull. 'You really don't need to worry about talking in front of me.' Her voice was so full of compassion I almost let go.

I wanted to trust Dr Clove, but she's too beautiful to be trusted.

Where does that come from, Connie? I blame school, and all the tall, blonde, sporty girls with their flicky ponytails and delicately freckled noses. If Dr Clove and I had been at school together, I feel sure she wouldn't have picked me for her netball team. She's the girl you most wanted to like you. You know, the one who's popular but also quite kind.

Smile at me all you like, Dr Clove, but we have nothing in common.

Well, maybe one thing. Isabelle Clove is also used to people staring at her in the street. Just for all the right reasons.

'It will be much easier for me to get to know you if we can actually talk to each other,' she said. There was the tiniest tug on the whiteboard, which I resisted. 'Maybe next session,' she said, releasing it.

Okay. Maybe. Then I drew a little face on the board, two eyes with a *u* shape underneath. That was probably the last actual smile I gave anyone.

Do you know why I wouldn't give it to her? It was because I didn't *want* her to get to know me. It was her job to ask me what happened. They needed to know if I'm an alcoholic, do you see? I needed to answer carefully, have time to think. That little whiteboard condensed all the frantic thoughts in my head and distilled them into a single word, or phrase, that even a clinical psychologist would be hard pressed to read much into.

She saw that whiteboard as a barrier, but I saw it as a shield.

Maybe it wasn't that I didn't trust Dr Clove.

I didn't trust myself, and what I might confess.

11:35 a.m. Bang on time. I have to swing the door wide open to hand Evgeni the enormous box. He sighs and rests it on the mat in the porch while he taps on his little black box.

'Sign,' he says, a little wearily.

So I do, a little squiggle. I've realized that any unintelligible hieroglyph will suffice, so I've started drawing a kind of little star, for Stella. I keep hoping that Evgeni will notice, but that may be asking too much. He always has somewhere else he needs to be, a van full of parcels destined for other people. I am only ever given a few seconds of his time.

He looks a little tired. The beard is still there, but today it looks more unkempt and dishevelled than rugged and manly. I hope he's just busy, rather than coming down with something. I should let him get on, but I don't want him to go. When he reaches out to take back his black device, I keep hold of it.

'Is Evgeni a Romanian name?'

He frowns and looks at me. 'I'm Bulgarian,' he says, still holding out his hand.

'Oh,' I say, but before I can think of a suitable response, he gasps and snatches his hand back. I blink at him a moment, shocked and suddenly panicked. Just now, I let the light fall on my face and didn't turn away, but only because I felt sure by now that he didn't find me frightening to look at. I quickly hand the box back.

Then he sneezes, forcefully and wetly, all over my hand.

I shut the door without taking a single breath. Then I wash my hands three times in a row and cover them with hand sanitizer.

CONNIE

'How is Marijo?'

Rosamie is ironing in the children's playroom while they are at school. In her first week, she had taken the ironing into her own tiny room, until Connie had discovered her. 'Why are you ironing in here?' she'd exclaimed, to a pink-cheeked and sweating Rosamie, while Mark's shirts hung all around, rotating like blank factory foremen in the stuttering air-con. It took a few tries to persuade her out of that steamy box, as if ironing their clothes in front of them would be unacceptable.

'I text her,' says Rosamie, running the iron over Alice's lemon-yellow sundress. 'Nothing back yet.'

'Do you think we should go and check on her?'

Rosamie shrugs. 'She's working, madam.'

Connie bends down to pick up some kind of car, or perhaps truck, that Ben has made out of Lego, boxy, with huge wheels, and what look like missile launchers fixed to the side. She presses it back together where the bricks are coming apart.

'Who's Marijo's madam, Rosamie?'

The iron sighs a hot, cloudy breath as Rosamie sets it on the stand.

'Please don't ask me questions, madam,' she says, pulling Alice's dress off the ironing board, and folding it neatly.

'Okay, I understand.' Connie places the Lego vehicle on the children's little plastic table, then starts to pick up toys scattered over the floor. Cuddly llamas and sloths, action figures dropped and abandoned, now lying in awkward poses so that the floor resembles a crime scene. 'But they do live here, right?'

Rosamie's lips purse, and she turns to place the dress on the pile of finished laundry.

'But she got to you so quickly after her madam scalded her,' insists Connie. 'She must live on this compound.'

Rosamie reaches down and unplugs the iron, draping the cord over the ironing board. 'Yes,' she says, resigned, 'they live on this compound.'

I knew it, thinks Connie. One of her own neighbours has done this terrible thing to a girl who lives with them, probably cooks their meals for them, and takes care of their children. She begins to think about all the women she has seen at the compound's pool. There's the woman with the high-pitched voice who's always shouting at her kids; there's the one who was so busy staring at her phone that she didn't even notice her toddler tip into the pool until someone else pulled him out. Was it one of them? Or maybe she's never at the pool. Perhaps she just glides in and out of the compound in her Mercedes G Wagon, hiding everything behind oversized sunglasses and tinted windows.

'Rosamie,' begins Connie, carefully, 'd'you think it would help if I talked to Marijo's madam?'

'Wah!' Rosamie's hands come down on the basket of laundry, now perched on the ironing board. A ball of socks rolls off and bounces on the floor. 'Madam, no, please!'

'Just to have a chat with her?'

'Marijo's madam not speaking good English,' says Rosamie.

'Where's she from, then?'

Rosamie straightens, drops the socks back into the basket. 'I really don't know, madam,' she replies. 'I only met
Marijo a few weeks ago. We haven't talked much.'

'I thought she was your friend?'

'Not friend, madam, *kababayan.*'

Connie knows that word. It means 'countryman', the
powerful sense of kinship that binds this diaspora.

Rosamie leaves the ironing and picks up a pile of books
from the sofa, handing them to Connie, who slots them
back on the shelf, in height order.

'Marijo was in the park with her family's little boy,' says
Rosamie, not looking at her. It's as if Rosamie's just talking to
herself as she bends and picks up a stuffed doll – all long, floppy
limbs and cute bunches – then arranges her on the edge of the
shelf, legs dangling over the side. 'She was alone and looking
sad. At first she not want to talk. She says her madam getting
angry if she sees her talking to other Filipinas. Then she telling me she always working, from early morning till late
nighttime, with no off day. Sometimes they not giving proper
food. I tell her they cannot do this. It is against the law.'

'But you're right, Rosamie. They can't do those things.'

Rosamie breathes out a long, frustrated sigh. The doll
stares back at her, its glassy button eyes reflecting a distorted, shiny version of the world.

'When she sent that text she had been fighting with her

madam. They still not giving salary. Her madam saying she has to pay back agency fees, Marijo saying this not right.'

'What happened?' Connie has stopped tidying the children's toys and is leaning against the wall, staring at Rosamie.

'She say her madam pull her ears. Then, after that, she always telling her she is stupid, calling her *hemar*.' Rosamie searches Connie's face for understanding. 'Donkey,' she translates.

Rosamie turns abruptly and scans the playroom. 'Children coming home soon,' she says, spotting the doll's twin wedged behind the sofa.

Connie stands up straight and follows Rosamie to the sofa. 'You can help her,' she says to Rosamie's back, as she reaches down for the doll. 'All she needs to do is file a complaint against them. You can even take it to the Ministry of Human Resources for her, if she can't get away.'

When Rosamie reappears from behind the sofa, clutching the doll, her face is grim. 'Those laws not helping Marijo,' she says flatly.

'But why not?'

Rosamie walks back to the shelf. 'There.' She places the dolls next to each other, alike save the colour of their outfits, and drapes their long arms round each other. Then she smiles. 'They are like little *kababayan*,' she says. 'Alice will like that.'

FOURTEEN

STELLA

Under my left breast there is a flap of skin that is not mine. Usually it doesn't bother me but today it's starting to itch. It's the beginning of an awareness, the very first sign that something may be wrong. The doctors attached it so they could take samples from it instead of marking my face. It's a sentinel, there to alert us to impending rejection, but so far I've ignored it. If I was the kind of person who picked up on warning signs, things would never have turned out the way they did.

Are you wondering how I became more Bonnie and Clyde than Mills & Boon?

It wasn't just the Victoria sponge that brought me back to my mother. The odd behaviour and the lost words were the pull, but there was also a push.

Remember the pretty little terrace a few streets away? I didn't live there alone. I moved in with a man called Tom, whom I met at a pottery class. He was quite a lot older than me and he used to wear brown corduroy trousers, a little faded and worn. His glasses were speckled with tiny spots of clay from where he had been hunched over the wheel. I liked all this. It made him seem real, unpretentious, as if he was not trying to be anything other than the man he was: slightly shabby and flecked with slip. We started learning pottery at the same time, at an adult-education class, bashing out lumps of clay, then pinching them into misshapen mugs with untrustworthy handles. During the fourth week, I accidentally let go of my coil pot while I was dipping it into the cobalt glaze. We got talking when he tried to fish it out for me.

He was at that stage in life when he was able to start trying all the things he had always wanted to do. Not just pottery, writing poetry as well. His wife had died unexpectedly a few years before and he had decided to stop the commuting, the soulless grey days working in the City, and enjoy life because if it was all going to end suddenly, he told me, he sure as hell wasn't going to be on the 6:07 a.m. to London Bridge when it did.

By the second term, the whole class was desperate to stop the pinching and coiling and get onto the pottery wheel. There's something about watching someone try to throw a pot for the first time. It's incredibly humbling, a window into their vulnerability, their capacity for failure. Once you've seen someone try to keep a slippery ball of mud on a spinning wheel, seen the walls of their pot emerge then fragment and collapse, over and over, it's like you know them. You can share anything after that.

By the third term I felt able to mention him to my mother.

'Never trust a man who writes poems, Stella,' was all she said.

I should have known then that it wouldn't end well.

When I think about Tom, what I remember most are the textures of him. The tufted ridges of his corduroy trousers, the fuzzy feel of his jumpers, the way the skin on his jaw was soft and bristly at the same time. I remember the first time I touched him. We were packing up after a lesson and we both tried to hang our aprons on the same hook. There's a leather armchair in the living room that catches the sun as it moves round the garden. The brush of the back of his hand was like the feel of that chair in the late afternoon. Warm and smooth to the touch, but slightly faded and cracked, covered with tiny fault lines of clay.

We laughed, embarrassed, and pulled our hands back, but the touch of another human being breaks something down, some invisible barrier, and he asked me if I had to rush off, whether I wanted to grab a coffee at the little café on the top floor.

I'm never rushing off, Connie. That would imply I always had somewhere to go, or someone to meet, and I can assure you that is not the case. But I still said no. It was instinctive, a knee-jerk rejection. He looked a little crestfallen, so I said, 'It's my mother'.

'Your mother?'

'She wouldn't like it.'

'Oh.' He raised an eyebrow, his expression somewhere between concerned and amused.

How ridiculous that sounded from a woman of over thirty! It's just that it's hard to have a relationship when you're *selfish*, like me. It was selfish of me to leave my mother on her own in the evenings, do you see? I was terribly self-centred, planning to go out or wondering what I was going to wear. If I had only spent more time thinking about others, rather than myself, my mother might not have been so miserable. I know what you're thinking: it might have been easier if I'd moved out of her house. But to do that I would have needed more than a teaching assistant's salary, and by then I had just about given up on becoming a teacher as I'm *not good at things*. It was better that I was a TA because *ambition* leads to *disappointment* for *people like me*. Further, small children can be very forgiving and, unfortunately, I have a tendency to *alienate people*.

'She's not well at the moment.'

The amusement faded and the concern took over.

I don't like lying, Connie, but sometimes it's just easier that way. I wish I hadn't said it now, because it wasn't long before it turned out to be true.

We didn't have that coffee until the end of the next term, and even then it was only because the whole class went. It was almost Christmas, and at Christmastime any group of people, engaged in any common activity, will always feel compelled to have a group outing. So there we all were, having our Class Christmas Coffee Get-together at 11 a.m. on a Wednesday morning. By 1 p.m., there was only me and Tom left. By 3 p.m., I was calling my mother and telling her I had stayed in town to do some Christmas shopping.

'Who do you have to buy presents for?' she said.

The sentinel flap is looking a bit red. Red is never a good sign. It's the colour of fire and blood, of severe weather warnings and terrorist threats. I know what it signals – another separation. The fourth time in my life that someone I'm close to is going to leave me. First my father, second Tom, third my mother. Next, you.

The side effects of immunosuppressant drugs are hypertension, headaches, diarrhoea, vomiting and cancer. That, and the constant terror that there will be some germ on someone's hand, or some virus in the air they exhale, that is inconsequential to them but deadly for me. Is it any wonder that I stopped taking them?

The problem is, though, Connie, they're what's keeping us together. Dr Clove made that clear during our many talks. You have to keep taking the drugs, Stella. Can you do that? Can you make that commitment? Yes, Dr Clove, yes, I can. I'm like that alcoholic I told you about, swearing blind they'll never drink again. Are you a smoker, Stella? No, I've never smoked, Dr Clove. I told her everything she wanted to hear. I wonder what she would say if I told her that, just once in a while, I like to go out into the garden and sit in the still, dark night turning my face up to the gentle stars and their benevolent gaze. That sometimes I light a cigarette and watch the tip glow red against the blackness and the curling smoke mingle with my misted breath. That I try to clamp the filter between lips that refuse to cooperate and suck hard, until my lungs burn, my head spins, and my blood races with the illicit thrill of it. And what if I told her that I do it just because I shouldn't, that ever since that day with the gun there's something about staring at death and blowing smoke in its face that intoxicates me?

It's happening, I can feel it. First we recognize someone as different from ourselves, then we reject them. That's what happened with Tom, and now it's happening with you. The sentinel flap is trying to forewarn me. It's like it doesn't belong any more – it's cleaving from me, signalling our separation.

Why is it that we push away the people who try to help us most?

CONNIE

Ben's hand feels soft and warm in her own, like a little creature curled in her palm. They are walking in the mall, shops on one side, vast windows flanking the other, all under a huge vaulted dome. Cathedral-like, a shrine to commercialism, among fountains, potted date palms and spectacular light fittings.

She knows this moment is precious. It makes her want to grip Ben's hand even tighter, as if by doing so she can hold on to the little boy who is growing up so fast. Ahead of them, Alice is squeezed into one of the mall's kiddy-cars with a shopping bag and handle attached, being wheeled round by Rosamie so she doesn't have to walk. 'These are for little kids,' Rosamie had chided when Alice said she wanted one. 'But I'm *tiiiiired*,' Alice had insisted. Ben knows he's far too old for them, but still eyes his sister with a certain regretful envy as she twists the steering wheel round and they turn the corner.

Ben shifts his hand in hers, their pressed palms getting a little sticky. She has the sensation of cupping a little bird in her hands, hoping it will stay, but knowing it's about to fly away. A woman with a pram passes them, large, fretful baby in the front, whingeing toddler perched on a buggy board at the back. The mother looks fraught, teeth gritted behind a forced smile as she tries to explain to the toddler that they have only one more thing to get, while trying to get a dummy into the baby's mouth as he thrashes his head from side to side. Where do they go, those years of barely coping? Sometimes Connie feels as if she has wished them away during nights haunted by endless screaming, or let them disappear down the plughole of a thousand bath times, scrubbing scummy rings from the tub while Alice weed on the changing mat waiting for her nappy and Ben smeared Sudocrem on his pyjamas.

Gently, Ben removes his hand from hers and slips it into the pocket of his shorts, strolling along, nonchalant, quite the little man. There he goes, the bird escaping from her fingers and fluttering away. She feels real sadness at the loss of the little boy she once found too clingy, clutching her hand all the time, refusing to walk on his own. How is it possible to grieve for the children they were when they're both right in front of her? What she wouldn't give now for one single night with them still babies, hauling their damp, chubby bodies from the bath, wrapping them in fluffy towels and holding them while she kissed away the bubbles still clinging to their hair.

It's December and a Western Christmas has infiltrated the mall, hanging golden stars from the glass balustrades and gigantic shiny baubles from the expansive ceilings. A huge, perfectly conical Christmas tree stands in the central atrium, covered with lights flashing different colours.

'I'm hungry.'

Frank and Julia are arriving tomorrow. Connie wouldn't normally bring the kids to the mall after school, but she has too much to do and last-minute shopping to get. She'd rather press on, but the avenue they have turned down is lined with food outlets. Ben stops and turns to his mother. 'Can we have something to eat?'

Ahead, Alice is climbing out of the bright red kiddy-car while Rosamie is still pushing it. '*Ay, maganda!*' Rosamie exclaims, stopping abruptly. 'Be careful!'

'I'm hungry too,' says Alice, planting her feet on the shiny mall floor then skipping back to her brother.

'I want McDonald's,' says Ben.

'So do I,' confirms Alice, nodding sagely.

'But it's only four o'clock,' says Connie. 'What about your packed lunch at school?'

'I didn't eat it,' says Ben.

Connie sighs, exasperated. 'Okay,' she says, 'but not McDonald's.'

They park the ridiculous kiddy-car, loaded with their shopping, next to a banner saying *Happy Holidays* in English and Arabic, then sit down at a generic-looking pizza/pasta place.

Connie orders the only thing Ben will eat from the children's menu, and coffees for herself and Rosamie. At least she won't have to feed the kids at home, she thinks. When their drinks arrive, the waitress puts a little plate of carrot and cucumber sticks and a creamy dip in front of each of the children.

'Kids' starter,' she says.

'Mmmm,' says Connie, encouragingly.

Ben casts a dismal look at the vegetables.

'Just have a few,' says Connie.

'No,' says Ben, sliding the plate away from him.

'You can't have anything else until you've eaten some.' Almost immediately Connie wishes she hadn't said it, hadn't opened a negotiation she couldn't win. She hears Julia's voice in her head: *Don't make food a battle, Connie!*

'Yes, I can,' says Ben, 'or you'll have to throw it away, and you hate doing that.'

'I'll eat it,' says Connie.

Ben folds his arms across his chest, sits back in his chair.

Rosamie takes a sip of her coffee and Alice grins, munching a piece of cucumber. Connie puts forward another offer. 'Just eat one of each, that's it.' To confirm her intentions, she isolates a carrot stick on the side of his plate. 'Ben, you have to eat *some* healthy things *sometimes*,' she says, her voice nice and calm. Just bloody eat it, she thinks, as she stares hard at her son.

'Here you go, guys,' says a chirpy waiter, placing two pizza Margheritas on the table. 'Shall I take these?' he asks, his hand hovering by Ben's starter.

'Yes/no' say Ben and Connie in unison.

'I'll leave it then,' says the waiter, clearing Alice's dish.

'Right,' says Connie, sitting forward. 'This looks delicious!' She pretends to reach for Ben's plate.

'Have it,' says Ben. 'I'll just have some of Rosamie's biscuits.'

Rosamie's biscuits? What does he mean, *Rosamie's biscuits*? Rosamie carefully spoons at the froth on her coffee.

'What biscuits?' says Connie.

'The ones Rosamie gives him,' says Alice, gleefully. 'When he doesn't like his dinner.'

Every meal with her son used to be a carefully brokered event. Tiny florets of broccoli traded for chips. Single peas — just to try — exchanged for an extra sausage. And if the meal is not eaten, THERE IS NO PUDDING. But recently she has been leaving Rosamie with the kids while they're eating, taking a moment to sit down with a cup of tea, and scroll through her friends' posts on her phone.

'Rosamie?'

Rosamie places the spoon on her saucer. 'I cannot let him be hungry, madam.'

'So you give him biscuits?'

'Just sometimes, madam.'

'But he has a proper dinner to eat.'

'He won't eat the dinner.'

'Well, that's because he knows you'll give him biscuits.' Connie tries to speak levelly, but her jaw is set in annoyance. Rosamie inspects her coffee.

'Mummy,' says Alice, 'why are you being mean to Rosamie?'

'I'm not. I'm just—' Connie puts her head into her hands. She still has so much to sort out and here they are, having yet another cheese and tomato pizza in a mall. She sits up and runs her hand through her hair. 'Just eat it,' she says, pushing the plate towards Ben, who immediately removes the sprig of fresh basil leaves from the top.

★

Rosamie has offered to take the children to the mall's soft-play area while Connie finishes her shopping. It was a good idea. Alice wouldn't get back in the kiddy-car, *I'm too old for that thing!*, and Ben was like a horse refusing the jump every time she tried to go into another shop. And she needs to get Frank's Jack Daniel's which involves going to the liquor store, right at the end of the mall, with its plain door and blacked-out windows. Non-Muslims only, a necessary evil hidden in the mall's backwaters.

I hope I've got Mark's alcohol licence, she thinks, as she rummages in her bag for her purse. Ben and Alice, both clearly possessed of a second wind, are running round the arcade games outside the soft-play entrance, pressing random buttons, making lights flash and horns honk. Ghastly place, thinks Connie, suddenly feeling better disposed towards Rosamie and her biscuits.

She pays, then signs the children in, carefully writing out their names, ages and her phone number. Then there's the last box to fill in. Is her maid allowed to leave the play area to go to the toilet? She writes *Yes* in the box.

An image of Marijo, and her resilient, trembling smile, comes into her mind. Marijo and the other maids who might claim to need the toilet, then run, still dressed in their neat uniforms, down the perfectly buffed and polished galleries of the mall and out of the door, disappearing into a hot, dusty possibility of freedom.

Who are they, she thinks, the people who write *No*?

FIFTEEN

STELLA

That Christmas I spent getting to know Tom was the best I've ever had.

It was almost like having an affair. Snatched meetings and being secretive with my phone, making excuses to get out of the house. It wasn't that my mother didn't know about *that Tom*, as she called him. It was more that if she knew I was meeting him, she would suddenly develop a migraine, or remember that she needed help turning her mattress. I sometimes had to cancel my plans with him and was often late. It was easier to just slip out, even on Christmas Day. Especially on Christmas Day.

I wasn't even expecting to see him. I was busy with my mother and he had told me he was going to his brother's house for Christmas lunch. Then, in the afternoon, my phone vibrated in my pocket. My mother and I were watching television after our lunch, sitting on the sofa with a bowl of easy peelers. *Mine wasn't very easy to peel, Stella. Was yours?*

163

I could see my mother was about to nod off, so I said I'd go and clear up the kitchen.

Park? said his message, when I pulled the phone out of my pocket. *15 mins? xx*

He meant the little park at the end of my road. Not much more than four squares of lawn, with paths in between, set round a huge copper beech in the centre. I quickly loaded the dishwasher and wiped down the surfaces. I felt so nervous and excited that I almost put the leftover turkey in the cupboard and the packet of gravy granules in the fridge. Then, when the kitchen looked reasonably tidy, I grabbed my Puffa jacket from the coat rack in the hall and slipped out of the door, closing it ever so quietly behind me.

Outside it was almost deserted – just the occasional dog-walker – and the roads were strangely silent. As I approached the park, I could see Tom's car, an old Lotus Elan, parked in the road. He was sitting on a bench beside a bed of roses pruned back to sparse stalks for the winter. He got up when he saw me, opened his arms wide.

'Merry Christmas, Stella,' he said, then wrapped his arms round me and squeezed me so tightly that my face was pressed into the folds of his grey wool scarf, soft and scratchy against my skin, holding the scent of him, like parchment paper does the smell of a freshly baked cake. It made me want to unwrap and inhale him.

'Merry Christmas, Tom,' I said, lifting my face up to look at him. Then he kissed me and for a moment the world was just warm mouths and cold noses all pressed together.

'I couldn't not see you today,' he said then. 'I hope you don't mind?'

'Of course not,' I said, taking his hand and sitting down with him on the bench. 'I was so happy to get your text.'

I've never thought of that park as a particularly magical place, but it was then as we sat talking on the bench in the last of the silvery winter sunlight, holding hands and watching two grey squirrels chase each other through the skeletal branches of that magnificent beech. There was such stillness to the world, a seeping feeling of peace and warmth. Strange, that I felt the warmth sitting in the bleak landscape of a freezing park, but not in the suffocating closeness of my mother's house, its picture frames draped with shiny tinsel, and the red-cheeked Santa in the hallway, plastic face eternally jolly, trapped for ever in the joy of Christmas.

'I know you'll have to get back soon,' he said, 'but I just wanted to give you something.'

I drew in a quick breath of surprise and slight embarrassment. 'I thought we weren't exchanging gifts?'

He grinned at me, reaching inside his tweed jacket. 'You haven't seen it yet,' he said, laughing and pulling out a palm-sized parcel from his inside pocket. 'It's just something small.'

His gift was wrapped loosely in tissue paper, already unfurling, like a blooming flower, in my hand. Inside the folds of tissue was a white ceramic star, the glaze riven with tiny cracks, like parched earth. At the end of one of the points was a hole with a silver ribbon tied through it.

'For your Christmas tree,' he said, picking up the star by the ribbon so that it hung in front of me, rotating slowly in the cold air.

'Tom, it's lovely, thank you.'

'I decided to use a crackle glaze to make it look like it was twinkling,' he said, frowning at it, 'but I'm not sure I've quite pulled it off.'

'It's perfect,' I said.

By the time the terracotta pots outside Tom's house were full of tulips, he had asked me to move in with him. Telling my mother was like breaking up with a lover; gentle words, carefully spoken. I didn't actually say I was leaving, just that he had asked me. To her credit, she didn't try to persuade me not to go. Instead she provided me with helpful observations to aid my decision-making.

'You have to ask yourself,' she said, soon after I told her, 'what that Tom sees in someone like you.' We were in the living room and she had made a quite spectacular lemon-frosted pistachio cake, dripping with confectioner's sugar and sprinkled with ground almonds and orange zest.

'What do you mean?' I asked her.

'Well,' she said, cutting me a large slice, 'didn't you say he got rid of his first wife?'

'No, Mum, she died.'

'All the same, why hasn't he found someone else his own age? What is he – *fifty*?'

'Forty-nine,' I muttered, but she ignored me.

'If I were you, I'd worry that in a few years he'd trade me in for someone even younger. Men like that don't want real women. They're just addicted to youth and beauty.' She handed me the cake and studied me briefly before she let go of the plate. 'Well, youth at least.'

I dug my spoon into the cake. It was satisfying, the way it sliced through the pale layers and thick buttercream. For the few seconds it was in my mouth, my world was just sweetness, a joyful citrus pop.

My mother sighed. 'You know what you're like, Stella.'

And when the sweetness dissolved, it was like a loss. It left an emptiness that had to be filled.

'People don't exactly warm to you, do they?'

So I carved out another mouthful, let the fuzzy sponge fill my mouth, like white noise in my ears.

'I'd worry that you'd move in and then be terribly hurt when it all went wrong.'

The sourness of the lemon, the bitterness of the peel, all made bearable by icing so sweet it hurt my teeth.

Did you know that in the original version of *Snow White*, it was the mother, not the stepmother, who poisoned Snow White? The published version was changed to make the story more palatable to little children. I guess it's too bad for me that I've never had a fairytale existence. I realized that day that those beautiful cakes my mother baked to perfection, stuffed with buttercream and sprinkled with chocolate flakes, were her poisoned apple. I haven't had a single slice since.

★

I think I have a fever. I'm shivering and sweating at the same time and my whole body aches. I have been trying to do my exercises – press, release – but everything feels even more numb and swollen than usual. And it hurts, Connie, it really hurts. I'm a little annoyed with Evgeni. That sneeze. Disgusting! He must have given me the flu.

I want to lie down, but I'm worried that then the thoughts will come. The bad ones. The ones I suppress. *Persistence*, the memories that never leave you. I keep them penned most of the time, but when I feel low, or tired, they're able to trample my flimsy defences and strut unhindered round my mind.

Tom, lovely Tom, with his kind blue eyes and jumpers smelling of woodsmoke and cinnamon. He was the one who could have saved me from all of this. Why did I push him away? No, *not* lovely Tom, *hateful* Tom. The Tom who betrayed me. The one person I thought was different, but who abandoned me anyway.

Which is he, Connie? Am I making any sense? I think I'm going to be sick.

In bed now. The pillow is cool and soft, but my face is so swollen I can't lie on my side, so I rest the back of my head against it and look up at the ceiling. It's a blank white canvas and my memories project onto it like an old cinema reel. I lie here and watch them, trying to make sense of what happened.

I remember moving in with Tom in colour. The first thing I saw as we got out of his car was the intense purple of the tulips in huge pots outside his house, so dark they were almost black. Then the chequerboard pattern of the old terracotta and cream tiles on the porch, where Tom put down my bags to open the front door, then laughingly tried to pick me up. And that paint, a beautiful Regency yellow, which we used to repaint the kitchen. He told me I could choose the colour, put my own stamp on the place, then spent the whole time we were painting saying, 'Are you *sure* about the colour, Stella?'

I was right about it, and by the time we'd finished even Tom had to agree. We planned a special dinner in our redecorated kitchen to celebrate my moving in. I can remember him even now, sautéing onions and garlic in that heavy cast-iron pan of his that I could barely lift, while running his finger over a page of the recipe book, crinkled and spattered by previous attempts at *easy coq au vin*. It was a mild spring evening and the French windows were open. Tom had laid the table outside and lit tea lights all along the little brick walls of the courtyard garden.

He was just opening a bottle of red wine when my mother called.

I took my phone out of the kitchen to speak to her. When I came back in Tom was tucking an extra bay leaf into the bubbling sauce. 'Chicken's on,' he said. 'Ready for some wine?'

He grabbed the bottle and poured me a glass without waiting for an answer. Then he picked up his own and handed me mine. 'To us,' he started saying, 'may this be the first of . . .' Then he stopped. 'What's the matter?'

I put my wine on the kitchen counter. 'It's Mum,' I said, circling my hands round his waist in a placating gesture. 'I just have to pop over there really, really quickly.'

'Right now? Can't it wait till tomorrow?'

'She says she can't work the smart TV and her favourite programme's on soon.'

I had bought her the smart TV as a parting gift. She hadn't wanted it, but I'd thought it might distract her, help fill the evenings with me gone. *Look, Mum, you can watch whatever you want, whenever you want.* Even so, she couldn't get out of the routine of watching certain shows on the day they aired.

'But what about dinner?' Tom stepped back, easing himself out of my arms.

'Doesn't it have to simmer for a while?'

'Well, yeah, I suppose so.'

'She was really upset, Tom, very tearful. I don't think it's just about the TV.'

Tom sighed. 'Of course you should go,' he said. He glanced doubtfully at his wine. 'D'you want me to drive you?'

'I'll walk, it's fine,' I replied, then leaned over and kissed him. 'I'll be half an hour, promise.'

I may have been a little longer than half an hour. It may have taken me a while to work out what she wanted to watch over the sobs and reproachful glances, and then she may have asked me to stay and watch a bit of it with her. *Just five minutes, Stella, please.* I may have had to make her some cheese on toast and a cup of tea before I left.

By the time I got back, Tom was sitting at the kitchen table with an empty wine bottle next to him. Most of the pretty tea lights had gone out, and on the hob a sticky sauce lay like a shroud over the chicken.

'I'm so sorry,' I said.

There is a noise. It knocks at my consciousness, like a chisel on stone, over and over. It's my phone. It rings, then stops, then starts ringing again moments later. What if it's Tom? I have to answer it. I roll over to reach for my mobile, but it's as though the pillow is covered with hot embers. As soon as skin touches linen, the pain is unbearable. But still I reach because I need to ask him why he did what he did. I grab the phone and drag it towards me. A glass of water topples off the edge of the bedside table, spilling on the carpet, turning the pale beige dark brown. What have I done? Another *almighty mess*. I'm sorry, Mummy, I'll clear it up right now. *I'll write to you, Twinkle, I promise.*

The phone's stopped ringing. Don't go, Tom, please don't go.

I touch the screen and it springs into life. Two missed calls from Dr Clove and a text, *You okay, Stella?*

Not Tom.

It's not been Tom for more than five years.

I should send her a message back – tell her not to worry, that it's only the flu – but my fingers don't seem to work any more. I've dropped the phone into the folds of the duvet and now my clumsy hands can't find it.

CONNIE

'I wish I'd had a maid, eh, Frank?' Julia elbows her husband playfully in the ribs.

Frank takes off his reading glasses and looks at Connie. 'Quite the lady of leisure, aren't you?' he says.

Connie shifts from one foot to the other in tennis shoes that now seem clumpy and awkward. 'I'll just be an hour or so.'

'Goodness!' exclaims Julia. 'It must be wonderful to have so much free time. Tennis lessons, indeed!'

Frank chuckles. 'Can't imagine many mums with two young children in England having tennis lessons.'

It was true. Her life in England had been a blur of trying to finish work on time to pick up Alice and Ben from nursery or school. Getting them fed, bathed and in bed, then logging on again after dinner with Mark, catching up on emails and finishing drafting reports for the next day. Even when she'd gone down to a four-day week, it had seemed to make little difference, the work simply expanding, like a gas, to fill the empty space of the fifth day, or the four working days becoming so busy and stressful that she wondered if it was worth it. Yet, even so, she still missed working. Missed the adrenalin of it, the stimulation and the satisfaction of seeing one of their projects make a real difference to a community somewhere in the world. This person standing in front of Frank and Julia in a little white tennis skirt and matching top wasn't someone she even recognized, or had ever aspired to be.

'They were a present,' says Connie, a little defensive, 'from Mark. For my birthday.'

Julia becomes saccharine and looks at Frank. 'That was thoughtful of him.'

'It's quite the life he's made for you all out here,' agrees Frank.

Something in Connie bristles. Why is this life something that Mark has made for her? As if he were forging a life path and she were just following behind, with a small child clasped in each hand.

'I've been looking for a job actually,' she says, wanting to remind them that she had been someone else not so long ago, and that this other Connie hadn't gone anywhere.

'Have you found anything?' asks Julia.

'I'm looking at a few options,' says Connie, vaguely, but the fact was that Mark's employer had yet to find the budget for a corporate responsibility manager and nothing else had come up. But she didn't actually *have* to work. They could get by financially without it and she could be there for the children. Like her own mother had been there for her. It seemed almost disloyal to her to want to work, as if it implied that what her mother had done was somehow not good enough, when the reality was that there was no one she admired more. But she couldn't quite get used to talking about herself in the past tense at only thirty-eight – I *was*, I *used to be* . . . Or did she feel that she was letting her mother down by not working? *You can be whatever you want to be, Connie*, she had always told her. What would her mother say if she could see her now? How will her children see her in the years to come?

Frank hooks his glasses back on his nose and picks up the brochure in front of him. 'Look at these villas, Julia – spectacular!'

Frank shows his wife a developer's image of a brand-new villa set in perfectly landscaped gardens, with bushes like fluffy green clouds and shiny cars parked on the drive. On the path in front of the house, a brightly clad Westerner jogs past an Emirati man wearing a crisp white dish-dash, out strolling with his family. These villas aren't even built yet, just available to purchase off-plan in a new development. Still just a dream in the mind of both the developer and her husband. *Maybe we should stay a few more years, Con, buy one of these . . .*

Julia leans over and sucks air through her pursed lips. 'Oooh, Frank, look at all those balconies and verandas.' Julia plucks the particulars from Frank's hands and waves them at Connie. 'Can we take these,' she asks, 'to show everyone at home?'

There is something unsettling about the image that Julia holds up to her. It's entirely manufactured. There is nothing real about the villa, the greenery, or the smiles on the faces of the people. It's as if the development is being built in Fairfield County, Connecticut, and she will be planted in it, whether she likes it or not, a docile, robotic housewife in a flowery summer dress.

'Sure,' replies Connie, but Julia is now looking past her to the living-room door.

'Hello, Rose-Amy,' says Julia, sitting up.

'Hi, ma'am,' says Rosamie amiably.

'It's Rosamie, Julia.'

'Yes, but that's two names just squashed together, isn't it? Like – what do you call it nowadays – a mash-up.'

Connie cringes, but Rosamie just smiles. 'That's very common in my country. Like . . . Marijo. That's María Josefina.'

'See?' says Julia, pleased with herself.

'Sorry to disturb,' says Rosamie, 'but Alice asking if sir Frank will help her make a Lego sleigh, for Santa.'

'Love to,' says Frank, swiping off his glasses again, and jumping off the sofa, surprisingly agile for a man of his size.

'Right,' says Connie to Julia. 'I'm off now. Will you be okay while I'm gone?'

'Don't you worry about me,' says Julia, settling back on the sofa and reaching for the copy of the *Daily Mail* she saved from the plane. 'I'll be fine with *sir Frank* over there.' Then she laughs so hard it comes out as a snicker through her nose.

Josh closes his hand round Connie's. They are alone, on a raised area above the compound's gym, with all the clanking, rattling units that pump water and air-conditioning to the houses arranged in a neat grid round them. Beyond the rooftops of the villas, the sea is a hazy band of blue, punctuated by a Starbucks sign in the distance and the precise curve of a mosque's minaret.

But Connie isn't looking at the view. She's studying Josh's face. He is golden, this boy, with skin the colour of warm sand in the sunlight, and wavy hair turning almost white at the ends. Josh tightens his grip and moves to stand behind her. She looks down at his hand enclosing hers, at the tiny blond hairs and the braided leather band round his tanned wrist, all faded and worn against his smooth skin. There is something about the heat of his hand that is beyond the glare of the sun, and the humidity that makes their bodies gleam. It's the kind of touch she hasn't felt in years, made strangely electric by thoughts she knows she shouldn't be having.

'Like this,' whispers Josh, into her hair. He guides her hand back in an arc then accelerates it in front of her, so that the racquet finishes across her shoulder. 'You have to hit through the ball. Do you see?'

Connie nods, suddenly wishing she had paid more attention to what Josh was saying. She can't understand why she's so distracted by him, but lately her marriage has seemed like a bit of a vacuum, and into that void have crept the smallest gestures of attractive strangers.

'Great. Let's hit some balls, then!' Josh strides off towards the net, wedging tennis balls between the outside of his trainers and his tennis racquet, expertly flicking them up into the air, bouncing and catching them as he goes. Connie follows him, bending down to help pick up the many balls that seem to have colonized her side of the net, furry yellow snitches telling tales of her incompetence.

Josh is talking in his Antipodean lilt about the bar he went to last night. He is twenty-four and earning some money in Dubai as a tennis coach before he sets off on his travels again. It is lesson four of six, and Josh is more relaxed with her now, telling her about his friends, the beers he claims to have drunk and the girls he claims to have bedded, as if she were a big sister.

'What a skite, eh?' he says, grinning. Connie smiles back and empties the balls, balanced like profiteroles on her racquet head, into his basket. She's never heard of the bar he went to and he might as well be talking about life on Mars, so alien is that existence to her now.

They finish the lesson with Josh feeding her tennis balls from the other side of the net, nice, easy shots that drop perfectly near her feet ready for her to swing at them. *Hit through the ball*, she thinks, and she sends them flying out of the court, bouncing up against the wire fence that surrounds the two rooftop tennis courts.

'Next week we need to look at topspin,' says Josh, with a good-natured chuckle. 'Let's get the balls in.'

As Connie walks over to the opposite fence to pick up yet more tennis balls, the call to the *Asr* prayer begins. A wavering, nasal note, which swells to a lyrical chant that resonates through the mid-afternoon, suffusing the air as completely as the heat. This side of the court overlooks the little park, and when Connie crouches next to the scattered balls, she sees a girl standing by the patch of sandy grass, ebony hair long and straight down her back, hands stuffed into the pockets of her jeans. She is following a little boy on a trike as he pushes himself along the path that circles the park, legs working like chubby pistons. Connie rolls a few balls onto her racquet and the girl moves along the path, turning as it curves so that her profile emerges from the sheet of hair.

Connie recognizes her immediately. It's Marijo, swiping at her long, wayward fringe, tucking it behind her ear. Marijo looks at her watch, then bends down beside the little boy, speaks to him, tries to lift him from the trike, but he starts to scream and clings to the handlebars so that the little vehicle dangles from his clenched fists and bangs against Marijo's legs. She must be trying to leave, thinks Connie. Maybe she needs to get home to make more tea for the madam who scalded her, who pulled her ear and called her *hemar*. Don't get involved, says the voice in her head, but her indignation is like a tide pushing her forward, and she is already throwing the balls into the basket and grabbing her bag.

'Got to run,' she tells a bemused Josh, as she heads out of the gate and down the steps.

SIXTEEN

STELLA

It's funny, but I don't recall Tom ever calling me 'lady' before.

Yet 'Hey, lady!' is all I can hear, over and over. Tom must be shouting up at me from the front drive, then banging on the door, shouting again. I should go and let him in, but my body doesn't work any more, doesn't do anything I tell it to. I just lie here, and the only people with me are the ones in my head.

I haven't thought about Tom in years. Not really. I couldn't, not with what was happening to my mother, then happening to me. But he's with me now. It's like my mind is cleaving from my fretful, feverish body, taking with it only my memories. I'm leaving the real world and travelling to the hinterlands of my mind. They're all there waiting for me, all the people I've ever known. All the people I try not to think about.

Ahead of me is a corridor. It stretches out into the distance, disappearing into a white light that burns as brightly as a furnace. This can't be flu. I feel like I'm dying again, but this time there is no peace, no soothing oblivion. I'm haunted by my mistakes and bad decisions. A man is walking towards me, indistinct and fuzzy round the edges. My heart is beating fast in my chest. I cling to its galloping rhythm because that's how I know I'm still alive. At first I think he must be God, or whoever comes to take us from this world, but as his form resolves out of the light, I see it's Tom. Not Tom from pottery class, but another, older, Tom. The Tom I might have been with now, had things been different.

Is he here to tell me something? Or is this my chance to ask him why he left me?

It's like he knows what I'm thinking, all the questions I have. 'You left *me*, Stella,' he says, looking at me. His eyes are strangely light, as if I can see through them into the white infinity beyond. There is no emotion in them, no anger, no sadness even, just the endless emptiness of lost opportunity. And I can only stare into them, delirious with regret.

The end came a few weeks after that incident with the whisk and the Victoria sponge. Tom and I had arranged to go on a pottery weekend together. You know the kind of thing, a group of us in a nice cottage in the countryside, making pots all day, eating, chatting, drinking wine in the evening. I'll admit I wasn't particularly keen to begin with. I don't usually enjoy spending time with people I don't know, but Tom thought it would be good for us to get away for a few days, while developing our pottery skills.

We'd only been living together a few months by then and

some of my clothes were still at Mum's. I'm not sure why I hadn't moved everything to Tom's. He kept offering to drive me over there and load up the car, but I just made excuses. I kept hearing my mother's voice in my head: *It's too soon, Stella. You hardly know him.* I couldn't ignore it because she was right: I did hardly know him. Somehow it felt better to keep a foot in both camps.

It was Friday afternoon and I had finished work before Tom, so I went over to Mum's to get the things I needed. She was busy writing in her study when I let myself in, so I left her to it and started pulling some clothes out of my drawers and laying them on the bed. I was beginning to feel a little nervous about going. Would I be wearing the right thing? Would anyone want to talk to me in the evenings? Would they laugh at my attempts to throw a pot? I was just holding up a shirt with a floral print, trying to decide if it was pretty or garish, when I noticed my mother standing in the doorway.

'Where going?' she said. She seemed to know she had said it wrongly because she gave a frustrated little shake of her head and said it again, slowly, 'Where are you going?'

'Away for the weekend with Tom, remember? I'm just picking up a few things before we head off.'

'Oh, yes,' she said, but her voice was small, wavering.

I put the shirt down and sat on the edge of bed. 'Come here, Mum,' I said.

When she sat down next to me I took her hand. She had always been beautiful, ever since she was a child. No wonder her parents had thought she was destined for stardom. But now her almond eyes were wide with agitation, not ambition, and her once lithe body seemed fragile, as if she were shrinking to nothing under her clothes.

'Are you okay?' I asked her.

She gripped my hand tightly. 'You are coming back, aren't you?'

'What d'you mean?'

'You're not leaving me, are you? It's just I can't find him.'

'Find who?'

'Patrick.'

'Dad? He left years ago. Don't be silly, Mum.' I gave a little laugh, but really I felt as if my whole world had shifted, as if the bedrock of my life had been undermined.

She studied our clasped hands, but didn't say anything.

'Mum? What's the matter?'

'Nothing,' she said, but that didn't stop the percussion of anxiety in my chest.

'Maybe we should take you to the doctor's.'

She snatched her hand away. 'I don't need a doctor,' she said, getting up. 'I'm going back to my . . .' She paused, set her jaw and closed her eyes for a moment. 'You know, that room I write in.'

When she had gone I got my phone out of my bag and called Tom.

'There's something wrong with Mum,' I said.

I could hear him sigh. 'Yep, quite possibly,' he said.

'Stop it, Tom. I'm really worried.'

'Okay, what's wrong with her, then?'

'She asked me where my dad was when he's been gone for almost thirty years.'

He laughed. 'That's priceless. I can see why everyone thought she should have been an actress.'

'What?' The word came out as a snap, stinging and annoyed.

'Stella,' he said, his voice serious again, 'she is *always* doing this. I don't know why you can't see it.'

'She's not doing it on purpose! There's something wrong with her mind. What if she's got dementia?'

'She can't possibly have dementia. She's only five years older than I am!'

'Something else then. Maybe it's an infection in her brain. I'm not sure I should leave her.'

I listened, waiting for the fuzzy silence to turn into words.

'Why do you let her do this to us?'

I did try to find the words to tell him he was wrong, but they were lost somewhere in the guttering flame of a solitary tea light.

'I can't fight this any more,' he said. 'I know she's lonely, I know she needs you, but I need you too. Whenever we have something nice planned she tries to ruin it.'

'She's not doing that, Tom, I promise you.'

'Maybe it's you, then. I mean, did you ever actually intend to come?'

'I'm literally here packing!'

'Fine. I'm coming to pick you up in an hour. I'll wait for you in the car and it's up to you whether you come or not.'

I did intend to go, at least I think I did. I packed the clothes I needed and then I made a cup of tea and sat in the kitchen waiting for him. I watched Tom's green Lotus Elan pull up outside the house, saw him sitting in the front seat staring ahead of him. Then my mother came into the kitchen.

'He's here,' I said, standing up.

She looked out of the window, saw Tom in his car and the most incredible look of expectation, joy even, came over her face.

'Is that Patrick?' she said.

I did love Tom, but my feelings for him were just beginning. My love for her was different. It was biological, hardwired into my DNA, ingrained by years of living just the two of us.

In the end, it wasn't that hard to let him drive away.

Shouting outside again. The tunnel implodes and Tom is gone. That's what you get when your bedroom is at the front of the house, lots of street noise. My mother's room is at the back, above the living room and overlooking the garden. I could have moved in there after she passed away, but I couldn't bring myself to do it. That's where it happened, you see.

I can almost feel the whiteness coming again. It's billowing towards me, like a mushroom cloud, leaving a desolate brilliance in its wake that I could so easily step into, despite my useless limbs. Not many people get to die twice, do they? If this is it, and death really is opening up before me, like a chasm, then this is my last chance to talk to you.

I want to tell you I'm sorry, Connie. I wanted to make you proud of me. I was your second chance and I've failed you. I should never have stopped taking the drugs. Please believe me when I say that all I ever wanted was to be worthy of you. I'm crying, but these eyes barely shed tears. It's ironic, really. Not being able to smile might stop you being happy but finding it hard to cry doesn't stop you feeling sad.

I'm weak, you see. I'm that alcoholic, unable to refuse another drink. Death has become my addiction. The whiteness is blinding now, bleaching out the memories from my brain one by one. Suddenly it's 20 June again. There's Mum sitting up in bed in her nightie. I know this memory so well but this time I'm seeing it differently. The pink bed jacket is the same, but my mother has an old-fashioned frilly cap on her head, tied with an elaborate bow. Her nose is long and pointy. I lean in towards her and she smiles a sharp-toothed smile. 'What a big mouth you have,' I say.

'All the better to eat you with,' she replies.

Another bang on the door. 'You home, lady?'

Then a woman's voice below my window, asking the man what on earth he thinks he's doing.

'She's always in,' he insists. 'I have parcel!'

'Is there no answer at the door?'

'Why you think I'm standing here knocking?'

'Well, there's certainly no need to be rude.'

'You neighbour? You take parcel?'

'I don't care about the parcel! It's her I'm worried about.

Stella? Are you there, love?' The metallic clang of the letter-box swinging closed, then, 'Hang on. I'll try round the back.'

Their voices cut through the whiteness taking over my mind. I can hear them, but when I open my mouth to respond it's like it's full of snow. Choking, suffocating, white.

It wasn't my mother who was the big bad wolf, Connie. It was the dementia that had swallowed her whole. I was just the huntsman.

A voice threads up the stairs. 'Stella? It's Pamela Wilson. Can I come up? Just to see if you're all right?'

'Just go, why you wait?'

'What are you doing in here? Go and wait outside!'

Feet on the stairs, two pairs. Two voices whispering, squabbling.

The door creaks open – I never did oil the hinges. Some-one has taken my hand and is pressing it between their own, rubbing at my skin with their thumb. It feels so good to be touched.

'Wake up, Stella,' says kind Mrs Wilson, squeezing with her soft, worried hands.

'Are you sick, lady?' says Evgeni, his voice gentle like I've never heard it before.

'She's terribly hot.'

'I call ambulance.'

CONNIE

By the time Connie gets down the stairs and round the corner to the park, Marijo has already left and is walking down
the road, holding the little boy's wrist in one hand, the trike
in the other. He is whining and refusing to walk, trying to
sit down on the pavement. Marijo puts down the trike and
hoists him onto her hip, then picks up the trike again. They
can't have far to go, thinks Connie, not if they've come out
without a pram. Connie follows them, staying well behind
Marijo and her fractious charge. The road curves, taking
Marijo out of her sight. Connie starts to jog to catch her up,
her tennis bag bouncing on her back.

As she rounds the corner, Marijo is turning into the
driveway of a large villa occupying a corner plot. On the
driveway a man is washing a Nissan Armada, standing on
an upturned bucket to reach a soapy sponge across its
expansive windscreen. Marijo stops to talk to him, her
voice low and easy. The child squirms in her arms and she
sets him down in the garden.

For a moment, Connie just watches her. It is such an
ordinary scene of day-to-day domesticity. She is free,
thinks Connie. There are no chains; she's not imprisoned in
the house; she is chatting on the drive with another Fili-
pino, a *kababayan*. The man says something and Marijo tilts
her head back and laughs, flicks soap suds from the car
at him.

She doesn't need me, thinks Connie. She's about to turn

away when the child, toddling about the grass, veers off towards the street.

'Wah, silly boy, come back!' exclaims Marijo, snapping round to follow him. As she scoops the child back into her arms, she looks up and sees Connie. Initially her look is quizzical. Then she seems to recognize her and gives her a half-smile. Connie feels foolish and starts walking past the house, as if she were just passing by.

'Hello, Marijo,' she says, stopping beside her. 'How are you?'

'Fine, madam.'

'I was just . . . I thought I'd just . . .' Connie glances at the man, who politely turns away and takes up the sponge again. 'Well, I was wondering how your hand is?'

'Fine, madam,' Marijo says again, a practised automaton.

Instinctively, Connie's eyes slip down to Marijo's hand, clasped across the boy's back, holding him to her chest. Marijo sees Connie looking, but can't move her hand away. The skin over the knuckles has blistered and turned to scabs.

'Are you sure,' Connie says slowly, looking up towards the house, 'you wouldn't like me to talk to your madam?'

Marijo's pointed little chin is set firm, adamant. 'Sorry, ma'am, but I must go.' She nods towards the child.

'Of course,' murmurs Connie. Marijo turns and walks up the drive into the empty garage, then opens a door leading into the house and disappears through it with the little boy.

Connie is about to go when the man steps off the bucket

and walks round in front of the car. Standing close to her, he leans over the car bonnet with a cloth draped over his hand. 'Maybe you shouldn't come here again, ma'am.'

'What?' For a second Connie isn't sure he's talking to her as he keeps his eyes on the car, drying it with slow circles of his hand.

'It's better for Marijo if you don't,' he says.

'But I just wanted to see if she was all right.' Connie tries to keep her voice nonchalant, but it comes out with an edge to it that she did not intend. She sounds sharp, defensive.

The man stops wiping the car and turns towards her. His hair stands up almost comically straight from his head and his jaw is square with a slight dimple. If it weren't for his concerned expression, his boyish looks could have come straight from the pages of a teen magazine.

'I know, ma'am,' he says, nodding, 'but our madam is always watching her. She doesn't like Marijo talking to people.'

'Do you work here?'

'Yes. I'm the driver.'

'How do you find it?' Again, Connie's eyes lift to the blank, expressionless walls of the villa, tinted windows like veils, shrouding the inside from view.

He shrugs. 'There are better places to work,' he says, 'and worse, too.' He follows her gaze to the villa. 'My madam going out now. I need to get the car ready.'

Connie nods. As she turns away the man says, 'Don't worry, ma'am. I'll look out for Marijo.'

Connie walks slowly back the way she came, trying not

to think about Marijo. Instead she fills her mind with mundane thoughts of stocking presents, places to take Frank and Julia that they haven't already been to, and whether Christmas dinner will be quite the same with no pork. As she rounds the corner towards her road, the Nissan Armada rolls past, heading for the exit, and for a moment she sees herself reflected in its perfectly glossy exterior.

'Mummy, look!'

Alice is skipping towards her, holding aloft a structure made of yellow Lego bricks, all sharp angles and strange add-ons, like a clear plastic canopy and steering wheel.

'Santa's going to use this when he comes tomorrow. See, here are all the presents.' Alice pushes her finger into a pile of assorted bricks in Santa's sleigh.

'Wow, Alice, that's amazing. I particularly like this.' Connie points to a row of white bricks jutting over the back of the sleigh. 'What is that?'

'Snow, of course,' says Alice, frowning slightly.

'Oh, I see. I wonder what will happen to the snow on Santa's sleigh when he comes all the way to the desert to deliver your presents.'

Alice's eyebrows creep up her forehead, and she runs back into the playroom.

Frank and Julia are outside on the patio, under a sun umbrella. Julia is scrolling through the photos she's taken of the children, and Frank is behind Julia's newspaper.

'They've changed so much,' sighs Julia, when she sees Connie, 'even in a few months.'

Connie smiles, but says nothing. It seems more an observation on their decision to move abroad than on the children themselves.

'Have you seen Rosamie?' Connie asks them.

Julia shifts in her seat. 'She's upstairs, I think. I hope you don't mind, but I did ask her to give our clothes a quick press. They get so crushed in those suitcases.'

There's a rustle and Frank appears from behind the paper. 'She's in the kitchen,' he says, 'making me a cup of tea.'

SEVENTEEN

STELLA

The ambulance Evgeni and Mrs Wilson called took me straight to hospital. They did what they could to stabilize me, before I was transferred back to the specialist centre where they were better able to treat my Acute Rejection Episode. I'm much better now, but they want to know why it went wrong when everything had been going so well, what I was thinking and feeling. How we can make sure it doesn't happen again.

That is Dr Clove's department.

She is sitting on the edge of my hospital bed, legs crossed, hands neatly folded on her lap.

'Don't feel bad, Stella,' she says. 'Almost everyone suffers some rejection in the first few months. You did well to get to over a year.'

I nod, glad that I can do this now without pain.

She must think I need more reassurance because she leans forward and rests her arms on her knee. 'The skin is highly immunogenic,' she explains. 'It provokes more of an immune response than solid organs. It wasn't your fault.'

Wasn't it, Dr Clove?

She seems concerned by my silence. 'Do you want to talk about what happened?'

I miss that whiteboard. I liked the simplicity of it. With that on my lap, every question in the world could have a one-word answer. Yes/no/maybe. I know what she really wants to know: did I stop taking the pills? The tacrolimus, the prednisone, the mycophenolate mofetil. Immunosuppressants with big names and even bigger side effects.

Was it because I couldn't be bothered?

No.

Was it because they made me feel ill?

Yes.

Did I deliberately sabotage my own recovery?

Maybe.

After a moment, she takes a breath and sits up straight again, taps her hands on her thighs. 'Maybe you're not ready to talk,' she says, and starts to get up.

'I was thinking about an old boyfriend.'

Dr Clove smiles and sits back down. 'Oh, Stella, that's never a good idea.'

A laugh swells in my chest. Like a tide, it surges only to be washed up, spent and useless, on these lips. Still, the way she said it was funny. She's a little bit mischievous, Dr Clove, under that solemn clinical-psychologist exterior.

'Why were you thinking about him?'

'I was telling a friend about him.'

She's pleased with this, nods encouragingly. Dr Clove thinks it's good for me to have friends, people I can talk to. It helps with my re-socialization. I wonder what she would say if I told her that the friend was you, Connie.

'Would you like to tell me about him?' She fixes me with an endearingly earnest gaze. Looking at her, I find it hard to believe that Dr Clove would understand, that she has ever been left by anyone, but she's here to help me so I'll tell her.

'I'm not sure I was thinking about Tom, so much as a choice I made. I guess I was wondering whether I made the wrong decision, whether things could have been different.'

'Things could always have worked out differently. We just have to make the best decision we can at the time.'

'But what if it wasn't the right decision?'

'Why do you think it wasn't right?'

I pause. In my head, I'm clear about what happened, the rights and wrongs of it. What worries me is that saying it out loud might change that. What if it sounds different when I speak the words? What if I listen and think, You were wrong, Stella, you were so very wrong.

'Tom asked me to go away with him on a pottery week-end. He loved that kind of thing.'

'You didn't want to go?'

'Well, not particularly, but I knew he really did. The problem was Mum. She needed me.'

Dr Clove doesn't say anything, just sits and waits. Smiles her gentle smile.

'I was worried about her. She'd started saying odd things, forgetting words that anybody would know. Then, just before the weekend, she started talking about my dad as if he was still around when he'd left her thirty years ago. I think Tom thought Mum was making it up, doing things on purpose just to manipulate me.'

'Did you go on the weekend?'

I can't look at her now. My eyes slip away to the machines and the wires. The reading on the blood-pressure monitor starts to rise, 121, 122, 123. It's like being hooked up to a lie detector.

'I was going to, but then Mum saw him outside and thought he was my dad. It was heartbreaking.'

126, 127, 128.

'He only waited a couple of minutes, then drove away. I just stood there and let . . .' I don't finish the sentence. The length of the silence that follows is measured out in little beeps from the monitor.

'If you had truly thought he was the right person for you,' says Dr Clove, 'I don't think you would have let him leave.'

'Perhaps I didn't at the time, but I do now.'

'But was it fair of him to make you choose like that?'

She could be right. I'm trying to remember it all clearly, but the problem is, I can't remember what came before without the recollection being coloured by what came after.

'Or was there more to it than that, Stella?

'It wasn't just about the weekend, Dr Clove. I think he felt he always came second. He wanted me to show him that

I could put him first for once, and if I couldn't . . . then what was the point?'

'Perhaps, but ultimatums don't often work.'

She's definitely right about that. Everything imploded then, just like one of Tom's sticky-walled pots spinning on the wheel. First it emerged as something promising, beautiful even. Then it wobbled, and as soon as the balance was off, the whole thing collapsed.

I do try to remember Tom as someone kind, someone who wanted us to work, but that's not the whole story, Connie. I would only tell you this part, but the story didn't end there. Tom went on that weekend anyway, and you know who else did too? Susie from our pottery class. Sweet Susie, with her long gypsy skirts and her hair in little plaits, even though she must have been thirty-five.

I never did buy all that self-improvement stuff. I don't think he was ever really interested in poetry and pottery classes. He went because they were full of women. And quite often lonely women – or, at least, women looking for something missing in their lives. It pains me to say it, but maybe my mother was right. Tom just wanted to move on from me to the next perter, prettier potter or poet. That ultimatum was just a way to bring things to a head, so he could make the most of his weekend.

Or that's how I *choose* to remember him, because it suits me to think of him in that way. That's the next Sin of Memory: *bias*. My recollections of Tom are like the little blocks children play with. I can build him anew every time I think of him. How I put him together, and with which bricks, is up to me. If I wanted to, I could think of a different Tom. One who went to the pottery weekend feeling angry and rejected. One whose hurt feelings were smoothed over by a fey companion in a man's shirt slipping off one shoulder, with a potter's slippery fingers and a woman's sympathetic smile. But I don't, because this Tom would take on a hazy shape and look right through me with light, infinite eyes and a face telling of a future we'll never have. 'You left *me*, Stella,' he would say.

'It sounds like you've had a lot on your mind. Perhaps you got behind with the drug regimen,' ventures Dr Clove. 'Shall we leave it at that for now?'

I nod. 'I'm sorry,' I say.

'You look tired,' says Dr Clove, rising from the bed. 'I'll let you rest.' Then she hovers as if she wants to say something more. 'You have to try to accept it, Stella.'

For a moment I think we're still talking about Tom, but we're not.

'I think that's why you stopped taking the pills,' she continues, 'but you have to accept that the face is yours. Accept the person you are now.' She reaches over and pats my leg over the hospital-issue cellular blanket, then turns to go.

'Dr Clove?' I say, as she reaches the door. She stops, turns back to face me. 'How long will I be in here?'

She smiles. 'Don't worry, you'll be out in time for Christmas.'

CONNIE

Rosamie takes a step towards Connie and reaches for the tray in her hand. 'Let me help you, madam.'

'No, really, Rosamie, I'm fine. It's Christmas Eve, you shouldn't be working.'

'Don't worry,' says Rosamie, taking the tray from Connie, 'my friends not meeting till later.'

Connie glances round the kitchen. There are piles of carrots and Brussels sprouts already peeled, and rows of pale stuffing balls sitting in a dish covered with cling-film. On the hob, an onion studded with cloves simmers in buttery milk, sprinkled with nutmeg, so that the flavours can infuse overnight, ready to make the bread sauce tomorrow morning.

'Okay, well, thank you. I really appreciate it.'

With her newly free hand, she's able to grab the bottle of Prosecco standing chilled on the kitchen worktop. In the other, she has hooked the stems of four champagne glasses between each of her fingers so that the flutes cluster, like a glass flower, in her upturned palm.

'Why don't you join us for a Christmas drink?'

'Ah, no, thank you, madam. Shall I take these through to the living room?' Rosamie lifts the tray as a question.

Connie nods and, carrying the glasses and the bottle, like the orb and sceptre of celebration, follows Rosamie.

Julia is sitting on the sofa with Alice on her knee, tracking Santa on an iPad. 'He's just delivered his presents to all the little children in Port Moresby, which is in . . .' Julia pops on her reading glasses and peers at the screen '. . . oh, Papua New Guinea.'

'What about the children in England?' asks Alice, wrinkling her little brow.

'He's nowhere near them yet.'

'Does that mean I'll get my presents before all my friends from the England school?'

Julia thinks for a moment. 'Well, yes, I suppose it does.'

Alice looks pleased and slides off Julia's knee. 'What have you got, Rosme?'

Rosamie places the tray on a large footstool. Connie has managed to find real sausage rolls in Waitrose, hidden in a separate room behind the freezer section, with all the pepperoni pizzas, chipolatas and bacon.

'Yeeez,' says Ben, bouncing towards them.

'Just a few,' warns Connie.

Julia tuts loudly. 'Oh, *Connie*, it *is* Christmas.'

'Right then,' says Mark quickly, taking the bottle from Connie. 'Let's get started!'

'Hang on,' says Connie, 'I'd better turn the hob off.'

She hurries into the kitchen. The milk is swelling threateningly at the edge of the pan. She turns the knob and it exhales, settling to a filmy pool round a squishy-looking onion.

Rosamie walks to the door leading through to the utility room. 'I go now, madam.'

'Yes, of course. Well . . . merry Christmas!'

'Happy Christmas, madam.'

For a moment, they face each other a little awkwardly. Connie tenses her arms, as if to outstretch them for a hug, but she freezes, unsure whether it's the right thing to do. 'Have a lovely evening,' she says instead.

'You too,' says Rosamie, with a little smile.

Rosamie leaves, and Connie takes off her apron ready to have her Prosecco. When she turns to put it on the kitchen counter, there's a loud pop from the living room and a cheer from Frank. She stills, with her hand resting on the work-top. Julia is saying, 'Oooh, how lovely,' then there is the clinking of glasses and lots of merry Christmases.

Connie walks into the living room.

'Here you go, babe,' says Mark, handing her a glass of fizz.

'Merry Christmas, love,' says Frank.

Connie opens her mouth to say merry Christmas but what actually comes out is, 'You couldn't have waited for me?'

'What d'you mean?' asks Mark.

'To open the Prosecco? I said I was just turning the hob off.'

'You were gone a bit longer than that,' mumbles Julia, taking a sip from her glass.

'I was saying merry Christmas to Rosamie.'

'Well, you've got a drink now,' says Julia. 'Happy Christmas,' and she holds out her glass to Connie.

'Happy Christmas, Julia,' responds Connie, rather flatly.

After a couple of minutes of standing around chatting, Connie is filled with the urge to be alone with her children.

She wants to chatter with them about when Santa will get there and what he might bring. That morning they had made reindeer food out of oats, mixed with glitter and tiny silver stars. She has already got out their stockings and, after bath time, they will hang them at the end of their beds, then creep outside in their pyjamas to sprinkle a sparkly path of dust over the patio for the reindeer to follow. Just like she used to do with her own mother.

'Come on, kids,' says Connie, putting down her glass. 'Time to get ready for bed.'

Both children are unusually enthusiastic about their bath, and they gleefully race towards her.

Julia, who has already finished her Prosecco, intercepts Ben and puts her arm round his shoulders. 'How about I do all that, Connie?' she says, her cheeks little pink balls of Christmas cheer. 'Give you a chance to get on with a few things?'

Cranberry sauce, wrapping pigs in blankets, not to mention tonight's dinner. Yes, plenty to do, Julia, but she doesn't offer to help with any of that. Still, the offer is well meant and Connie thanks her.

'Can you give me a shout once they're in their pyjamas, please?' Connie calls after her, as Julia follows the two children bounding up the stairs.

Connie takes the lasagne she made a while ago out of the fridge and pokes it with her finger to see if it's defrosted. She'll just pop it in the oven and then she can get on with the final preparation for tomorrow. Mark can make a salad to have with it, she thinks, and goes to the kitchen door to ask him. Mark and Frank are on the sofa, refilling their glasses. Frank has bought a new car and they are having an animated discussion about brake horsepower. Frank is saying he can't wait to take Mark out for a spin in it. 'We'll do it this summer, Dad,' Mark reassures him, 'when we're all back for a visit.'

Connie goes back into the kitchen and starts to make the salad. They don't get to spend much time together, she thinks. Just let them chat. With Mark and Frank laughing in the room next door, Rosamie having some time off and the children upstairs with Julia, the kitchen seems oddly quiet. She puts on some Christmas music, but the songs are not enough to fill the emptiness. Christmas should be about celebrating everything you have in your life, but all Connie can think about is what is missing. The one person who will never be with her again. Frank and Julia seem larger than life, somehow. They fill the house with their James family bonhomie, till it threatens to overwhelm her. But they don't fill the void: they just make her feel the loss more keenly.

There's no Prosecco left, so Connie takes out a bottle of sherry from the cupboard. She doesn't particularly like it, but she has bought a bottle every year for the past four years. Every Christmas she pours herself a single glass.

'Merry Christmas, Mum,' she whispers.

EIGHTEEN

STELLA

If Dr Clove thought I'd be glad to be out of hospital in time for Christmas, then she was wrong. It's just an assumption that people who have family and loved ones make. It doesn't occur to them that Christmas for people who are alone isn't a time of busy preparations and frantic buying. It is unfilled time, unrolling like a red carpet in front of you, a gauntlet to be run while society stands by and hurls sympathy invitations your way.

Ah, yes, Mrs Wilson. The minute I came out of hospital, there she was on my doorstep, an effulgent smile on her face, inviting me to spend Christmas with her, Mr Wilson, their two children, the children's partners and poor Mrs Cummings, who's going through an awfully messy divorce. She really didn't know how she was going to fit everyone round the table! Nevertheless, she asked me to join them because more is always merrier at this time of year, isn't it? I tried politely to decline, at which point she looked aghast and said, 'You're not going to spend it alone, are you, Stella?'

This is a tricky one from an opposite neighbour. I couldn't just make up visitors when she would be able to see that they never arrived, and I couldn't very well pretend I was going out either. So I just had to be honest and tell her I was a Jehovah's Witness and considered Christmas to be a pagan ritual. She did give me a bit of a strange look, but she's left me alone since then.

So, here I am, Connie. By myself on Christmas Eve. I've thought about you a lot today. I like to imagine your Christmases and how they sparkle. Not just the tasteful decorations in shades of white and silver, but with love and laughter. They are filled with the excited squeals of your children and Nat King Cole crooning in the background. Your house smells of gingerbread, fresh out of the oven, which you have made into little houses for your children to decorate with colourful sweets and snow made of icing, while you and Mark watch them, smiling, already tipsy on sherry and sentiment. I stopped short of imagining it snowing in Dubai, though. That would just be silly.

I want to know if I'm right, so I'm scrolling through your December posts. There's nothing between a photo of Alice dressed as a star for her school Christmas show and a picture posted on New Year's Eve of you standing at the top of a sand dune, vast open desert behind and around you. This can't be right. Where are the pictures of Ben and Alice wearing cute Christmas hats in front of a Christmas tree piled with so many presents beneath that it's hard to imagine how you could know and love so many people? I flick back to November and look again, slowly this time. There's still nothing. The only thing you did in late December was to change your profile picture on Christmas Eve. It's a scanned image of an old photograph, grainy with muted colours. A woman in a long skirt with a little girl propped on her hip. The girl is playing with the woman's hair and the woman is turned towards her, smiling. It's you and your mother, I know it is. It's like the woman is looking at her mirror image, just from long ago. Her younger self, reflected back at her. Incredible, isn't it, how we can pass on our image to someone else?

I don't know why you haven't posted anything. I presume it's because you were too busy. You had too many visitors, too many invitations to the houses of your friends, too many Christmas parties to attend. This is what I will believe, because the alternative – that something spoiled your last Christmas – is unbearable.

The trouble with Christmas is that there really isn't much to do. That's a blessing, I suppose, for people who spend the rest of the year breathlessly hurtling through their to-do lists, but not so great for the people who live from one appointment to the next, sustained by a single weekly activity or favourite programme. I can't even have my parcels delivered. By the time I came out of hospital it was too late to guarantee pre-Christmas delivery. I haven't seen Evgeni since I was ill. Everything just grinds to a halt, lying dormant till the New Year.

One thing I did a while ago, though, was order a couple of special things for Christmas. The parcels are in my bedroom, stashed at the bottom of my wardrobe before I got sick as if I was hiding presents from a snooping child. They are my gifts to myself, no returning these. I'm wondering whether it's too early to open them. My mother never let me open anything until after the Queen's speech. Then it occurs to me that she's no longer here, that I have only myself to please. That, surely, is the beauty of the solo Christmas, so I walk into the hall to go upstairs.

I'm on the first tread of the stairs, when I see a shadow in the porch. It hovers there for a moment – the Ghost of Christmas Present – then peers through one of the obscure glass panels to the side of the wooden door. A face, slightly jumbled by the textured glass, materializes.

'Are you there, love?'

'Yes, Mrs Wilson.' I sigh.

On the doorstep Pamela Wilson is taking no chances with the weather. She is wearing a wide scarf wound twice round her neck and a bobble hat over her hair, which she usually wears in a wispy bob.

'I know you don't celebrate Christmas,' she says quickly, 'but I just wanted to bring you these.' She holds out a paper plate with some slightly misshapen mince pies firmly restrained under multiple layers of cling-film. 'There's nothing pagan about homemade mince pies, is there?'

I catch her eye and she presses her lips together as if she's trying not to smile.

If I could smile at her now, she would stop holding back. She would take her cue from me and know it's okay to give me a little grin and we would probably start laughing. But there are over a million nerve endings in these lips, and the nerves that feed them grow microscopically slowly and take a long time to regenerate. So, for now, it's like I speak by text message. Just the words, without the nuance of human expression. I should carry round my own emojis and hold them up when I speak. LOL, Mrs Wilson. Winky face.

'I'm not actually a Jehovah's Witness.'

'Well, I did wonder,' she replies. 'It would be hard to . . . you know, go through what you did and be a Witness, what with their views on . . . on . . .'

Blood? That blood is life and sacred. That once blood has been removed from a creature its only use is for the atonement of sin?

I nod to save her having to say it but, incidentally, she's wrong. It's just the blood they object to. Anything else is personal choice.

A sliver of silence, then, 'I do understand, Stella.'

I look at her blankly, partly because I always do, but this time I actually don't know what she means.

'That you'd prefer to be alone,' she continues. 'Heavens, sometimes I think I'd love a Christmas without Mr Wilson and the kids and all the faff.'

She passes me the mince pies but she doesn't release the

plate because she hasn't quite finished. 'I want you to know, though, that I'll never let it happen again. Being on your own on Christmas Day is one thing, but you mustn't think you're truly alone, because you're not. I didn't do enough before but I'm here for you now.'

Mrs Wilson's face disappears behind a huge pink-mittened hand. She pats at her eyes and brushes away bits of fringe escaping from her hat.

'It wasn't your fault, Pamela. You hardly knew me then.'

'Yes, but we're neighbours, and neighbours should look out for one another,' she says firmly. Then she takes a deep breath of frosty air. 'Best be off now, love,' she says, finally relinquishing the plate. 'You know where we are if you change your mind.'

Then she's halfway down the drive already and I'm glad she's gone because, although Mrs Wilson can't make me smile, she has made me cry.

I dig the boxes out from the back of the wardrobe and lay them on my bed. I open the biggest one first because everyone knows the smallest are always the best. Inside is a coil of fairy lights. I pick up one end and draw them out, unravelling them into a string of tiny bulbs encased in opaque stars. Three metres of starry light, dots of brightness in this dark world.

The second box is another of those smart ones, cream with a dark brown ribbon. I undo the ribbon like I'm undressing a lover, slowly and with care, thrilled with anticipation. I run my finger under the flap of tissue paper and the little sticker holding the edges together peels away. When I separate the folds of paper an expanse of velvet is revealed.

Teal. The gleam of a starling's wing.

This is what I'm going to do with my gifts. I will wait until it's dark, take the army blanket off my mirror and drape the fairy lights over it. I will put on my new dress, one-shouldered with a fitted bodice and full skirt. When I'm ready I'll switch on the fairy lights. Then, in the forgiving glow of a hundred tiny stars, I will look at myself and I will see the girl that I could have been. Then I will lie down on my bed and wait for Christmas to be over.

A Miss Havisham in teal, content in my magnificent solitude.

CONNIE

'All done!' sings Julia, coming into the kitchen.

'What's done?' asks Connie, drying her hands on a tea-towel.

'Everything! Bath, teeth, story,' Julia checks them off on her fingers. 'Then we put up their stockings at the end of their beds and took that stuff outside. What do you call it? Reindeer dust?'

Connie freezes, the breath caught in her lungs. 'But I thought you were going to give me a shout when the kids were in their pyjamas?'

'Don't worry, it was no trouble. In fact, I really enjoyed it. We didn't have all this Christmas Eve stuff in my day. My mother just . . .'

Connie's no longer hearing words. It's just background noise, like the Christmas songs and Frank's rumbling laughter from the room next door. She's watching Julia's mouth move as if they are both underwater. Drowning in misunderstanding.

'But I *wanted* to do it.'

Something about the tone of Connie's voice makes Julia stop. She gapes for a moment, then, 'Wanted to do what?'

Words collect in Connie's mind, like little arrows ready to be launched. 'I wanted to put the children's stockings up with them and scatter the reindeer dust. I told you to let me know when they were in their pyjamas.'

Julia blanches, swallows hard. 'I thought I was helping.'

'No, Julia.' She pronounces her mother-in-law's name carefully, arming herself with every syllable. 'If you wanted to help, then you'd be in here, peeling potatoes.' She doesn't know how much she's raised her voice until Mark and Frank appear at the kitchen door.

'What's going on?' says Mark, quietly.

'Oh, Mark,' says his mother, turning towards him, 'I'm so sorry, I *really* am.' Julia's voice breaks on the *really*, and her hand flutters up to her mouth.

'Sorry about what?' He looks at his wife. 'Connie? What's happened?'

Connie turns away from them. She still has the tea-towel in her hand and she starts to fold it very carefully, deliberately smoothing out the wrinkles as if she could do the same to the situation.

'Nothing. It's fine.'

'No, love, it's not fine.' Frank's voice is steely, with an edge to it Connie has never heard before. No more the amiable grandpa, all bear hugs and bristly kisses. 'Julia's almost in tears.'

Julia gives a little sniff, just to reinforce his point.

Connie gives up trying to make the tea-towel into a perfect rectangle, gives up trying to make this a perfect Christmas for everyone else. She faces the family she married into. Frank now next to Julia with his arm round her shoulders. Mark, standing in a kind of no man's land between his parents and his wife.

'I've been in this kitchen all day and not once have any of

you offered to help me. I don't care, I really don't, but the one thing I was looking forward to was putting the children's stockings up and doing the reindeer dust with them. Then Julia did it, even though I asked her to tell me when they were ready, and I didn't even notice because I was elbow-deep in a raw turkey preparing dinner for all of you!'

'It's a bag of porridge and some glitter,' says Mark. 'It's not a big deal.'

'It *is* a big deal,' she insists. 'That's the whole point of Christmas for me. Magical time with the children.'

'But we hardly ever see them,' bleats Julia.

'For Christ's sake, Connie, Mum and Dad see the kids a few times a year. Why can't Mum have that time with them?'

'So I'm stuck in here doing all the work and you all get to sit around drinking Prosecco and doing all the fun stuff? Great!'

Then Frank says something. Something that makes Connie realize it's not arrows she needs but a shield. 'Well, sorry you had to take time out of your tennis schedule to cook a few sprouts.'

'*What?*'

'I'm fed up with this,' Frank says, deliberately to Mark, not Connie. 'If she's so put upon, I don't know why she didn't ask her live-in *help* to do it.'

'I dunno, Frank,' says Connie. 'Maybe I couldn't because she's too busy ironing your bloody shirts for you!'

Julia gives a little gasp and Frank grips her shoulders more tightly. 'Come on, love,' he says, guiding Julia out to the living room.

Mark stands in the kitchen staring at his wife. Then he lifts his fingers to his brow and presses at his temples. 'What the fuck, Connie? What the actual fuck?'

'Me?' she says, in a vicious whisper, jabbing a finger into her chest. 'Why is this my fault?'

She knows, then, that her husband isn't going to step towards her and put a protective arm round her, like Frank did to Julia. That he won't try to comfort or reassure her, whispering in her ear that when his parents have gone to bed they'll open another bottle of Prosecco, just for the two of them. That next year maybe they could take the kids skiing for the first time instead and scatter reindeer dust from their balcony onto knee-deep snow. He isn't going to turn to the turkey, defrosting forlornly on the kitchen counter, push his sleeves up his arms and say, 'Right, you, causing all this trouble,' so she could laugh, then cry, and say, 'I'm so sorry, darling, it's just that I miss my mum.' And then he could pause and say, 'Of course you do,' and press her head onto his chest, so she could hear his heart beating and be reminded that there are still people in this world who love her.

'You know what?' Mark says. 'Why don't you stop worrying so much about the peasant farmers in Guatemala and think about how you treat people closer to home?'

The swimming pool in the dark glows like a witch's cauldron. Connie stares at the beams of white radiating from the underwater lights, illuminating floating fragments and drifting hair. Without the inflatable toys and squealing children, it's a mercurial expanse of shifting shades of turquoise and aquamarine.

She is sitting on the bare slats of a sun-lounger divested of its cushions, which are stacked against the wall of the little gym. She startles when someone comes up behind her, through the screen of hibiscus separating the pool from the houses.

Rosamie doesn't say anything, just drags another lounger closer to hers and sits down on the edge of it. She is wearing jeans and a pretty top. There are gold sandals on her feet showing off neon-painted toes. She looks beautiful, almost fawn-like.

'You look lovely, Rosamie.'

'Thank you, madam.'

'I thought you'd gone out?'

'I am going now. I was just getting ready.'

Something inside Connie twists. 'Did you hear . . .' she begins, then falters.

'I only hear sir Frank, madam. Boy, he has loud voice. Boom!' Rosamie claps her hands together in an exaggerated fashion. Then, when Connie's smile has faded, she says, 'You not seem happy lately. What's wrong?'

'Oh, it's just a silly falling-out with Mark's—'

Rosamie shakes her head. 'Not that, madam. You sad about something else. I feel it, for days now. Little things making you feel bad.'

Connie stares at the pool water, watching the myriad refractions of light, thinking she'll just say, *Nothing, I'm fine*, but then she looks back at Rosamie, her eyes the shiny black of a beetle's wing where she has followed her gaze to the water.

'My mum died a few years ago,' she begins. 'I miss her so much, particularly at Christmas. I guess it hurts how quickly other people seem to forget. Everyone thinks about it the first Christmas after, and maybe the second, but by the third, the fourth, it feels like I'm the only one who's still remembering her.'

'I understand. It's hard not being with the people you love at Christmas.'

'Oh, Rosamie, your son.'

How petty it all seems now. How ridiculous the reindeer dust. Tomorrow morning Connie will wake up and her children will pile into their room bringing their stockings and excitement with them. She only has to share them for a couple of weeks with other people who love them just as much. She hasn't had to give them up for a year, or maybe five, or even for ever.

Rosamie smiles, reaches out to Connie and touches her knee lightly. 'I'm sorry about your mum. For me, it helps to think that the people you love who are far away are still with you somehow. You know, the ancient people in my country believed that there was a sacred, magical tree, and that it was visited sometimes by a god, Pandaki. We call him the god of second chances because he can give souls a second chance. So maybe your mother is here in some way.'

And in the night, looking into the pool's ethereal depths, with the breeze rolling up from the open desert, bringing with it the first notes of the *Isha* call to prayer, Connie can almost believe that that could be true.

Rosamie stands up. 'I go out now, madam.'

'Of course.' Connie gets up with her, so that they are facing each other again. This time the hug comes easily, with no awkwardness or indecision. 'Thank you, Rosamie,' says Connie, squeezing her tightly before releasing her.

Rosamie grins. 'Maybe now you give madam Julia a second chance.'

NINETEEN

STELLA

Like everyone else, I intend to get fit in the New Year.

I'll be honest and tell you that my new exercise bike hasn't had much use, but in my defence I've not been well. That's all going to change, though, Connie. Just as soon as my new delivery arrives. I've ordered leggings, a T-shirt and a hoodie to train in, though you'd think that actual training was hardly necessary, given all the sculpting, lifting and firming these new leggings claim to do. I can't wait for them to arrive. In fact, I can hardly keep still. I go to the kitchen window every few minutes and look out onto the street – bleak and wintry, frozen somewhere between Christmas and New Year – looking for the white van with the big red box on the side. It's hard to believe how excited I am about getting these new leggings. And nervous, definitely that too.

I've tracked my parcel ten times today. I admit it's a bit obsessive, but that's the problem with the world nowadays:

too much information. I'm delivery eighteen out of eighteen. Why so busy, Evgeni? Damn those Boxing Day sales.

Check number eleven tells me he is now on delivery seventeen. My heart starts to clatter in my chest and my mouth goes dry. Almost here. My first delivery in weeks and he's almost here.

It's instinctive, when I go to check my reflection in the mirror. An overhang from a past life, when checking your appearance in a hallway mirror was something you did without thinking and the biggest problem you might face was lipstick on your teeth or bags under your eyes. But all I see when I glance at the wall is a little rectangle of pristine wallpaper, the pattern distinct, the colours bright. This house hasn't been redecorated in years and my mother was a smoker. I never realized how time and smoke had clung to these walls until I lifted that mirror off its hook and hid it.

It's not that I don't ever look in the mirror because I do – press, release. I. Like. Peach. Pie. It's more that I cannot be *surprised* by my reflection. I cannot be pottering around the house and happen to catch sight of myself. It's like being ambushed, as if someone you don't know is hiding round every corner ready to leap out at you unawares. It's not frightening, at least not any more. It's perplexing. A bit like getting old, perhaps. In your mind you have an idea of what you look like, then you see yourself in the mirror and think, Who is that woman? We all have to come to terms with losing the person we were. It's just that usually it's a gradual process.

So down came the mirrors and up went the army blanket. No nasty surprises, just a single uncovered mirror on the bathroom cabinet in my mother's tiny en-suite where I keep my medicines and do my exercises. When I go in there I'm prepared. I know who I'll see. The rest of the time I use the main bathroom on the landing, and the only other images of myself I happen upon are distorted apparitions in a rain-spattered window pane or the curve of an Anglepoise lamp.

It seems so unfair how time concertinas, expanding end-lessly when you're unhappy or bored, then compressing into an instant as soon as you're enjoying yourself. I'm only too aware that after all this tedious waiting the moment my parcel arrives will pass in the blink of an eye. That one min-ute he will stand on my doorstep and in the next breath he'll be gone. Unlike those months with my mother, near the end, which seemed truly interminable. The kind of time that just has to be brought to a close. One way or another.

It wasn't Alzheimer's, Connie. Don't make the mistake of thinking that. This dementia didn't even have the decency to wait for old age and took the one thing my mother cherished most. Words were my mother's friends. They were the tools of her trade. They entertained her when she had nothing to do and they kept her company when everyone else had gone. But, above all, they were her weapons.

I used to keep a diary, and in the early days with Tom I would write down the nice things he had said to me. One afternoon when I came back from school my mother started telling me that men could not be trusted, that they would say all sorts of things to women, especially the ones who *don't usually get much attention from men.*

'What do you mean, Mum?' I asked her.

'Just that you need to be careful. Don't believe everything people say to you. Just because a man tells you you're *elegant*, it doesn't mean he actually likes you. More likely, he's just seeing what he can get out of you before someone better comes along. You're far too *trusting*, Stella. I'm just trying to stop you getting hurt.'

Later, upstairs in my room, I opened my diary and the last entry was a few lines about when Tom admired a pot I had made. I can't take a compliment, I'm afraid, Connie, so I just mumbled something about it being a bit too simple and boring and he said, 'No, it's elegant and understated, just like the person who made it.'

There wasn't any point asking Mum if she'd been reading my diary. There was only ever one answer to questions like that: *You have a very vivid imagination, Stella.*

But this thief of words took the sting from her tail. If I had mentioned my diary then, she might have asked, 'What is diary?' or she would have struggled to find the word until she blurted out, 'That thing for writing in,' or called it a newspaper instead.

The doorbell makes me jump. I've been standing here too long just staring at this patch on the wall. I have to be careful not to think about my mother too much because I tend to binge on my memories until I feel sick, as though I've eaten too much cake.

I freeze for a few seconds because I can't open the door straight away. He would think I was literally right here *waiting* for him. Then I shuffle about a bit to make it sound like I've just arrived and open the door. I can see only the top of Evgeni's head, in his bright red beanie, while he taps on his little black box thingie. What is it called? I get worried, nowadays, when I can't think of the word for something.

'Hello, Evgeni,' I say, with confidence, opening the door wide.

He looks up, eyes slightly narrowed, like he's not entirely sure what I'm on about. 'You better now, lady?'

I nod.

'Good,' he says, offering me the black thing to sign.

Then it occurs to me that this is his last delivery: perhaps he doesn't have to rush off just yet. Maybe we have time to chat. I'm not much of a conversationalist, so I just say the first thing that comes into my head. 'What's that called?'

'What?'

'That black device.'

'A saturn.'

'Oh.'

A *saturn*. I didn't forget that word. I don't think I ever knew it in the first place.

'Happy New Year, lady,' he says, handing me the parcel.

'You too, Evgeni.'

Then he's trotting back down the path in his DPD-issue fleece and khaki shorts. Why do delivery drivers wear shorts no matter how cold the weather? I just can't fathom it.

I close the door and put the parcel on the chair in the hall. I cannot even summon the enthusiasm to open it. I just feel deflated, all the excitement suddenly over, snuffed out in one ten-second conversation.

I listen to the van door slam and wait for the sound of the engine. Then there is a movement in the porch and a red shape taps lightly on the bobbly glass.

Did I not sign properly? Has he given me the wrong parcel?

When I open the door again Evgeni is standing there with a little flowerpot in his hand. Inside is a hyacinth, still a tightly closed green fist.

'Almost forgot,' he says. 'I got you this from petrol station when I saw you on the delivery list.'

For a moment I just stare at his gift.

'Marks & Spencer,' he says encouragingly, nudging it towards me.

I take it from him. The pot is in a little basket with a sat-iny white ribbon round it.

'Thank you so much,' I almost whisper.

'Your friend,' he says, glancing behind him towards Mrs Wilson's house, 'she told me you've had bad time, so I hope this cheers you up and gets you well.'

I can't say anything, so I just nod mutely.

'So . . . I see you in couple of days, yeah?'

'But why?'

He nods towards the parcel on the chair. 'For the return, right?' Then he smiles, a big, broad grin that breaks, like a wave, over his teeth. And I try so hard to smile back because

I want him to know that I get his little joke, that I'm so incredibly touched by his gesture. There's definitely something there. A flicker of expression maybe, or perhaps just a twitch.

'I think I'm going to keep this one.'

'Whatever you say, Stella,' he says, still grinning. I'm a little wrong-footed by his use of my name. I almost miss the abrupt, *Bye, lady*, that has been his sign-off for the past few months. I'm trying to think when I introduced myself, then remember that my name is on every parcel, and a squiggly version of it has been scrawled across his saturn numerous times. He knows so much more about me than I know about him.

He holds up his hand as a goodbye. 'Till the next parcel then,' he says, and steps down off the porch.

When he's gone I put the hyacinth in the living room. He couldn't have made a better choice. It's tempting, at this time of year, to buy a poinsettia but that plant is just Nature's tinsel. A hyacinth is about spring and new beginnings. I go to the cupboard under the stairs and rummage about a bit. It's easy to find, leaning against a picture of *Padstow in the Rain* painted by a one-time friend of my mother's.

I wipe the glass with my sleeve, angling it slightly away from me, then take it to the hall and ready myself. When I hang the mirror back on its hook, there she is.

Not me.

Not you.

Just someone in between.

CONNIE

It's New Year's Eve in the desert and the sky is so clear that the black seems luminous. Strings of bright stars hang in the dark, like fairy lights. The heat of the day has gone, dissipated to nothing by the vastness of an empty night. They are sitting on the crest of a dune, the sand sliding away into a darkly undulating terrain behind them, while in front of them Dubai twinkles in the distance, a city of lights and promise.

'I love feeling cold,' says Ruby, retreating into the fuzzy mohair of her roll-neck jumper.

'Rubbish,' says Adrian, though his tone is good-natured. 'You did nothing but complain about it in England.'

Ruby and Adrian are sitting between Connie and Mark, helpful colonizers of the distance that has separated them since Christmas Eve, human buffers to Mark's barbed words and Connie's prickly glances. They had acted out the rest of Frank and Julia's visit as a kind of mirthless pantomime, each quietly nursing their own grievances, papering over the tension with the children's chatter and excitement.

'We could go back to the camp-fire?' suggests Connie.

Below them, at the base of the dune, a collection of small tents is pitched round a glowing fire, a tiny settlement of their tribe.

'No, it's okay. I like it up here. Maybe I just need more wine.' Ruby holds out a plastic cup to her husband, who has a bottle dug into the sand between his knees.

'I hope the kids are all right,' says Connie.

'Of course they are,' says Mark, slightly impatient. 'They're asleep.'

'No, they're not,' says Connie, under her breath, watching the light from a torch dance round the inside of one of the tents, like a firefly.

'Probably telling each other scary stories,' says Ruby.

'God, I hope not,' says Connie, bracing herself for a pyjama-clad Alice to crawl out of the tent, wailing, *Mummy! Are there really sand-monsters here?*

'I can't believe they haven't all conked out.'

Their four children had spent the whole afternoon climbing huge dunes, then sliding or rolling down them. As the sun set, the sand had turned warm shades of red, ochre and terracotta, the breeze making ripples, like tides, over the surface of a landscape that harks back to a more pristine age.

'What time is it?'

Adrian peers at his watch. 'Eleven fifty-ish.'

'It was a brilliant idea to spend New Year's Eve in the desert,' muses Ruby. 'I've never done anything like this before. I'm so glad I'm not at some hotel buying overpriced drinks and trying to find a taxi.'

'I know,' says Connie. 'It's like there's nothing out here, but at the same time, everything that matters.'

There's a silence, then Ruby giggles. 'Have some wine, Connie,' she says, taking Adrian's bottle and passing it to her.

'What are your New Year resolutions, then?' says Mark, an outlier in the conversation.

'Never agree to do any school events with Liz again,' says Ruby, solemnly.

Connie sniggers. 'That's a good one.'

'No, really,' says Mark, 'what are they?'

Ruby is silent, staring out into the distance as if inspiration were written in the stars. Surely Ruby's life is charmed, thinks Connie. What could possibly need resolving?

'Oh, I dunno, Mark,' replies Ruby. 'Drink less maybe. Seriously, I'm so drunk I feel like I'm gonna fall off the dune.'

'I read an article once that said expats drink more than other people and engage in more risky behaviours,' announces Adrian.

'You are so random,' says Ruby.

'I just thought it explained a lot,' he replies. 'If you think about it, we do stay up later, spend more money, drink more. I dunno, it's a bit like being on a permanent bloody holiday or something.'

Speak for yourself, thinks Connie, watching the children's tent move, changing shape, like a sack full of puppies. 'Shall we get them to say Happy New Year since they're not asleep?' she asks.

'Good idea,' says Ruby, 'but if I go, I don't think I'll be able to get back up.'

Connie stands, dizzy for a moment with wine and the odd sensation of the world shifting under her feet. Part of the dune gives way, sending a small avalanche of sand tumbling down towards the tents. She is on a cusp. The New

Year is barrelling up towards her from the desert. Like a sandstorm, it will engulf her, blind her to the truth, and change her course. Yet she welcomes it without question, as if ushering a stranger through the door, without thought to who they really are, or what they bring with them.

Connie starts to half step, half slide down the dune.

'I'll come with you and get ours,' says Adrian, starting to shuffle down without even standing up.

In the distance, a firework explodes into the sky, then another and another, unfurling in the night like anemones.

'Shit!' Connie hears Ruby say from the top of the dune, 'We've missed it! Ade, I thought you said we had ten minutes?'

Adrian stands up next to Connie and looks again at his watch, squinting at it and moving his wrist backwards and forwards. 'Can hardly bloody see it, to be honest,' he mutters.

In front of them the tent births a litter of children as they spill out onto the sand.

'Is it time, Mummy?' squeals Alice, standing up and running towards her.

'Yes, sweetie,' says Connie, catching Alice in her arms. 'Happy New Year.' She and Adrian hug all the children, then take a child in each hand. 'Come on, guys, let's watch the fireworks.'

Then she turns to start the climb back up the dune. There, at the top, are Ruby and Mark, arms round each other, faces pressed together, making a momentary silhouette that is far more striking to her than the shimmering, exploding sky.

It's New Year, Connie tells her skittering heart. It's okay to kiss your friends.

TWENTY

STELLA

I want to tell you about book number sixty-seven.

My mother's final novel was titled *The Harlequin's Bride* and, about ten thousand words in, it stopped making sense. The characters, usually so biddable in my mother's hands, became like errant children, refusing to do as they were told. Their rebellion took the form of nonsensical dialogue and strange behaviour until they would do nothing at all. They stopped tripping up the heroine on her path to true love with their double-crossing antics and became shadows of themselves, moving formlessly through the pages. Just puppets hanging limp on their strings with no one to animate them.

None of this stopped my mother continuing to work on her novel. She still thought she was writing *The Harlequin's Bride*. Every morning she would get up and go into her study to write a book she would never finish. But the true story of my mother's changing brain is told by book number sixty-six. Although it was finished and published, it is strange compared to the rest, both woolly and scattered. Reading it now I can see the subtle changes in syntax and vocabulary written into every line. As a love story it's banal, but as a portrait of a faltering mind it's compelling. And it's littered with adverbs, one of the quirks of semantic dementia. I'm glad she was spared an awareness of that, at least.

I remember the shock on DC Bains's face when I wrote *Mother did it* on my whiteboard, how he leaned forward and rubbed slowly at his bristly jaw with his fingers.

'Did what?' he said. 'Found the gun?'

No. Pulled the trigger.

You must be wondering how she could have done that, given how sick she was. DC Bains did too because when I wrote that he narrowed his eyes at me and said, 'I thought she had Alzheimer's?'

You see? I told you people are always doing that.

Semantic dementia.

'Right,' he said, shifting awkwardly, a little out of his depth. 'But still she was very poorly, wasn't she?'

She hummed.

'Hummed?' He looked confused.

And tapped.

I don't know why I chose to tell him about the humming, when I could have told him about the other stuff. The binge-eating, the snatching food from me and trying to eat the egg-timer like it was an apple. The fact that we labelled all the cupboards and the doors of every room but she still couldn't work out which one was the toilet.

'You've gotta help me out here, Stella. What's humming got to do with you getting shot?'

We'd had a bad day.

He nodded slowly. 'You were her carer?'

Yes.

Because I had to be. My mother's care was considered to be *social*, not a *primary health need*. By then we were at the mercy of the changing tastes of the romance reader and royalties had slowed to a trickle, but she had the house and that was enough to mean that we would get little help with the cost of care. Only spouses and dependent children get to stay in family homes, so my choice was to sell the house to pay for a care home or care for her myself.

'Did you get any help?'

Some.

The Admiral nurses who tried their best but whom my mother detested. She couldn't understand who they were or why they were in her home. She either fought them or became so distressed that it was almost easier to care for her myself.

'That's not easy. I'm sure we'd all understand if things got a bit . . . on top of you.' He paused, rested his hands on the arms of his chair and leaned back. 'Did they?'

Yes.

The pen hovered. He didn't rush me, just sat calmly in that ridiculously squishy chair.

I wiped away the yes.

I did something I should have done months before.

'Go on.'

Quick wipe, then: *Told her she had to go into a nursing home, that we would just have to sell the house.*

'How did she feel about that?'

Don't think she really understood.

I was very angry.

(I scrubbed out angry and wrote *upset* instead.)

So I packed her suitcase right in front of her.

I did do that, Connie. I stormed into the spare room and dragged my father's old suitcase out of the wardrobe. I brought it into her room and tipped the contents out onto her bed. Then I started throwing her clothes into it. Not *packing*, dramatically chucking things in, like a wife who's discovered an affair. You might have laughed in spite of yourself, had you seen me. All sorts of things were landing in that case – a pussy-bow, flutter-sleeve dress from the 1970s, a maillot swimsuit with cut-out sides – not really the kind of attire she might need in a nursing home. I think I was just making a point. I didn't mention anything to DC Bains about my mother's pink bed jacket, though. I couldn't begin to explain how I felt about that.

The gun was in the suitcase.

Carefully stored in that beautiful oak-tanned leather box. I wince even now to think of a gun bouncing out onto my mother's mauve paisley eiderdown.

DC Bains was sitting very still, alert like an animal.

It was in a box, could have been anything inside. Didn't check, too upset.

He nodded slowly, not believing necessarily, just accepting, letting me go on.

I left the room, took a few deep breaths, then went back in to tell her I was sorry

So much to say, I was running out of whiteboard.

I left her room because I wanted to calm down, to get away from the eternal humming that made me want to stuff her mouth with a tea-towel, and the foot-tapping that made me want to tie her, like a hostage, to the chair. Terrible thoughts I was having, Connie.

'So what happened when you went back in?' prompted DC Bains.

I wiped the board clean again. *Do you know what utilization behaviour is?*

Bains shook his head.

It's when you see an object and start using it. Right action, inappropriate place or time.

I didn't know what utilization behaviour was until I'd taken my mother to a National Trust property not long before. We were walking round a Jacobean stately home, with its velvet rope stanchions and script font *Do Not Touch!* signs. We were part of a crowd shuffling through the bedroom of the lady of the manor when my mother spotted a vintage hairbrush on the dressing-table. She reached out, grabbed it and started enthusiastically brushing her hair with it. The kids behind us thought it was hilarious. I don't think the hairbrush was actually from the seventeenth century, but that wasn't really the point.

She touched everything. Fiddled with things.

Anything she saw she would pick up – fluff on the carpet, a toothbrush.

It may sound as if this conversation was quick, but it wasn't. It unfolded in a laborious way – my pen squeaking over the whiteboard and my letters losing their shape, dissolving into squiggles and lines – with DC Bains creeping further forward in his chair until he had one elbow on my bed, his eyes flicking from the board to my face, almost as if he had forgotten what he would see.

If she found something she would act out what it was used for.

'So what are you trying to say?' asked Bains, sitting back and running his fingers over his bald head.

When I came back in she had the gun in her hand.

'Jesus,' breathed DC Bains.

Just now, I picked up a peach from the fruit bowl. It had been sitting in the sun and something about its velvety warmth made me think of human skin and I sat there for a moment, rubbing my thumb over its soft, fuzzy surface. It's been a long time since anyone touched me. I'm not talking about doctors or therapists, I'm talking about real human contact. Love, affection, sex. You almost get used to it, until something reminds you: that peach, even someone washing your hair at the hairdresser's. A picture you posted made me think about the things that are missing in my life. You're not even in this one, Connie. It's just a shallow box, with the lid sliding off. It caught my eye because it's the kind of box that the things I order come in, all thick ribbons, crisp tissue and glossy cardboard. We just get a tiny peek inside, something pale and silky tumbling over the side of the box, edged in lace. *Something to welcome Mark back from Oman with!* you say. I'm trying to remember how thrilling anticipation feels, but it's almost easier not to, so I distract myself with your friends' funny responses to your post.

I'm looking to see what Ruby has to say, but she's been strangely silent about this one.

CONNIE

While Mark is in the shower Connie changes into a silk-satin camisole and matching shorts. The silk is the same oyster white of her wedding gown, and the neckline is edged with Leavers lace. She lies down on the bed, reclining against the pillows. No, too artful. She shouldn't just lie there, it looks staged. He should open the bathroom door and just happen upon her doing something, but in a silk camisole and looking very sexy. But doing what? Sorting the laundry pile? That's hardly romantic. Painting her nails? Far too messy and wet nail polish would be very inconvenient. Reading, then. Connie glances at the pile of unread books on the floor beneath her bedside table. There were so many started but not finished that she had begun to borrow the children's bookmarks, decorated with scratch art smiley faces and a crocheted squished rat.

When did she last actually finish a whole book? She used to love reading, but it had begun to feel like a chore, something she had to make time for. Every night, when she climbs into bed, she thinks, *It's been far too long, I really ought to read a chapter of my book.* Sometimes she even picks one up and opens it, reading a few paragraphs until lethargy overwhelms her. It wasn't that she didn't like reading any more, it was more that it was impossible to read during the day, and by nighttime she was just too tired to summon the desire to pick up a book. And then there were the children. Who wants to be in the middle of reading a good book and be asked for a glass of water by a six-year-old? Or perhaps, somewhere along the line, she had just grown a little tired of reading the same old stories.

She listens for the sound of running water. Mark is taking ages. If he doesn't come out soon, her resolve will weaken. She will slip the barely there straps of her camisole off her shoulders and step out of the French knickers. She slides a hand under the pillow and feels around. Yes, there they are, her favourite pyjamas, freshly laundered and smelling of Bounce. She resists the urge to put them on. They need this. Mark has been in Oman with work for almost a week, but even before that Connie had taken to going to bed before him and couldn't always stay awake until he came up. Or was it Mark who had taken to staying downstairs, watching box sets and checking emails, until he knew she would be asleep?

After a page of one of her books, Mark opens the bathroom door wearing a towel wrapped round his waist. He glances at her and raises his eyebrows, 'Nice, er, outfit,' he says, then walks over to the chest of drawers, pulling one open and riffling through it.

'Oh, thanks,' says Connie, tossing the book onto the bed. 'This is what was in the parcel from the UK that came to your office.'

She observes him. He has started running again, watching what he eats. The contours of his muscles are re-emerging, rippling under his skin as he reaches further into the drawer. She slides off the bed and walks over to him, putting both hands on his back and kissing the nape of his neck, still wet from the shower.

Mark turns, a pair of lounge joggers in his hand. 'Well, it's lovely. Really suits you.' He leans over, pecks her on the mouth, then slips out from her hands. For a moment he seems a little awkward, then turns away from her and starts to climb into his joggers, holding on to the ball of the metal bed frame to steady himself.

'Hey,' she says gently, walking round to face him, 'you don't need them.' Then she steps on them before he can put his foot in. 'I missed you while you were away.'

'Really, Con,' he replies, 'I'm pretty tired after the trip and I need to go back downstairs and finish some work stuff for tomorrow.'

'Surely it can wait?' She keeps her voice soft – with the same gossamer seductiveness as the silk-satin camisole, which is beginning to feel just a bit ridiculous – even though her skin is prickling with rejection. She tugs the towel from Mark's waist. Before she can stop it, something between a laugh and a shocked exclamation comes out of her mouth. 'Goodness,' she says, 'how very . . . millennial.'

Mark, angry, snatches the towel back from her. 'For fuck's sake, Connie.'

'Sorry, it's just . . . I mean . . . seriously?'

'What?'

'Nothing, it's just that you've never bothered before.'

He picks up his joggers and pulls them on, snapping the elastic waistband.

'Yeah, well, I've never lived in a hot country before. It's just more hygienic and comfortable this way.'

'It's not for my benefit, then?'

Mark sighs, runs his fingers through his damp hair. 'Listen,' he tells her, 'I'll just nip downstairs and finish this work thing, then I'll be back. Okay?' He circles her waist with his arm and gives it a quick squeeze. 'Don't go anywhere.'

The full-length windows of the master bedroom open onto a little balcony. Connie twists the grating lock and pushes on the door, which she has never thought to open before. The balcony tiles are slippery with dust under her bare feet. In the corner a metal chair, left behind by some long-departed tenant, is relinquishing its paint in peels and flakes, offerings to an insatiable sun god. But now the air is cool, shifting round her, like a restless spirit. It's a good thing, she thinks, that she decided to change into her pyjamas, or she would be cold. There will be only a few more weeks of these gentle nights with their balmy breezes. In March the weather will start to turn, and by May the temperature of the days will barely drop below forty degrees. This is the wettest month. Earlier that day a few drops of rain had fallen and dried almost instantly, giving the balcony's film of sand the look of a pockmarked skin.

It's late but she cannot sleep. She's already been downstairs to see what Mark was doing but stopped at the top of the stairs, silently watching him on the sofa, grinning at his phone, tapping away, waiting, then tapping again, a glass of wine on the table beside him. He had looked up then, seen her standing there, startled slightly and put down his phone. 'Won't be a minute, babe,' he'd said. 'Just checking in with Mike about our meeting tomorrow.'

She feels the need for space, room to organize her jumbled thoughts without Mark, or the kids, or her in-laws. But there is nowhere to go, so she stands like Juliet on her balcony under a starry sky, looking not for someone but for answers lost in the darkness.

Beyond the patio, with its elderly frangipani and rusting barbecue, the path from the pool winds past their villa. As she watches, a couple is caught in the electric haze of the streetlamp, arm in arm, chatting in Tagalog. The man stops and pulls the woman towards him, kissing her with an urgency that cannot wait even another step, his fingers breaking through the silky black sheet of her hair, cradling the back of her head. For a moment she thinks the woman is Rosamie, slender in her smart jeans and top, but then she breaks away – smiles at the man and touches her finger to his lips – and she sees that it isn't.

Their simple display of unguarded affection touches Connie, makes her feel wistful, nostalgic for another time when love was something powerful and all-consuming, not something to be worked at. But as soon as she realizes who the couple is, the sentimentality runs cold in her veins. She wants to shout to them, *Hide your feelings – don't let anyone see you*, but they are already walking away, merging as one into the darkness.

★

She is about to go back into the bedroom when Mark appears in the doorway. She feels a little surge of hope when she sees him, assuming he has thought better of spending his evening on the sofa arranging meetings, and come to join her. Then he steps out onto the balcony, and the light from the streetlamps illuminates his face. It is rigid, unsmiling. His jaw is locked in annoyance.

'What's wrong?'

'Why d'you do it, Connie?'

'Do what?'

'This.' He holds up his phone to her, showing the post about her new camisole set. 'It's really inappropriate.'

She laughs, incredulous. 'It was just a joke!'

He walks over to her, stands so close she can smell the wine on his breath. How many glasses has he had?

'It's not a fucking joke. It's . . .' he struggles to find the word '. . . *cringeworthy,* just embarrassing. I don't want our private life plastered all over social media.'

'Sorry,' she says, but she's not quite sure what she's apologizing for, feels the need to explain herself. 'I thought you'd be flattered.'

And she had thought that. In fact, she still can't understand why he's so annoyed. It had been tasteful enough, hadn't it? It hadn't shown anything, just hinted at something. Why would a husband not want his friends to know that he and his wife are close? That they have a loving relationship?

'Flattered? Are you for real? I don't want people we know to see this.'

'What people?' Now her voice is steely, her gaze fixed on his face.

'I dunno.' He flounders. 'People from work.'

'It's Ruby, isn't it?'

'What?'

'That's why you're annoyed.'

'I have no idea what you're talking about.'

'She's the one you didn't want to see it. What have you told her about us, Mark?'

'You're crazy – you know that, don't you?' He leans further towards her. Instinctively, she leans back. The top of the balcony railing presses hard into her lower back.

'Were you messaging her?' Connie has only to whisper it. 'Did she see the post and give you a hard time about it? *But you told me you two didn't have sex any more!*' She says the last sentence in a deliberately petulant voice, bitter and whiny at the same time.

'What is your problem with her?'

'It's not just her, it's both of you!'

'Why? Because I like her? Because being with her is *easy* and *fun*?'

'What's going on, Mark?'

'For Christ's sake! Nothing!' He's right up against her, spitting the words into her face. She goes rigid with shock. He's been angry before, of course he has, but she has never seen him so venomous. To her, his vitriolic denial feels like confirmation.

'Show me your phone.'

He pulls away from her. 'What? No!'

'Show me!' She moves suddenly, grabbing at the phone. The wine has made him sluggish, and she pulls it from his hand.

His eyes widen and he lurches towards her, swiping at her hand. She leans back sharply, holding the phone above and behind her. Then, suddenly, the centre of her world shifts. There is a grating sound as the end of the railing – weakened by the relentless sun, and unused to the weight of two people pressing against it – begins to move away from the concrete wall. It is enough to send her off balance, and she feels herself falling back, grabs vainly at the air.

For the briefest of moments, before she feels his hand grip the top of her arm and pull her back, she wonders if he will just let her fall.

TWENTY-ONE

STELLA

The lava lamp in Dr Clove's room reminded me of something. Something I wanted to tell her. It was the way the shifting patterns drew me in, mesmerized me. The orbs of lava spinning towards each other, then melding together, as if their path was predetermined and they, like all of us, would just become the light in the end.

'I died,' I told her, the second time we met, when she was just beginning her *psychiatric evaluation*.

Have you ever tried to speak when you're nearly frozen with cold? That's how the words came out, lipless and clumsy, with my precious whiteboard tucked firmly between Dr Clove's thigh and the arm of the sofa. My face was still a strange construction of hip bone and leg muscle then, held together with titanium plates and screws.

She must have thought she'd misheard me as she leaned forward, a little swirl of wrinkles on her forehead.

'Tried to what, Stella?'

I shook my head. '*Died*. When it happened.'

She nodded slowly, then sat back. 'Okay, tell me.'

So I did. I told her about the light and being able to see *everything*. I told her I could hear my mother speak to me, although I couldn't bring myself to repeat what she'd said. All explained in short, staccato sentences. I wanted to know if she'd take me seriously, if she was prepared to believe me.

'That's fascinating,' she said.

'Do you believe I died?'

She pressed her lips together, then drew a deliberate breath. 'I believe in the authenticity of your experience, certainly, but there is a medical explanation.'

I don't know why people say that doctors don't have all the answers, because in my experience they almost always think they do.

'In that situation,' said Dr Clove, looking at me carefully to see if I wanted her to stop, 'your brain would have released chemical signals that can activate specific areas, particularly those involved with vision and feelings of peacefulness. This can lead to a very . . . *vivid*, and quite possibly comforting, experience.'

'So you don't?'

She smiled. 'I didn't say that. I believe that your experience was real, but I can't tell you why it happened or what it means.'

Except that she has. Everything I have ever felt, all my hopes and fears, all my love and rage, reduced to little bursts of electricity. Chemical signals pulsing along a synapse. Disappointing, really.

'I'm not scared to die, Dr Clove. Not after what I saw. What I felt.'

She paused for so long the silence seemed to congeal round us.

'What about before that, Stella?' she said. 'How did you feel about dying then?'

It blindsided me, this question. I didn't know what to say, so she continued, 'I've read DC Bains's report,' her face was serious, her gaze level. It made me prickle, as if I was about to be peeled apart, layer by layer, 'but I'd like you to tell me what happened in your own words.'

It wasn't a question, so I didn't say yes or no. Dr Clove put her notebook down on the table and sat back in her chair.

'So,' she said, 'you were upset and you lost your temper. You went outside the room to calm down, and when you came back your mother had the gun in her hand. Is that right?' I nodded. 'So what happened then?'

'I was shocked, terrified. I didn't even know if it was loaded, but I had to take it from her.' My words sounded breathless, husky, like they were coming from the back of my throat. I wondered if she could even understand me, but she was staring right back at me, head slightly tilted, waiting for me to go on. 'I could have just run out, called the police, but I couldn't leave her. What if she hurt herself? So I tried to talk to her, said, "Give that to me, Mum." I took a step towards her, but instead of handing the gun to me she seemed to stiffen and her eyes grew wide, as if I were about to hurt her. She raised the gun higher, pointed it right at me. I kept talking to her, the way you'd talk to a nervous horse. I thought it was working. She seemed to relax a little. I was close to her then, so close I had only to reach out and close my hands round the gun.'

I wasn't looking at Dr Clove, I was staring at the lamp, watching the globs of lava collide and merge. Everything seemed fluid then, capable of being endlessly reshaped. Even memories. Even the truth.

'The first thing I did was to angle the gun slowly upwards, so that it wasn't pointing right at me. Then I tried to take it from her. She almost let me do it, right to the last moment when the gun was about to slip from her fingers. Then there was a noise from the street, someone putting their bin out, I think. It spooked her and that was it. She pulled the trigger and the bullet caught the edge of my face.'

Dr Clove took a deep breath and shifted position. Her movement dragged my gaze back towards her. She seemed almost to sink into the sofa, as if her sadness had a weight to it. 'You do understand why we're having these sessions, don't you?' she said.

'I think so,' I replied.

'I need to know how you came to have the injuries you do. Not because I'm investigating any possible crime, like the police, but because we want to support you, and do whatever we can to make sure nothing like that happens again.' She reached for her notes, flipped the page and spent a few seconds reading what she had written there. Whatever it was seemed to give her courage. She sat up a bit straighter and became almost matter-of-fact.

'I understand what you say about your mother's utilization behaviour,' she said, 'because that's quite common in her type of dementia. But grabbing a toothbrush and acting out brushing your teeth is very different from firing a gun. One is straightforward and the other is complex. Firing a gun requires planning, loading the cylinder, turning off the safety, pulling back the hammer. I'm not sure your mother would have been able to implement the series of steps necessary to fire a revolver.'

She glanced at me to gauge my reaction, a human habit, but my engineered features gave nothing away.

'Then there's the question of gunshot residue,' she continued. 'If your mother had pulled the trigger, there would have been residue on her clothes, but Forensics found the residue primarily on yours, not hers.'

'We were so close the residue could have got anywhere.'

She nodded slowly. 'Possibly, but then there was the path of the bullet. To have grazed the front of your face like it did, it would have had to be fired upwards. Probably held pointing under your chin.'

Silence then. Just the futile rise and fall of the lava in the lamp, constantly morphing into different versions of itself. It made me think of an Henri Bergson quote: *I change, then, without ceasing.*

'It can't have happened the way you described, Stella,' she said, so softly her words fell like snow between us.

CONNIE

'Look, Mummy!' Alice is holding out a bloody tooth for Connie to inspect, her broad grin revealing a wide arc of gum.

Connie gasps and squats in front of her daughter. 'Oh, my goodness,' she says, taking the little tooth, 'that's both the front ones now. How are you going to eat your raw carrots?'

Alice is thrilled and fascinated by the thought, while her brother looks hopeful. 'Will I lose these again?' he says, tapping his own front teeth with a finger.

'Fraid not, Ruben,' replies Connie, standing up. 'No excuses for you.'

Mark is in Oman again, advising on new developments pushing up from the desert, their appearance almost improbable, like snowdrops nudging out of the January earth. When he's away, Connie eats with the kids at six o'clock, sitting round the little kitchen table. There is something liberating about not having to make an adult meal, and an evening to herself seems almost a treat, especially given how they have been getting along recently.

'There you go,' says Connie, handing Alice back her tooth, rinsed and wrapped in kitchen roll, 'you can put it under your pillow later.'

Connie turns back to the cooker where a saucepan of peas is coming to the boil. The children sit at the kitchen table chattering about the Tooth Fairy and swinging their legs back and forth.

'*Coya-coy, coya-coy,*' sings Rosamie, when she comes into the kitchen and sees them.

'What's that mean, Rosme?' asks Alice.

Rosamie stops and looks thoughtful. 'It means . . . just hanging out, kicking your heels.'

Connie smiles, 'That's a nice phrase. Would you like to eat with us, Rosamie? I can offer you fish pie and peas?'

'Aww, fish pie.' Ben visibly deflates and props his head on his fists, squishing his cheeks up towards his eyes.

'No, thank you, madam. I am already making chicken adobo. You like, *gwapo*, eh?' says Rosamie, playfully pinching the top of Ben's cheek.

Life has a certain simplicity to it when it's just Connie, Rosamie and the children. The kitchen feels warm and happy, full of food, songs and friendship, so when the shrill ringtone of the phone begins, it makes them all jump.

'Sorry, madam,' mumbles Rosamie, delving into the pocket of her loose cotton trousers.

'Don't worry,' says Connie, but Rosamie has already turned away and is opening the door of the kitchen leading to her room. As she disappears through it, Connie hears her begin to speak in rapid, urgent Tagalog.

Once the children are in bed, and the tooth safely under Alice's pillow, Connie returns to the kitchen. She takes her purse out of her bag. How much does the Tooth Fairy pay in Dubai, these days? she wonders, then puts a little pile of dirhams on the kitchen worktop to remind herself to take them with her when she goes back upstairs. Alice has left half of her pudding and Connie can't resist sliding her finger round the inside of the pot and licking it. She's about to get a spoon to finish it off, when Rosamie hurries back through the door. Her head is bent and she doesn't look at Connie. Instead she grabs a cloth and starts wiping the kitchen table, her hand moving in quick, agitated circles.

'I'll tidy kitchen, madam,' she says, picking up Ben's abandoned fish pie and cleaning underneath it.

'What's wrong?' asks Connie, quickly throwing the pot into the bin now that Rosamie is there.

'Nothing, madam,' says Rosamie, but her voice cracks and when she looks up her eyes are tearful.

'Is it Marijo?'

Rosamie nods, stricken.

'Where is she?'

'In my room, madam.'

Marijo is sitting on Rosamie's bed hugging her legs, with her chin resting on her knees. She is wearing a domestic worker's uniform, navy blue trousers and tunic, with a white collar and piping on the sleeves. On the floor by the wall, the chicken adobo simmers on the single hot plate, flavouring the room with soy, garlic and bay. It could almost be cosy, were it not for the swelling under Marijo's left eye, forcing it closed in a permanent humourless wink.

Connie realizes she is holding her breath. She lets it out slowly at the sight of Marijo, trying to collect her racing thoughts.

'I'm sorry, madam,' says Marijo.

Connie sits down on the edge of Rosamie's bed and takes one of Marijo's hands in hers. 'What did she do?' she asks, squeezing Marijo's hand, but Marijo just shakes her head, tears dropping onto her nylon-clad legs.

From over by the door, Rosamie's voice is deliberate. 'She beat her with a mop.'

Instinctively, Connie tightens her grip on Marijo's hand. She tries to keep her voice level when she says, 'You must go to the police now. I'll take you there myself.'

Marijo snatches her hand away. 'No, madam.'

Connie turns to Rosamie with a bewildered expression. Rosamie sighs then walks over to the bed and sits down opposite Connie, next to Marijo. She takes a deep breath and tilts her head back against the wall. After a moment, she stops staring at the ceiling and looks back at Connie.

'Marijo cannot go to the police.'

'Why not?'

'Because Marijo doesn't have proper visa. If she go to police she will get in big trouble. Deported.'

'But surely—' Connie starts to say, but then Marijo sits up and crosses her legs in front of her, leaning forward and starting to speak with an urgency that stops Connie's words.

'You don't understand, madam.' Marijo's voice wavers,

despite her desire to speak. 'I am single mother. I have baby back home. I have many brothers and sisters, but none working. Just me giving money to my mother. If they send me back, how will I get money for my family?'

'But you cannot stay working for someone who hurts you. Seriously, Marijo, what happened this time? Was it the tea again, or did you cut her sandwich into triangles instead of squares?'

Marijo sniffs and presses a tissue tentatively round her swollen eye. 'I have been there almost two years. I need to go home this summer to see my little girl. I am asking for trip home, but madam saying no. When I tell her it is my right to go home every two years, she telling me I cannot go home because she has bought me. I telling her, "I am a person, not a dog. You cannot *buy* anyone." Then she take mop and hit me with it.'

Connie clasps Marijo's hand again. 'I'm sure we can sort out your visa,' she says.

'Not just visa, money too. I go to recruitment agency in Manila. They pay for my flight and my visit visa. They say I have to tell Dubai authorities I am visiting my aunt. They promise me good job, with good pay. I already told them, "This not good job! No off day, Madam shouting all the time, no salary." But they say I have to give them seven thousand dirham if I want to leave, as they spend all this money on me already, and Madam paying big recruitment fee. If I go to police, that's it.' Marijo slices her hand through the air to indicate the finality of the outcome. 'I get deported, maybe banned for working on a visit visa. Then who will take care of my family?'

Marijo takes a breath, something between a gulp and a sob. It's not even that much money, thinks Connie. Marijo is trapped for less than the cost of a term's school fees, or a family holiday.

Connie leaves Rosamie and Marijo to eat the chicken adobo. She goes to the computer and looks again for answers, but women working illegally on visit visas don't have the protection of the law. She thinks about offering Marijo the money herself, but these bogus agencies are crooks and seven thousand dirhams would become ten, then fifteen, and Marijo would never be free of them while she doesn't have the right visa. Better, surely, to go through the proper channels.

Connie presses a button and a single sheet of paper slides out of the printer. She finds a pen and writes *Connie* followed by her mobile number at the top. Then she goes back to Rosamie's room and hands it to Marijo. 'Here's a couple of places that might be able to help you,' she tells her. 'Promise me you'll call them at least. Even if you don't give them your name, just explain your situation and see what they say.'

Marijo looks at the piece of paper with the contact details of the Ministry of Human Resources and the Dubai Foundation for Women and Children printed on it. Then she nods. 'I will try, madam.'

'And if anything else happens call Rosamie or call me. Okay?'

★

Later Connie lies in bed thinking what she would do if she were Marijo, following each option to its conclusion, trying to find an outcome that doesn't end in punishment or further abuse. But her mind just whirs, clouded by fatigue. Things will be clearer in the morning, she tells herself; there must be a solution.

She is awoken the next morning by Alice standing at the foot of her bed, a tear-streaked spectre that startles her.

'Mummy, have I not been a good girl?'

'What d'you mean, darling? Of course, you have.'

Alice holds out a scrunched ball of kitchen roll in her hand. 'But the Tooth Fairy didn't come,' she whispers.

TWENTY-TWO

STELLA

I've just popped a card through Mrs Wilson's door to thank her for the mince pies and all her kindness recently. I even suggested that she might like to come over for tea again soon. I admit I was wrong about Pamela Wilson. I thought her interest in me was the ruthless curiosity of the freak-show voyeur, but she just wants to help me. I hope she comes soon. I, more than anyone, know how important it is to stay connected to people.

Social isolation. That was a phrase Dr Clove used last year when we were talking about what can happen when you're a carer for someone. I never even thought of myself as isolated – why would I when I had someone with me all day, every day? – but it crept up on me, as insidious an attack on me as my mother's dementia was on her. I began to disentangle myself from the world, unravelling the flimsy bonds I had with people, one by one. Tom was the first to go, and with him went the weekly pottery class I had enjoyed. Then, as I watched my mother's behaviour grow increasingly bizarre, I had to give up work, so I gradually lost touch with the teachers. I missed the children with their constant chatter and little fingers sticky with clay or paint sneaking round my waist for a hug. They always wanted to cuddle me. I found it surprising at first, as if hugging me was an odd thing to want to do: me, the icicle child, the one made of glass. But I grew used to it, until it delighted me, even fatigued me sometimes. *I'm not a teddy bear*, I used to tell them. Without those small interactions, my world narrowed to a pinhole.

I was surprised by how much I got used to. The piles of newspapers in the corner, and the collection of threadbare scouring pads hidden under the sink, because my mother refused to throw anything away. I had to wait until she went to bed to put the empty plastic milk containers into the recycling. She became obsessed by routine, doing everything in the same way, at the same time, taking the same precise route round the house over and over. I developed little ways of adapting, like vacuuming all the time to stop her constantly bending down to pick up some tiny bit of something off the carpet.

Thinking about all this now reminds me of the very first time we invited Mrs Wilson to come over. She had just moved in opposite us and I thought we should introduce ourselves. I also hoped it would be good for my mother to have a visitor, something to break up the endless routines, for my sake if not for hers.

I asked Mrs Wilson to come mid-morning so that my

mother could still have her coffee at exactly 11 a.m. We made a cake to go with the coffee, which wasn't easy because my mother had taken to switching everything off. I would try to start the mixer and find she had turned it off at the wall. When I put the radio on, a moment later she switched it off. I kept a close eye on the oven and somehow we managed a basic fruit cake that I left my mother to ice while I tried to tidy the living room without it looking like I'd thrown anything away.

It turned out that mid-morning is open to interpretation. Mrs Wilson rang the bell at nine thirty, when I was just wondering where to put the white unicorn with the multi-coloured mane that my mother had inexplicably insisted on buying the last time we were out shopping. I squashed it onto one of the shelves at either side of the fireplace and ran to the door.

Mrs Wilson looked a little nervous, which I found reassuring in a way: it wasn't as if we had a lot of visitors ourselves. She offered me a bunch of daffodils that she told me she had cut from her garden. My mother refused to entertain in the kitchen, so I tried to take her straight through to the living room, thinking I would then bring my mother in to meet her. But as we passed the kitchen door, left ajar, my mother shouted, 'Who that?' and Mrs Wilson stopped.

'It's Mrs Wilson from across the road,' I called. 'She's come over to have a cup of coffee with us.'

'Not time coffee,' my mother said.

'If it's not convenient?' Mrs Wilson whispered.

'No, it's fine,' I said. It seemed rude not to introduce her to my mother now that she had made her presence known, so I told Mrs Wilson, 'I'll just put these lovely daffodils in some water,' and opened the kitchen door.

My mother was sitting at the kitchen table. In one hand was a large lump of cake and in the other was the spoon from the icing bowl, which she was licking. Not licking in a normal way, but rather *mouthing,* like a baby might chew on a teething ring. Icing was smeared over her cheeks and her lips were shiny with saliva. All that was left of the rest of the cake was a few crumbs scattered over the plate.

'Goodness,' said Mrs Wilson.

'Mum, we were waiting for Mrs Wilson to have the cake, remember?'

My mother put the spoon down, got up and walked over to Mrs Wilson. Then she put her arms round her, squeezed, and planted a firm kiss on her cheek.

'Oh, my!' exclaimed Mrs Wilson, stepping back and patting at her cheek, now sticky with icing.

'I'm so sorry,' I said. 'She does that sometimes.'

'No, really, it's fine,' said Mrs Wilson, opening her handbag and pulling out a small packet of tissues.

'I'll put the kettle on,' I said, handing the flowers to my mother. 'Mum, look what Mrs Wilson brought us,' I said brightly, then turned to Mrs Wilson. 'There are some profiteroles in the freezer,' I told her. 'They'll defrost in no time. We can have them.'

'Don't go to any trouble on my account,' she said, wiping

the tissue across her cheek and inspecting it with a dubious expression.

'No trouble,' I said. 'We're just glad to meet you at last. Aren't we, Mum?'

I turned back to her. 'Mum?'

My mother was staring at the daffodils, touching the leaves and fiddling with the trumpet heads. Then she walked over to the bin, pulled it open and dumped the flowers into it. 'Don't like tulips,' she said.

Sometimes you have to look for small positives. I was right about the profiteroles at least. They did defrost in no time because, when I opened the freezer door to take them out, I discovered that my mother had switched the freezer off.

There's a Persian word, *taarof*, I read about once, which means 'social politeness'. The kind of situation where someone might offer an invitation to their home in the expectation that it will be politely refused, perhaps many times, despite the would-be host's show of genial insistence. I don't think it's just the Iranians who do this. Over the months that followed, Mrs Wilson sometimes looked up from deadheading her shrubs and talked about popping over to see how we were managing, or me coming in for a cup of tea, but I just smiled and nodded. Even if she was the only other person I had spoken to that week. Even if all I really wanted to do was walk out of my mother's house and never go back. It was just *taarof*. I knew I wasn't actually meant to accept.

★

The humming started a little after Mrs Wilson's visit. Not a tune, with variations of pitch and tone, but a single constant, reedy note, like the bugle call of the vanguard. A warning, a sign of things about to change.

Anyone would understand if you felt there was no other way out. That was what Dr Clove had said and she was right. As far as I was concerned there was no other way out.

CONNIE

Whenever Connie goes to the pool, or the little gym next to it, she walks the long way round, past the large house on the corner with its Nissan Armada parked on the drive. She doesn't know what she's looking for, or whom, but she keeps watching as if the house might let its secrets slip in the rustle of the date palms that flank the house, like guards, or in the peevish cries of the hoopoes squabbling on the windowsills.

It's Thursday: she has dropped the kids at school and been for a run. She walks past the house again, pausing as she sees the Nissan slowing in the road as it approaches. For a moment, Connie has a clear view of the windscreen. Behind the wheel is a woman, her face a perfect oval enclosed by draped black cloth, glancing at Connie with a passing interest before she swings off the road and crunches up the drive. Connie waits while the car engine shuts down, then watches the woman get out of the car. She is wearing a floor-length black *abaya*, which hangs open at the front, revealing skinny indigo jeans and gold stiletto-heeled sandals. She dips back into the car and takes from the front seat a bright yellow handbag with big gold buckles, which she hangs on the crook of her arm.

'Hello,' says Connie, and she starts to walk up the drive before she changes her mind.

'Hi,' says the woman, taking a few steps towards Connie. 'Is something the matter?' She inspects the back of her vehicle.

'Don't worry,' says Connie. 'The car's fine.'

'I thought you were going to tell me I had oil pouring out or something.'

'No,' says Connie, 'nothing like that.'

'Then how can I help you?'

Connie hasn't really planned this. She feels intensely awkward in front of this elegant stranger. The woman pulls her *abaya* closed at the front, gold bangles sliding down her wrists. It makes Connie feel self-conscious in her running shorts and racer-back top.

'I'm a friend of Marijo's,' she says.

The woman raises her eyebrows. They are perfect black arches, tapering across her brow. Under them her eyes are lined with kohl, lifting to a cat's eye flick at the outer edges.

'Well,' clarifies Connie, 'she's a friend of my ... um, domestic worker. We're both quite worried about Marijo because there have been a couple of incidents recently.'

'Incidents?'

Connie takes a deep breath, tries to appear calm even though her heart is racing. 'Marijo has been hurt and I ... I was wondering if you knew anything about that?'

The woman narrows her eyes. 'What do you mean, hurt?'

'Scalded,' Connie says, 'on her hand.'

The woman looks concerned, confused. Then she says, 'Oh, do you mean the tea?'

Connie is suddenly wrong-footed. The moral momentum that had propelled her up the drive is starting to falter. She had been so convinced of her own rectitude that there hadn't been room for anything else, another version of events.

'We were very sorry about what happened to Marijo's hand,' the woman says. 'My aunty is not in good health and needs quite a lot of help moving around. She asked Marijo to hold her tea while she got up, but she stumbled, grabbed Marijo and the tea spilled on her hand. It was an accident.'

'Oh,' says Connie, 'I see.'

'Is that what you came to ask me?' The woman looks faintly incredulous, on the brink of annoyed.

Connie should just say she's sorry, that she got it all wrong, and then leave, but she has a memory of Marijo that won't go away. A girl in tears, in pain. If you scald someone, you help them, surely.

'It wasn't just that,' says Connie, carefully. 'She had a black eye, too.'

'I don't know anything about a black eye. I've been away for a few days and I've only just got back.' The woman looks genuinely bemused. Connie had an image in her mind of the woman who was capable of doing those things to Marijo, an image that she now sees may have been built of her own preconceptions. An almost comic stereotype, a pantomime baddie.

'What exactly are you suggesting?' The woman's voice is beginning to break, revealing fault lines of distress.

'I'm not suggesting anything,' says Connie, quickly, trying to reassure her, backtrack from a place she'd rushed headlong into. 'I'm just saying that I saw Marijo's face and she had a very nasty injury, that's all.'

'I'll see how she is when I get in, but Marijo can be quite clumsy, you know. She's probably slipped or fallen.'

Clumsy? Connie looks at the woman. Clumsiness doesn't explain what she saw, but the woman's measured response has unnerved her. She doesn't know what to say in the face of this calm denial.

'These girls,' says the woman, matter-of-factly, 'sometimes they say things.'

'Why would she make something like that up?'

'I don't know. Attention, money? Do you think your housemaid has never said anything bad about you?'

The suggestion stops Connie in her tracks. She has never considered what Rosamie might say about her. Which of her faults and least appealing habits might be discussed, or laughed about, during a barbecue in Safa Park on a Friday afternoon.

'Marijo has a child in the Philippines.'

'Yes, I know.'

'She wants to go home, I believe, to see her baby.'

'And she will. Just as soon as we sort out her visa.'

'Her visa?'

'Yes, we are trying to sponsor her properly but Marijo prefers to work *khalli walli*.' The woman studies Connie's blank face, then says, 'How would you say it? *Flexibly?*'

Shock blooms on Connie's face, a blush of something

shameful. What does she know about Marijo, really? What does Rosamie even know about her? And if what Marijo had said was true, then surely she would just have gone to the police, whether she had the right visa or not. Yet there Connie was, standing on a neighbour's drive practically accusing her of doing terrible things. The woman sees Connie's reaction and gives a short, slightly mocking, laugh. 'I can't imagine what she has been saying about us.'

'Nothing,' says Connie. 'It was me who must have misunderstood.'

'I think maybe you have,' says the woman. 'Now, if you've finished all your questions, I need to get back to my aunty.' Then she turns away, stepping carefully up the drive on the slender heels of her sandals, leaving Connie with nothing but a sense of unease.

Around midday Connie's phone rings. A mobile number she doesn't recognize. When she answers it, there is silence at the other end of the line.

'Hello,' she says. 'Who is this?'

A faint rustling sound, perhaps a laboured breath, then a click.

The line goes dead.

TWENTY-THREE

STELLA

It's hard to interpret hyacinths. On the one hand, it's the kind of gift you might give to your grandmother. It's hardly a romantic flower. If roses say candlelit dinners and trips to Paris, hyacinths suggest support stockings and a copy of *Country Living*. I don't even think it's a particularly beautiful flower, but we forgive its clumsy blooms and thick, fleshy stems because it smells so wonderful. It's not the pretty girl that all the boys like, it's the plain one with the great sense of humour.

Still, it's been years since a man gave me a present. Over the past few days the green buds have opened. I was curious to know what colour it would be – blue or pink – a little like awaiting the birth of a baby. Then it surprised me by being white. Looking at it now, I see something strong and proud about the thrusting stem with its bulbous cap unfurling into starfish clusters of splayed white flowers. There's no question about it, the hyacinth is oddly erotic.

I'm expecting a parcel today but I don't know when he's coming. I've had no email or text with a delivery slot, no tracking number, so when the doorbell goes it makes me jump. I'm not ready! I haven't thought what I'll say. Should I mention the hyacinth or not? For a second I'm tempted to not open the door – *Sorry we missed you!* – but he knows I never go out, and what if he leaves the parcel with Mrs Wilson? Then I won't even get to see him. Or, worse, he could think I'm sick again, come round to the back door and see me cowering somewhere, behaving like an idiot. No, there's only one thing to do, and that's take a deep breath and open the door.

It happens so quickly I can hardly take it all in. There's a flash of neon yellow tabard and a parcel hits my stomach. The cardboard is so smooth it's almost slippery and I cling to it as it slides between my fingers, pressing it against my body to free a hand to squiggle on the saturn. Not *his* saturn, someone else's. Then it's over and I'm left reeling on the doorstep, clutching a pair of pompom-embellished, shearling-trimmed ankle boots that I didn't even want.

Yodel?

I mean, seriously?

Sometimes it's the small things that keep you going. One single thing in your day to look forward to. That's what he is to me now. Just the anticipation of him is enough. The pleasure of opening the door to see his face.

Our faces define us. They are the centre of our identity, announcing our age, our ethnicity and the vagaries of our shifting moods. Our most basic human interactions are with each other's faces. It's not about beauty, the spacing of our eyes, the contour of our cheekbones or the fullness of our lips. It's about expressiveness. Without a face we are mute, unable to look at another human being and say, *You make me happy*, just with the upturn of our lips. Without a face I couldn't speak. I couldn't tell the world what I wanted to say.

Even after reconstructive surgery I lived in constant pain with *significant functional deficits*. I had lost everything, including all hope. Then the surgeons told me about something I hadn't even thought possible. That they could give me a new face. Not one moulded from the rest of me, like I was made of plasticine and bits could be pinched from my legs and stuck on my head. A *real* face, with features perfectly coded by DNA to become lips or a nose, and smooth skin, freckled by the sun and covered with gossamer hairs. I cried when they told me, Connie. I cried with relief and the sheer joy of fresh hope.

Medicine is a balancing act, a question of whether the benefits outweigh the risks, and this wasn't a matter of life and death. Not like a heart or a liver or kidney. I was alive and likely to stay that way. The question was how much value we put on our social interactions. Is being able to walk down the street, unremarked upon, worth the risks of infection and malignancy that come with immunosuppression? What chances would you take to be able to smile, or kiss the person you love? They don't do something like this just for vanity's sake, or to pander to society's sensibilities about disfigurement. They do it to restore function, the ability to eat, speak, blink and smile.

They had just launched a face-transplant programme when I arrived at the specialist centre. During the months I spent there they did what they could to reconstruct my face, but they were also evaluating me to see whether I would be a suitable candidate for the transplant. Not just because of my injuries, but emotionally and psychologically. At the same time the surgeons were preparing for the procedure, practising with 3D imaging and virtual surgery, mapping out my nerves and the actions they controlled, like a blueprint of my future functioning.

They told me I could be on the transplant register for months or even years before a suitable donor became available. They had to find someone just the same as me, same blood type and antigens, with skin the same colour, density, tone and texture. The same hair and facial shape. Twin flames, you see, mirror souls. How long till you find the other half of you?

Six months, two weeks and three days.

That's what all those sessions with Dr Clove were about. She had to be sure that I was stable enough psychologically to cope, resilient enough to accept a new identity. Then, at the end of it all, she asked me, *Is this what you really want?*

What do you think I told her?

There was one thing that Dr Clove didn't explain, and that was how haunted I would feel. How you would be with me every minute of every day. How I would see a lifetime of your smiles and laughter in the creases round my eyes, and how your experiences would be written into every tiny flaw on my skin. Human beings crave connection: we want to merge with the people we love. We even inhabit each other's bodies for moments, or months, but nothing – not sex, not pregnancy – could join two people in the way we have been joined. I don't know where you end and I begin.

It's your birthday soon and I plan to celebrate it alongside my own. It's *our* birthday now. I'll order something beautiful and we'll wear it together, illuminated by the brilliance of a hundred fairy lights.

High-end retailers only, Connie, I promise.

I'm not taking any chances with the delivery this time.

CONNIE

At 12:43 Connie's phone rings again. Same number.

She snatches it off the kitchen counter, speaks into it urgently, trying to keep her voice confident, *Who is this?* But it's like calling into the wind, her words swallowed by a static silence. When it rings again at 13:07 she ignores it, puts her phone on silent. By 14:22, she has five missed calls, all from that number.

She runs through a mental list of people it could be. Innocent callers alongside other, more sinister, explanations until she is in the realm of conspiracy theories and true-crime programmes. She chides herself for being silly. Next time she will just try answering it again. Maybe Mark has lost his phone and is trying to contact her from Oman with someone else's mobile, but the connection is bad. It could even be Rosamie. Now she thinks about it, she hasn't seen her since this morning.

Connie opens the kitchen door and walks out into the utility area. A pile of wet washing sits in the laundry basket in front of the washing-machine, its door yawning open, lights still blinking. A T-shirt straggles over the cylinder's rubbery lips, and one of Mark's socks is stuck to the back of the drum. It looks abandoned, as if someone hastily dragged out the load, then just left it there.

'Rosamie?' Connie hears her voice wavering, coughs, tries again. 'Are you there, Rosamie?'

She walks towards Rosamie's door, which is slightly ajar, calls again and knocks on the door, which swings open. The room smells of ginger and annatto seeds. A chopping board sits on the bed, piled high with shredded greens, but Rosamie is not there.

It's strange that she hasn't had lunch by almost two thirty. Worried, Connie is about to go out to look for her, when the door to the garage opens and Rosamie rushes in. She looks startled when she sees Connie, misunderstands why she is looking for her.

'Sorry, madam,' she gasps, kicking off her outside shoes, 'back now.' She slips on a flip-flop and chases its pair across the tiles with the other foot. Then she shuffles over to the washing-machine, squats and collects the washing into the basket.

The fluorescent lights of this windowless space pick out the sheen on Rosamie's skin. Her hair, usually as smooth and shiny as a conker, is roughly tied back and strands of it stick to her neck. As she tilts her face up, reaching into the drum to retrieve Mark's sock, Connie sees the fraught lines etching her brow.

'What's going on, Rosamie?'

To her astonishment, Rosamie crumples. She leans forward, puts her hand on the edge of the washing-machine and rests her forehead against it.

'What's the matter?' Connie swoops down and puts her hands on Rosamie's shoulders, gently pulling her back and

SONIA VELTON

turning her towards her. Rosamie's foamy flip-flops slide out in front of her and she sits down heavily on the tiled floor.

It seems instinctive to sit down with her, not try to get her up, so Connie grabs a couple of beach towels from a pile by the dryer and sits on one, her back against the wall. She offers the other to Rosamie, but she just shakes her head, closing her eyes, as if deep in thought. For a few seconds they sit there like nursery-school children, cross-legged on the floor. When Rosamie opens her eyes, they seem unusually bright, the pupils shrinking in the fluorescent glare.

'Marijo's madam found out she has been saying bad things about her.'

Connie's senses seem suddenly heightened. She notices the flicker of the lights and their incessant hum. She feels the tiles press cool against her calves, even as the air around her begins to feel unbearably humid, making the skin under her arms prickle and her back turn damp against the wall.

'How do you know?' She hears her own voice as if it comes from somewhere else, tinny and echoey in this bare space, the question bouncing, unanswered, round the walls. Connie has the sensation that she is lurching, or perhaps the world is shifting around her, sent spinning by her own stupidity.

Rosamie rubs at her face with her hands and draws them back over her head, pushing away the loose strands of hair. When she looks up again, Connie sees how tired she looks, almost defeated.

'She is calling me all the time, madam, but I don't know what to do to help her.'

'What's she saying?'

'Her madam came into her room, very angry, asking her why she telling people lies about her.'

Connie imagines the woman she met on the drive going inside and storming into Marijo's room, demanding to know what nonsense she's been telling the neighbours, but something about the scene doesn't seem quite right. The woman's image is like a puppet that doesn't move when the strings are pulled. Connie cannot make her do the things she's accused of.

'Marijo was scared,' continues Rosamie. 'She trying to tell her she said nothing.' She pauses and looks down at the bright pattern on the sole of her flip-flop. When she looks up, Connie feels pinned by her gaze. Pressed against the wall by the weight of responsibility for what she knows is coming. Already she is imagining herself this morning, walking back from her run, seeing the huge Nissan rolling towards her, exchanging that glance with the woman driving, then just letting the car drive past. Not stopping, not interfering, just keeping on walking.

Rosamie takes a breath then says, 'I think maybe her madam believed it's not Marijo's fault, that someone just saw her eye and thought something must have happened. But then her madam see something on the table next to Marijo's bed.'

'What did she see?' Connie sounds impatient, willing this story to materialize, to take on a shape she could recognize and deal with.

'The piece of paper, madam. The one you gave her with the details of those places that could help her.'

Despite the heat building in the tiny cell-like room, a strange chill slides over the back of Connie's neck. It wasn't just those details that were on it, thinks Connie. Her phone number was there too.

'I didn't even think . . .' begins Connie.

'I know, madam,' says Rosamie. 'You were just trying to help. Marijo knows that too.'

Connie almost doesn't want to ask anything else, doesn't want to confront something that she has played more of a part in than even Rosamie realizes, but she swallows and tries to sound calm when she says, 'What did she do when she saw it?'

'She saw your number and she tell Marijo that she is going to call you. Find out what Marijo really saying about her. Did she?'

Connie nods slowly. 'Yes, lots of times, but she hung up when I answered.'

'Maybe she just want to hear your voice, find out where you from.'

Connie suddenly feels uncomfortable. Not just her crossed legs, but her whole involvement in this. She wishes the woman had spoken to her so she didn't have to keep hearing everything second hand. She stands and picks up the towel from the floor. Rosamie follows suit, taking the towel from Connie and putting it on top of the dryer.

'Rosamie,' says Connie, 'I'm not sure about all of this. I

mean, I'm confused, that's all. There are some things that don't seem to add up.'

Rosamie slides the laundry basket to one side with her foot and closes the door of the washing-machine. 'What, madam?'

'I met Marijo's madam and . . . I dunno, she just didn't strike me as someone who would do any of these things.'

'You don't believe Marijo?'

'Of course I do,' she responds quickly, but the assertion sounds empty, as bald as the walls and the concrete floor they're standing on. 'It's just that her madam explained some things. The scald was an accident. Yes, it was tea, but not how Marijo said it happened. Connie's voice is fluid now, the natural hesitation to say something that Rosamie might find difficult to hear has gone, dissipated by the fact that, said out loud, everything sounded so plausible. 'And as for the black eye, her madam says she hasn't even been at home for the past few days, so it's hard to see how she could have had anything to do with that.'

Rosamie bends down and picks up the laundry basket, resting it on the edge of the washing-machine. 'Marijo's madam never leaves the house.'

'Of course she does. She was driving home when I saw her.'

Rosamie shakes her head and lifts the laundry basket onto her hip. 'That was madam Hala. Marijo's madam is madam Dina. The aunt.'

'The aunt?'

'Yes. Marijo helps look after her.'

'Oh.'

'She very clever, that aunty,' says Rosamie, almost to herself as she walks past Connie and opens the kitchen door. 'Marijo not *hemar* in front of her niece. She not pulling Marijo's ears and slapping her face when anyone else is there. Then, when Marijo's hand all red and peeling, she just say, wah, accident! So sorry!'

'But the visa?' says Connie, following along behind her. 'Hala said they are trying to sponsor Marijo, but she *wants* to work *khalli walli*.'

Rosamie stops and snorts, turning back towards Connie. '*Khalli walli!* There is nothing "take it or leave it" about Marijo working there!'

'Why doesn't she get a proper visa then?'

Rosamie sighs, shifting the basket to her other hip. 'If they sponsor her, Marijo stuck there when all she wants is her passport back, and to leave. So she make excuses to madam Hala.'

'But Hala seemed kind. Why doesn't Marijo just tell her what's going on?'

'Tell her what? That her aunt is calling Marijo names, beating her, hurting her? Who will she believe? Her own family or a housemaid? Then madam Dina just making even more trouble for her.'

'Rosamie, I'm so sorry.' She's not even sure what she's apologizing for. That she was the one who stirred up trouble for Marijo? That she didn't believe her? Or is she just sorry that Rosamie is probably right?

'Not your fault,' Rosamie's voice is bright again, back to the singsong tones that call her daughter *maganda* and her son *gwapo*. 'Can I ask a favour, madam?'

'Of course.'

'I think someone should check on Marijo, just see if she okay.'

'Do you want me to go over there?' Connie's voice is eager, grasping at the possibility to make amends.

Rosamie smiles and shakes her head.

'No, madam, Marijo is my *kababayan,* I will be the one to go to her. I just want to leave early this afternoon.'

TWENTY-FOUR

STELLA

When I bring the tea through, Mrs Wilson is standing by the fireplace. In her hand she has a framed picture of me from when I was about sixteen. There aren't many pictures of me as a child, Connie – I don't know why – but in this one I'm sitting on a wooden stile, hands either side of me on the top of the fence, feet resting on the tread. I'm wearing denim shorts with bare legs and wellies. Countryside stretches out behind me, teetering on the brink of a new season, hazy with late summer, yet ripe with the promise of autumn. Something has made me laugh but whatever it was is lost now, only ever existed for that moment, then disappeared. Like the person I was then.

'Gosh,' says Mrs Wilson, turning the photo towards me, 'you were so pretty.'

It's an awkward moment, those few seconds it takes Mrs Wilson to realize what she's said. She snatches in a breath. 'I didn't mean . . . It's not that . . . I was just . . .' She gives up.

'I'm sorry,' she says, and carefully places the photo back on the mantelpiece.

I put the tea on the table. 'It's okay, Pamela. I know what you meant.'

I'm glad she accepted my invitation to come over again. I'm hoping we might even become friends. It's good for me to see people and practise speaking. The more I try to move these muscles, the more the connections will establish themselves and the closer I'll get to having a face that is a willing participant in everything I do, one that can show people the person I am behind this expressionless veneer.

Pamela reaches for her mug and settles back on the sofa. There's no teapot now, no china tea cups and bone-handled pastry forks, just two women at opposite ends of the same sofa, having a chat.

'You look amazing, Stella. You do know that, don't you?'

I look down into my tea, studying the tiny ripples on its surface.

She has opened a conversation that we need to have. Any new person I meet will be able to take me for who I am now, but Pamela has seen the before and the after and is understandably curious about the in between. One of the things I have struggled with most for the past eighteen months is to make sense of the person I have become, and I suppose, if we're really going to be friends, she needs to make sense of who I am too.

'It's like a movie,' she says, 'almost science fiction. I can't imagine what it would be like to wake up and suddenly be someone else, what it must have been like seeing yourself for the first time.'

I remember that moment, Connie. They wouldn't let me look until three weeks after the transplant. The whole team gathered round my bedside to watch as my surgeon handed me a mirror. Instead of gaping, puckered holes and a prosthetic nose, I saw the smooth contours of a normal face. A nose, smaller and flatter than my own, and lips with a pronounced bow, a fuller curve, all set into a perfect plane of skin that joined my own in a seam that ran under my eyes and across the bridge of my nose. It was both reassuringly familiar and terrifyingly different. I couldn't speak so I put the mirror down and reached for my whiteboard. They wanted to know what I thought of my new face, this astonishingly dedicated group of people who had spent years of their own lives preparing for this moment.

The strange thing is that it's not the sight of my own face that I'll never forget, it's the sight of my lead surgeon's. I handed him my whiteboard and he read out what I had written for the rest of the team. He was composed at first, but his voice faltered on the first word, *Incredible.* Then he looked up at his team and I was completely humbled by the emotion in his voice, and the way he had to pause and swallow before he read out the rest: *Better than I ever could have hoped for.*

It made me see quite how much of other people there is in this face.

'Can I ask you something?' Pamela gives me a searching look, tries to gauge how I might feel about being asked what

I presume will be a personal question. But there's no nuance in this face of mine, no hints given away by an unguarded expression that speaks before I do. So I have to just say it, 'Yes, you can.'

'Do you ever think about her?'

Even though she prepared me, the question still makes my heart skip. Almost as if she has been able to look inside my mind and see you in there.

'Yes.'

Every minute, of every day.

'Do you know who she was?'

'I didn't at first. It's all strictly anonymous.' I put my tea down. I still don't like drinking in front of people, even friends, and I can't concentrate on sipping carefully as well as talking about something like this. 'All they told me was that she was a woman a year or so older than I was, nothing more. Then I wrote to her husband. A thank-you letter, they call it. Not directly, of course, but through my transplant coordinator and the donor records department. I think, initially, he found it incredibly hard. I wanted to know all about her, you see, and I don't think he was ready for that. But over time, if you both agree, you can start to exchange more information. I think knowing something about her helps me. It's as if I need to understand her, and what happened to her, in order to be able to accept it. Accept *her*. Does that make any sense?'

Pamela nods, just the tiniest inclination of her head.

'And I suppose I hope that knowing about me might help

him too. If it were me, I think I would find it comforting to know . . .' Here I pause because I cannot find the words. I cannot even begin to express what her gift has meant to me. It was life-changing, a miracle, a rebirth, but all I can manage is '. . . that their incredible generosity has given me a second chance at life.'

But Pamela understands. She nods more vigorously. 'I'm sure he does, love.' Then she fiddles with the hem of her jumper and looks up at me again. I know she has another question.

'What is it, Pamela?'

'I was just wondering . . . Do you . . . *look* like her?'

I think this is what people want to know most about us, Connie. Would an old acquaintance of yours see me in the street and do a double-take – *Isn't that Connie*? Is there more than just a passing resemblance? Would even your nearest and dearest look at me and see you standing there, as if there could be both life and death in one face?

'Maybe a little. When they selected a donor, they were looking for someone as similar to me as possible. She had to be a similar age, and the size and shape of her face had to be the same. But that doesn't mean I will actually look like her, because our facial structures are different. The face is both her *and* me. A hybrid, if you like.'

Pamela looks quite pale and puts down her tea.

'Sorry, is this too much for you?' I ask her. 'I know it's a bit . . . icky.'

'No! Not at all. I mean, it's quite something to get your head round, I'll give you that. But icky? No. I find it absolutely fascinating, if I'm honest with you. Must have been an awfully tricky operation. Not like my bunions!' She snorts softly and picks up her tea again.

Actually, it took nine surgeons, fifteen specialists and a small army of nurses fifty hours to complete. They made a metallic mask the exact shape of my face, put it over yours and traced round it. They removed the skin and the subcutaneous tissue, the cheek fat pads and facial bone up to the orbital floors. For a brief moment your face lay alone on a table, clamped and pale, bereft of either of us. Then they transferred it to me, connected your nerves and mine, our veins and arteries. Then the blood vessel clamps were removed and your face flushed pink with my blood.

'Quite tricky, yes,' I say.

Pamela does something strange then. She reaches up to her own face and touches her fingertips to her cheeks, pressing them gently, almost protectively.

'Are you all right, Pamela?'

'Oh, yes, love, it's just . . . I don't know. As wonderful as I think it is, I'm concerned that they would just . . . take my face.'

'You really don't need to worry about that. This isn't a routine transplant and it's not covered by deemed consent. Novel transplants require specific consent.'

'That makes sense,' she says, relieved. 'Still, I doubt anyone would want this face!' She chuckles to herself and reaches for a biscuit. 'It's not like I've ever been much of a head-turner.'

When my surgeon explained the transplant to me, he told me a successful outcome would be not being noticed. No stares or whispers. No one turning their head deliberately either to look at or away from me. He said he wanted to make me *just another face in the crowd*. As perfectly – no, exquisitely – ordinary as Pamela Wilson is.

'Have you ever met him?' Pamela asks.

'Who?'

'Her husband.'

'No, never.'

Then I think about his most recent letter. The one sitting in the kitchen, leaning against the fruit bowl.

'Not yet,' I say.

When she's finished her tea, Pamela exclaims, 'Oh, I almost forgot!' and pulls out a small bunch of tulips from her tote bag, their stems secured loosely with an elastic band. 'From the garden,' she says. 'No daffodils this time.'

She knows she shouldn't really make a joke about the time she tried to bring me daffodils, but she grins anyway. That's what I like about Pamela Wilson. There's always a kernel of humour in everything, and she doesn't mind digging it out.

And right then, I feel absolutely determined to smile back. To show her that I agree, that no matter what either of us has been through, there would still be a moment when we could catch each other's eyes and smile. So I do. It's a forced contraction of the zygomatic major, no more than a rictus twitch, really – a true Pan Am smile – but just that movement, that electric connection of muscle and nerve is enough to send a message to my brain that I might actually be smiling. And in return, it releases the smallest burst of endorphins, an opium firework exploding through my blood to tell every cell in my body that . . . I'm happy.

Pamela reaches across the sofa and grips my hand. 'Oh, well done, love!' she says, and I can see that telltale shine to her eyes, that glossy brightness of genuine emotion. 'You're almost there.'

CONNIE

Connie is toying with her phone. After 14:22 there was one more missed call, but nothing in the last few hours. Why had Marijo's madam called just to hear her voice? What had she given away the minute she said hello? Her gender, her nationality? Was there apprehension in her voice when she said, *Who is this?* Why all the missed calls? Just a nuisance, probably, a warning shot fired in the air: don't make my life difficult, or I'll do the same to you. Maybe she should just call Dina and have a chat with her, clear the air. She touches the number in her call records and the screen springs to life, *Calling* . . .

Connie ends the call before it connects. Just leave it, she thinks, then distracts herself by calling Mark. He answers straight away.

'Hi,' he says.

'How's Oman?'

'Hmm,' he says, 'kinda hot.'

'I know,' she replies, 'same here. I guess summer's coming already.'

They chat for a while about the sleek buildings appearing in the shadow of Muscat's ancient craggy mountainscape, and what the food's like at Mark's hotel. Normal stuff, skirting round the rows they've been having, layering over them with the banal and inconsequential.

Then Mark says, 'You okay?'

'I'm fine,' though she knows she doesn't sound it.

There's a brief silence, but before Connie can find the

words to tell him about Marijo, Mark fills it by saying, 'Kids driving you crazy? Fed up with being on your own? Not missing me, surely.'

She hears his throaty chuckle at the other end of the line and finds herself desperately wishing he were there. She still feels she needs him, wants to be able to tell him that she's done something silly and have him unpick it with her. She is the catastrophizer; he is the one who could always stop the sky falling.

'There's this friend of Rosamie's,' she begins. 'She's saying that her employer has taken her passport, that they don't give her proper time off, even physically assault her. It's really bad, Mark.'

'Call the police, then. Or report them to the Ministry of . . . Something.'

'It's not that simple. She's working illegally on a visit visa. And I met one of the women she works for and she seemed really . . . I dunno, reasonable, I guess.'

'Christ, Con. Sounds a mess to me. Don't get involved, that's my advice. Can I talk to the kids, or are they having tea?'

'Tea's finished,' she says. 'They're in the playroom.' Connie slides out from where she's sitting at the kitchen table ready to take the phone to the children. Then she stops. A text from Rosamie interrupts the call, flashing up on the screen.

'Mark? I'll call you back, okay?'

madam dina has called the police
Connie types a reply. *What happened?*

We trapped in Marijo's room!

What?? I'll come get you!

You must stay with kids, madam! i'm just telling u why i not back yet

This is crazy Rosamie!

She waits for a few minutes, checks her phone several times in case a text notification was lost in the sound of the tap filling the sink, or the beeps and honks of the children's toys from the playroom. Nothing.

She takes the kids upstairs to get them ready for bed, skipping the bath and reading the shortest story. 'But, Mummy,' complains Alice, 'you didn't do the funny voices.'

'I know, sweetie,' she replies. 'Mummy's just got a lot to do this evening.'

When they're in bed, she checks her phone again, then sends another text.

I'm worried. What's going on?

No point staring at the screen. She flips open the lids of the children's insulated lunch containers and puts pieces of fruit and snacks inside ready for the morning, then fills their water bottles and puts them into the fridge to chill.

A ping.

Connie grabs her phone and inhales sharply when she reads Rosamie's text.

marijo has run away!

A few minutes later Rosamie is sitting at the kitchen table sipping the glass of water that Connie has given her. She looks tired and shaky. In the microwave, a wedge of cheesy pasta bake rotates, bathed in yellow light.

'What on earth happened?' asks Connie.

'Oh, madam, I worried the police will come and take me too.' Rosamie's face crumples.

Connie takes a deep breath. 'Let's have something to eat. Then we can talk about it.'

Rosamie nods mutely and Connie leaves her for a moment to go to the fridge and take out a few things for a salad.

'Your text was a bit of a shock,' she says, pulling open a bag of salad leaves and shaking a pile onto two plates. 'Everything seemed pretty calm when you came back at lunchtime.'

'Because madam Hala was there. Then she go out and madam Dina go crazy!'

'Were you there then?'

Rosamie nods. 'I was sitting on Marijo's bed. We hear her coming, tap, tap with her stick. Marijo tell me to hide in the bathroom. Her madam getting angry if she has friends in her room.'

'So what did Dina do when she came into Marijo's room?'

'She hold up your paper, then point her finger at your number. Like this!' Rosamie jabs her finger in the air, making an almost comical grimace.

'Could you see her?'

'Yep, the bathroom door not close properly and madam Dina very busy, not looking at me! Then she say to Marijo, are you telling this *Connie* lies about me? Marijo say no, but madam Dina saying, "I don't believe you!" Then she take Marijo's phone and start looking at her texts.'

Connie's hands still as she stops halving the cherry tomatoes. 'How dare she? Why didn't Marijo just grab it back?'

'Too late. Madam Dina already see something bad. Very bad.'

Connie puts down the knife and wipes her hands on a tea-towel. 'What was it?'

Rosamie lowers her eyes. 'I am ashamed to tell you.'

Connie sits down at the table. 'It can't be that bad.'

'In this country, madam, it is that bad.'

Something triggers in Connie's mind then, the memory of a girl smiling under the light of a streetlamp, her finger pressed against a man's lips.

'She's seeing someone, isn't she?'

'How d'you know?'

'I saw her, late at night, walking along the path leading to the pool.'

Rosamie's breath comes out in a short, exasperated sigh. 'That silly girl,' she says.

'Who is he, Rosamie?'

'Worst person it can be. Madam Dina's driver.'

Of course, the man she had seen washing the car, with his boy-band looks, smiling and laughing with Marijo.

'When you say texts, Rosamie, what kind of texts were they?'

Rosamie takes a deep breath and looks at Connie. 'I didn't see them, but maybe they sending photos. Madam Dina not understand Tagalog but still she looking like her head going to explode, screaming and saying words I didn't understand.'

The microwave gives a ding. Connie goes to open it and put the food onto the plates. She places the cheesy pasta bake in front of Rosamie, who stares at the rigid square of steaming pasta, bound by an anaemic sauce.

'Sorry,' says Connie. 'It's just that the kids love it.'

'Oh, no, madam,' replies Rosamie, gamely. 'It looks very delicious.'

'What about the driver? Where was he when all this was happening?'

'He not live-in. Danilo share a room in Diera.' Rosamie takes a fork and prises a tube of pasta from its sticky prison. Connie is surprised by the speed at which she starts to eat, then she remembers the uncooked food in her room from lunchtime. Rosamie may not have eaten since breakfast. When she has finished, Connie asks what made Marijo run away.

Rosamie puts her fork on her plate and takes a sip of water. 'I tell her to.'

'Why?'

Rosamie shrugs. 'Madam Dina take Marijo's phone. She say it is evidence, that she calling the police and reporting her under *zina* law. She say they will take Marijo away and lock her up, and that what she deserve!'

Zina: the crime of illicit sexual intercourse. Connie wants to reassure Rosamie, tell her that nothing will happen to Marijo, but they live in a country where you can be imprisoned for kissing in the street, where sex outside marriage is illegal but marital rape is not. She puts Rosamie's plate on top of hers and takes them to the sink.

Rosamie swivels round, following her with her eyes. 'What could I do? When madam Dina leave she lock the door. We can't just wait for police to come, so I tell her, go! Go now – better be deported than go to jail!'

'But how did you get out?'

Rosamie gives a little grin as if, despite the gravity of the situation, she is a little pleased with herself. 'AC, madam. Marijo have old slide-out unit, so that what we did. We slide it out and climb through hole.'

Rosamie is looking at Connie, her lips pressed together and her eyes bright. Connie stares at her for a moment, and then they are laughing.

'Crikey, it's like *Prison Break*!'

Rosamie snorts. 'I loved that show.'

Connie looks at her. 'You're one hell of a *kababayan*, you know,' she says. Rosamie just smiles and lowers her eyes, picking at the remains of a sticker left on the table by one of the children.

Connie breathes deeply and sighs with relief. All the tension of the day is dissipating. She walks over to the fridge. Maybe there's still some wine left in the bottle.

'Is she okay now, though?' she asks, opening the fridge door. Nothing. She'll have to open a new one.

'Yes, madam. She take a bag with her and I give her some money. Then I put her in taxi. We show the driver your piece of paper and tell him to take her to the women's shelter. She said she would use their phone to call when she get there.'

Connie shuts the fridge door and glances up at the clock on the wall. 'When was that?'

Rosamie looks at her watch. 'Quite a while ago now.'

TWENTY-FIVE

STELLA

I ordered an off-the-shoulder, scalloped twill gown for your birthday, Connie. It arrived this morning. I was waiting in the kitchen, scanning the road, looking out for his van. I knew DPD was bringing it. I'd had the email and tracked the parcel. I knew my delivery slot, *14:17 to 15:17*, and all I needed to do was wait for him to come. It reminded me of that day over five years ago when I sat in the same place watching Tom waiting in his Lotus Elan, then driving away. Now I think about it, that recollection was prescient somehow, as if past separation could predict future loss.

I saw the van coming down the street. From a distance it can be hard to tell one white van from another, so for a few seconds I held my breath, thinking about emergency changes to the delivery company due to unforeseen circumstances. Then, as it came nearer, I saw that big red box on the side of the van. I know I said that red usually foreshadows danger, but not the bright red logo of a DPD delivery

296

van. That red announces excitement. The thrill of a new parcel. The rustle of organza and the whisper of silk-chiffon. The sight of someone, walking down your drive, you can connect with in some tiny, fleeting way.

He pulled up outside the house. I thought he might like to see how his hyacinth was doing, so I went into the living room to get it. Oh, that smell, that glorious, treacly scent. It filled the room like sunshine.

A knock on the door, a machine-gun rattle. Not his usual cheery ring, or light tap on the glass. I hurried out of the living room, put the hyacinth on the little wooden chair and opened the door. The red beanie, the uniform, the cardboard box. It was all so familiar, Connie, yet at the same time utterly shocking.

'Where's Evgeni?'

The man looked at me, handed me my parcel, held out the saturn.

'But where is he?' I insisted.

'I don't know anyone called Evgeni.'

'But you must! This is his area.'

'I'm sorry, but could you just sign, please?'

I feel as if the walls are closing in on me again and I'm in free-fall. I know you probably think that this is a small thing to get so upset about, considering what else I've been through, but it doesn't work like that. Sometimes we're so focused on coping with the big things that it's the little ones that blind-side us. Devastate us out of all proportion.

I haven't felt this bad in a long while. I haven't felt this desperate since that day in late June, when the daisy heads in the garden were closing, and the birds were just beginning their chorus of the dusk. The day my mother kept asking for her pink bed jacket but I just couldn't find it.

CONNIE

Connie is on the sofa watching a TV programme that doesn't hold her attention. She has half an eye on the door, waiting for Rosamie to pop her head round and say, *Marijo's fine, madam, she called me just now,* but the door stays shut and, save for the canned laughter of the TV show, the house is quiet.

She's tried calling Mark a few times. This is too much to deal with on her own. There are too many versions of this story playing out in her mind, and she can no longer tell which are likely and which fantasy. She imagines telling him one, hears him in her head saying, 'Why on earth didn't you just call the police?' But then, at the end of another version, a twenty-one-year-old girl, with a baby and an extended family to support, ends up in jail for being naive, for being human. At the end of that one, Mark just seems incredulous and says, 'Why did you get the police involved? You must have known it wouldn't end well for that girl.'

She's tired and she needs a sanity check, but his phone keeps going to voicemail, as if it's turned off. No battery more likely, she thinks. He's not good about charging his phone.

When her phone finally rings, her first thought is Mark, but it's an unknown number. She stares at it. It's not the number she thinks is Dina's either. She mutes the TV and answers the phone with a slightly tentative hello.

'Madam Connie?' The voice sounds thin and insubstantial. The line is poor and breaks up momentarily, before reconnecting.

'Is that Marijo?'

'Yes, madam.' She cannot see the tears, but they are threaded into Marijo's voice, in its pitch and the way it fractures with relief at the sound of her voice.

'Are you at the shelter?'

'No, madam.' Actual tears now, carried down the line.

'Where are you?'

'Bur Dubai.'

'Why? What happened?'

'Taxi driver bring me here. First he is kind, asking me if I am okay and why I going to the refuge. Stupid me, I tell him everything. Then he say the refuge is closed but he can help me because he has Filipina friend in Bur Dubai. He says she have nice apartment and I can stay the night. He promise to take me to Philippines Consulate in the morning. I didn't know what to do, madam!'

'It's okay,' says Connie, but something inside her contracts with fear.

'When we get to apartment,' continues Marijo, fitting her words around sobs and gulps of air, 'I ask him where his friend is, but there is no *kababayan* here. Then another man come and they are talking together. Now I know that man not real taxi driver! They lock me in room with other girls, tell me I have to work there now. But it not housework, madam. It not that kind of work.'

'Marijo.' She tries to hold her voice firm so that it cuts through the sobs.

'Yes.'

'Whose phone is this?'

'One of the girls'. She see that I'm upset and let me use it if I promise not to tell those men. I want to call Rosamie but I only have her number in my phone. So I call you because your number on this paper. So sorry, madam.'

'I'm glad you called me. But I want you to hang up now and call the police.'

'No, madam,' Marijo's voice is hushed. She can almost imagine her cupping her hand over the phone and turning away, shielding herself from the gaze of the other girls. 'They not let me call police. If I do they get in big trouble.'

'I'll call the police for you, then.'

'Don't send them, madam, please!' Marijo's voice is as high and fragile as a child's. 'Madam Dina making trouble with the police for me.'

'You can't worry about that now, Marijo. Just tell me where you are.'

'If police come, I will get arrested, same like the other girls.'

Connie hears a woman's voice saying something in a language she doesn't recognize.

'Madam? I not have much time.'

Connie pauses, but she's only thinking of how to tell Marijo that she's going to call the police anyway. Then Marijo says something that changes her mind, something that makes her think they cannot wait for the police to organize a raid, or decide whether to send a patrol car out to a housemaid in Bur Dubai who went willingly to a man's apartment.

'A man is coming for me, madam.'

Connie sucks in her breath, decides in that moment that if there is something she can do she has to do it. 'What do you want me to do, Marijo?'

'Taxi driver man think I have no one to help me. He think I cannot even ask police to help me because I in trouble myself. But then I tell him, I don't just work for one person, I have another madam, and she will be looking for me. I tell him this madam will be angry at what he has done. But he just laugh and say, "Tell this madam to come get you then".'

The line hisses and crackles. In the corner of the room, the TV performs a mute pantomime, the actors' silent laughter mocking her predicament.

'Can you do that, madam?' whispers Marijo. 'Can you come get me?'

When Connie knocks on her door, Rosamie is already in her night clothes.

'Are the children sick?' she asks, grabbing a cotton dressing-gown and wrapping it round herself.

'No, they're fine. I just need to go and pick up Marijo.'

'Marijo? She call you?'

'Yes, she only had my number. The taxi didn't know where to take her, so she ended up in Bur Dubai.'

'Bur Dubai! Why—'

'I need to go quickly,' interrupts Connie.

'I will go and get her,' says Rosamie, already shrugging off her dressing-gown.

'You'd have to get a taxi,' insists Connie. 'It's easier for me to go and get her in the car. Can you come in, and listen out for the kids in case they wake up?'

'Of course, madam.'

Connie gives her a thin smile. 'Thanks. I'll be back soon.'

TWENTY-SIX

STELLA

There's one last sin of memory. *Suggestibility.*

It is flawed eye-witness evidence and false confessions. It is summoning demons from your past that were never there to begin with. They even did an experiment to prove that we're able to conjure up memories like rabbits out of hats. A boy was asked to recall being lost in a mall aged five, even though the event had never occurred. At first, he had no memory of being lost but, after a few days of being encouraged to remember it, he was able to give detailed recollections. Terrifying, really, that you can suggest to someone that something happened and they can begin to remember it clearly. Even if that wasn't what happened at all.

Dr Clove once told me that people are more effective mirrors than glass. She was talking about how our identity comes not just from our appearance, but from how others respond to us, and how that shapes our view of ourselves. I remember thinking that a similar thing happens with our memories. Our perception of them can be moulded by others, depending on whether these memories are encouraged or dismissed. So the more Dr Clove nodded during our sessions before the transplant and said, *I thought you had*, or *That makes sense*, the more I thought that what I was telling her must be true.

When I told Dr Clove that I found it difficult to cope with caring for my mother, she said, *Of course*. When I told her there were days I felt so tired and lonely and ground down by the relentlessness of it, she said, *I understand*. It made me feel they must have been right, those memories, because she encouraged them, validated them with her sympathy. She already knew I was vulnerable, she already knew the gun was in my hands not my mother's, so there could only be one explanation for what happened. The girl made of glass finally shattered.

'Have you ever tried to hurt yourself before?' she asked me.

I shook my head, no.

'Do you want to talk about what made you feel you had no alternative at that time?'

Still no.

Dr Clove gave me an understanding smile. 'You don't need to worry, Stella. I'm just here as a psychologist. I've spoken to DC Bains. They won't be pressing any charges. I'm not here to get evidence. I just want to understand more about your state of mind, and to offer you support so that you'll be safe in the future.'

She sat forward then and clasped her hands round her knee. She was looking at me intently, not challenging me, but rather perfectly open as if there was nothing that couldn't be said in this room of hers.

'I thought I was able to cope,' I said.

'But you couldn't?'

It was strange, but I almost couldn't tell if she was asking me or telling me. Then she said, 'Being a carer is exceptionally challenging. You have to deal with so much. Social isolation, lack of sleep and the distress of seeing a loved one suffer. It's no wonder that carers can experience episodes of depression and feelings of hopelessness, despair even. Anyone would understand, Stella, if, in a moment of exhaustion, you felt that there was no other way out.'

Anyone would understand. Wasn't that what DC Bains had said? Everyone says they understand but no one does. Not really.

'And if that was what happened,' I said, feeling my way carefully, 'would it mean that you wouldn't allow me to have the transplant?'

'No, it wouldn't mean that.' Dr Clove's voice was reassuring. 'I think we would accept that you acted on impulse and that, free of those difficult circumstances, you wouldn't be likely to attempt it again.'

'I did feel there was no other way out, Dr Clove,' I said. 'The gun was almost reassuring. I knew there was a way for it all to end, that I could escape the grief and the pain. I wasn't thinking straight when I picked it up. I was tired and something had really upset me. There was no logic to it, no rational thought. I didn't sit down and think sensibly about getting more help, I just knew it had to end. Right then. Right that minute. It was like all the pain I'd ever experienced my whole life, all my darkest thoughts, came bearing down on that one moment.'

CONNIE

Bur Dubai glows with the phosphorescence of commerce. The darkness of the evening is broken by the glitter of beaded saris draped round headless mannequins, hanging by the doors of shops filled with bolts of silken fabric in every pattern and hue. It is illuminated by the gentle brilliance of Arabic lamps, laid out in rows, crusted with an endlessly refracting mosaic of coloured glass. The shop windows are heavy with gold, lengths of chain wound thickly round spools, and bangles clustered on poles, like abacus beads.

Connie's car edges slowly through the traffic. This is not a place made sleepy by the advancing hour, it is just getting started. Restaurants line the streets offering food from India, Pakistan, the Philippines and Bangladesh, and minimarts with bright neon signs cater to the myriad tastes of the diaspora.

She has vague directions to an apartment block near Al Rolla Road. It's off the main street, on a side road above a pharmacy. Not helpful, thinks Connie, as she scans a roadside peppered with pharmacies. This isn't a part of Dubai that she usually comes to, especially not at night. She has only wandered round the old buildings in Bastakia, taken the kids on a wooden *abra* across the creek to visit the spice souk and inhale the scent of cardamom, cloves and *oud*, which lingers in its narrow alleys. But this is neither old Dubai nor new Dubai – it's a kind of bridge between the two. The buildings are low-rise, in shades of yellow and cream, with laundry hanging on the balconies. It makes the place feel strangely real, as if there is a certain authenticity in these signs of humanity.

She loops back onto the main street again, then turns down the next side-street. It's quieter than the other road, with a bank on the corner, long since closed, and an electronics store with a security grille pulled across the shop front. Then something makes Connie pull over sharply. Marijo said something else, that she can see a restaurant from the balcony. She grabs a piece of paper from the passenger seat and looks again at the hastily scribbled directions and landmarks that she has been trying to follow. Khandani Brasserie, that was it. A grand name, she thinks, for the establishment she has parked outside, with its plasticky interior and grubby pictures of food in the window. She gets out of the car and walks over to the restaurant. The smell of *shisha* creeps from the doorway. It's overwhelming. A sweetly cloying cherry scent, strangely out of place in this gritty urban sprawl.

She turns and looks up at the building opposite. Only four storeys high, with a parade of shops at ground level, including a pharmacy. Rows of windows stare back at her blankly, framed by arches and white metal railings. Why aren't you looking out for me, Marijo?

A man comes out of the Khandani Brasserie, glances at Connie curiously, then crosses the road to the apartment block. The drumming in her chest starts up again. Is this what they do, these men? Eat, then head over the road?

Connie doesn't know what to do next. It's almost like

she's in one of those *Choose your Path* books she used to read as a child. She acknowledges something then. She's scared. What is she even doing here? She has children at home, a husband, and they all need her. *I'm sorry, Marijo,* she says silently to the building's blank facade, *but I can't help you.*

She turns and walks back towards her car. She is about to pull open the door when her phone rings, same number as before. She almost doesn't answer it. Then she wonders, what if the man she just saw is *the* man? The one Marijo has been told to expect?

'Hello?'

'I can see you, madam.'

'Really? How?'

'Other side.'

She turns, stupidly, and looks behind her towards the Khandani.

'No! Other side of the block.'

To the left of the apartments is a small side alley. She crosses the road and skirts round the building. When she gets to the alley she looks up. The windows are smaller on this side, with tiny balconies no more than a thin strip outside the windows. Marijo is standing on one, looking down at her.

It's almost too easy. She is only on the first floor, in the corner apartment, which fronts both the road and the alley. Directly below the balcony is a flat roof over the entrance to an underground car park. It wouldn't even be hard to get out. Why aren't these girls just climbing over the balcony railings and running away?

'Are you coming up, madam?' Marijo has put the phone down and is speaking to her directly.

'I'm sorry, Marijo, but I can't.'

I'm not the one to save you, she thinks. I wish I was, but I'm not that person.

There is an air-conditioning unit, with a huge fan, like a propeller, on the wall next to the balcony. It hums and spins, sucking Connie's words from the air before they reach Marijo.

'What, madam?'

She opens her mouth to say it again, then thinks, Surely we have to try *something*.

'Just jump out onto the roof.' She speaks louder this time, points to the flat surface above the car-park entrance.

Marijo gives a vehement shake of her head.

Things look different from the ground. Distances seem smaller, drops less precipitous.

'Look, there's a ledge here. Step on that first.' Connie indicates a narrow platform just below the edge of the balcony, made by the row of signs above the shop front.

'Yes, but how do I get down from there?' Marijo's voice has a shrill quality that carries it down to Connie over the dull roar of the AC.

She's probably right: it's too high. Connie knows if it were her standing on the balcony, she wouldn't want to do it. She steps back and looks round the side of the building. Then she sees that there's a metal roof-access ladder on the side of the car-park entrance.

'There's a ladder,' she shouts to Marijo.

But the answer's still no, an even more panicked shake of the head.

Connie feels frustrated. There's nothing more she can do. Marijo needs to be brave now. She looks back up at her, ready to tell her she's leaving, that all she can do is call the police, but Marijo isn't looking at her: she's staring across the street. Connie follows her gaze to the Khandani where a man is standing, watching them.

The sight of him seems to shift something in Marijo. Suddenly she swings one leg over the balcony, then the other until she's clinging to the outside. Then she is cautiously lowering herself, feeling with her foot for the ledge.

'That's it,' says Connie. 'You're almost there, just a bit lower.'

Marijo's foot makes contact with the ledge. She transfers her weight onto it, tests it to see that it's sound, then uses it as a foothold, before dropping down onto the roof. For a moment Connie is euphoric. She did it! Then something makes her look round. The man is crossing the road, a brisk walk, breaking into a jog.

'This way!' Connie runs to the ladder to show Marijo where it is. Marijo starts to run across the roof but twists her head to look at the man who is running towards them, then stumbles and falls.

Connie is starting to panic. 'Hurry!' she shouts at Marijo.

Marijo gets up, scrambles to the edge of the roof, then turns her back to Connie and starts climbing down the ladder. But her progress isn't helped by her flip-flops. By the time she reaches the ground, the man is already standing next to them.

'Where you taking her?' The man is wearing a baseball cap pulled down low over his eyes.

'Let's get in the car,' she says to Marijo.

'Hey, wait!' shouts the man, as they walk away. 'I tried to help you!'

Marijo snaps round, indignant. 'No, you locked me up!'

'Just don't speak to him,' mutters Connie.

'I say you can go anytime.' The man is trailing them, crossing the road right behind them.

The two women speed up, stopping abruptly to allow a car to pass. 'That's my car,' says Connie to Marijo, pointing her key towards it and unlocking it. 'Get in,' says Connie. 'Hurry!' She opens the driver's door but the man is right there, his hand on the door, blocking it.

'Where you going?'

'Get out of my way, please.' She clutches the car key tightly because her hands are shaking.

'You going to police?'

'We're just going home,' Connie tells him.

'So you not telling police?'

'If you don't move, I'll call the police right now,' she says, with an assertiveness she doesn't feel.

'Hey, no problem,' The man holds up his hands, palms facing her, in a calming gesture, then steps back onto the kerb.

Connie slides onto the driver's seat. She reaches out to pull the door shut, but before she can close it, the man wedges his foot against it, rests his hand on the roof of the car and leans in towards her.

'If you go to police, I kill you.'

TWENTY-SEVEN

STELLA

It started with my mother's pink bed jacket. I couldn't find it. I'd just washed it and left it neatly folded on top of the laundry pile, ready to put away now that the weather was warmer. I bought it because it was meant to be comforting for people with dementia to feel cosy, meant to make them less restless. My mother had taken to getting up during the night and walking around. A few months ago I had found her sitting at the bottom of the stairs in her nightie. When I sat down beside her and put my arms round her shoulders – said, 'Mum? It's nighttime, best come back to bed now' – her skin had felt cold, like putting my hands on a chicken straight out of the fridge. I couldn't make her understand the difference between night and day, but I could at least make sure she would be warm if she wandered about. But by then it was 20 June. The summer solstice. The day of the maximum tilt of the earth.

I'd looked in the drawers, under the bed, in the airing

cupboard, but I still couldn't find it, so I went into the living room to look in the Hoarding Box. It was an old wicker picnic hamper, with 'Empire Made' written on the front. When my mother wanted to keep something safe, something important like yesterday's newspaper or the cuddly unicorn she'd bought, then this was where she was meant to put it. It was a good idea for me to check it every day, anyway. Especially before I'd labelled where the toilet was.

Not only was it not in there, but my mother wasn't in the living room either. I'd left her sitting in her chair, with some music on and the room smelling of the lemon balm that was wafting from a diffuser. I was trying to do everything right, Connie. I thought there was a bargain to be struck, that if I found out how to care for her properly – react in the right way, give her everything that might help her – we'd get through it. But negotiating with dementia is like making a pact with the devil: you acknowledge it as your master then get nothing in return.

I walked into the kitchen and noticed that the back door was open. There was a rustling sound from outside, like a fox scavenging in the night. I put my head round the door and saw my mother rummaging in the dustbin, her hands soiled by the incontinence pads she now relied on because labelling the toilet hadn't made the slightest difference, and potato peelings stuck to her forearms.

'Mum! What are you doing?'

She looked up. 'Doing.'

'Come on,' I said, gently shaking her arm to make her let

go of the sticky black tray of a ready meal. 'Let's get you back inside.'

She was about to step into the kitchen when she stopped and said, 'Where's Patrick?'

She asked where my father was about ten times a day. I had stopped explaining he had left as this just made her confused and upset. Sometimes I simply ignored the question or talked about other things, and sometimes I just stayed silent, unable to face the relentless tedium of maintaining a constant reassuring monologue. It was beginning to get me down, if I'm honest with you. The music and the lemon balm weren't just for her, they were for me too. I was trying to drown the humming and the endlessly repeated questions, calm myself, focus on anything rather than the constant toe-tapping. While I was looking for a way to cope, something to try that might help, I read some advice that suggested talking to her about Patrick and remembering him together, rather than simply telling her he was gone.

I washed her hands and arms carefully and took her upstairs. When she was settled in bed, propped up with some pillows, I got my father's old suitcase from the spare room. I'd only found it a few days before, and I thought the things in it might trigger some memories. I took them out, one by one, and described them to her. 'This was Patrick's favourite cardigan. He used to wear it in the evenings when he watched TV. Do you remember?'

I don't know if it helped her, what flicker of recollection there might have been deep inside a mind I could no longer reach, but we went through everything, even the pyjamas. Then I pointed to all the stickers on the case and asked her if she had been with him when he got them, talked about the cruise liners he had worked on, the adventures he must have had.

'This might be worth something,' I remember saying, as I picked up the oak-tanned leather case. That was when I still thought the gun had belonged to Bonnie Parker. I opened the case and carefully took it out, handling it with that blend of reverence and wonder we reserve for guns and newborns. I ran my finger over the ridges of the dull nickel cylinder, then turned it over, looking for the remains of the medical tape.

'D'you know what Dad told me once? He said that this sticky stuff was left by the medical tape Bonnie Parker used to strap the gun to her leg, underneath her skirt.'

Nothing, just that low, reedy hum.

'I had no idea you still had this, Mum. You're not allowed to keep guns at home, you know.'

An echoey vibration, a meaningless resonance neither agreeing nor disagreeing.

'We might be okay because it's an antique, but we can't keep it. I'm going to hand it in to the police.'

I was planning to go to the police, Connie, but what I didn't tell her was how oddly comforted I felt by having it there. Just for a little while.

It was my very own fleecy bed jacket.

★

By the time we finished it was mid-afternoon. I had ironing to do and the dinner to prepare. Her symptoms had worsened, and I needed to make some calls and fill in some forms to see if we might be eligible for more help.

'Would you like a nap, Mum?'

I knew that sleeping in the afternoon wasn't a good idea because then she wouldn't sleep at night. I guess it's like having a baby. You know you shouldn't let it sleep too much during the day, but it's so very tempting to just let it carry on napping. Those few peaceful moments to get something done or have a blissfully solitary cup of tea and read a magazine are just too precious. They will be worth the night that follows. Or, at least, that's what you think at the time.

The lack of sleep made me want to crawl out of my own head. It turned the world into a sludge I had to wade through. I began to see everything as if it was reflected in a fairground mirror, distorted and ugly.

She didn't answer so I took the extra pillow away from behind her and tried to get her to lie down, but she suddenly started screaming, clawing at me. I drew back in alarm, touching my hand to my lip where it was bleeding. I tried to stay calm, tell myself she didn't mean it, but all my fatigue, frustration and fury seemed to combine and I couldn't stop myself.

'Just go to sleep!' I shouted at her.

Then suddenly she was quiet, almost childlike, sitting up in her bed, staring at me in mute surprise.

'We'll both feel better,' I said, through gritted teeth, 'if you can get some rest.'

I decided not to try to touch her again, so I just backed out of her room, talking what was meant to be soothing nonsense but came out as a taut string of words, high-pitched and slightly breathless. I was almost at the door when she looked at me, eyes wide, and said, 'Coat!' then started clutching at her arms.

She wouldn't sleep without that wretched bed jacket, Connie. That was the problem.

I started looking all over again, even checking in the bathroom vanity unit, crazy places that I knew it couldn't possibly be. As soon as I left she got out of bed and started following me from room to room, a duckling imprinted on an unlikely mother.

I should have just left the house. Gone out for the paper I'd never read, or the pint of milk we didn't need, but I didn't. I was almost addicted to stress by then, as if the cortisol running in my veins kept me going.

I went into the kitchen to start to look there, yanking open the drawer of Things That Might Come In Handy and slamming cupboards.

'Coat,' my mother pleaded.

'I don't know where it is!' My voice was escalating, coming out so forcefully that it scratched the inside of my throat. I knew I had to calm down, so I tried to focus on my breathing, while the sound of 'Una Paloma Blanca' filtered in from the living room.

Then I saw that the kitchen door was still open. When I went over to shut it, I spotted the bin lid lying on the grass.

As I replaced it, I noticed something pink under the netting from a bag of fruit and some empty crisps packets.

I drew out the bed jacket slowly – oddly thrilled by the unspeakable things stuck to its fuzzy material – and held it up to her.

'Well, there it is,' I said.

'Where's Patrick?' she said.

That bed jacket was the little thing I couldn't cope with, Connie. It was no more than annoying, really, but I just couldn't tolerate it because I didn't have anything left after dealing with the bigger things.

'You'll need this,' I said, my voice more vicious than it had ever been before, 'in the nursing home.' Then I ran upstairs with it, and she followed with a slow, shuffling gait. I grabbed my father's suitcase, carefully repacked, and tipped out the contents onto her bed. Then I packed it for her in the dramatic fashion I had described to DC Bains, soiled bed jacket and all.

CONNIE

When Connie climbed into her car outside the Khandani Brasserie, she'd noticed a white hatchback parked a little way behind: it had followed her when she pulled out into the road. She lost sight of it once they were back in the melee of Al Rolla Road, but now that the other traffic has dwindled she thinks she can see it again, a solitary white car in her rear-view mirror, almost eclipsed by its own headlights.

The evening has given way to night, and route E44 stretches out before them into an empty landscape. They have left the city, and passed the new developments that bleed into the desert. There are few cars, and little by the roadside, save scattered clumps of broom bush. Marijo is using Connie's phone to call Rosamie to let her know they're okay, and on their way to the women's shelter. She chats to her with a breathless relief that Connie herself doesn't feel. When Marijo puts the phone down, Connie asks her if she recognizes the car behind.

Marijo twists to look back at the road, squinting against the glare of the headlights. 'Hmm, maybe,' she says. She watches a while longer, then turns back and seems to slump down into the passenger seat. 'Not sure, but it could be the taxi that took me to Bur Dubai.'

'But it's not a taxi.'

'I took unofficial taxi. Cheaper than proper taxi.'

'I think he's following us.'

'Best get to refuge quickly,' says Marijo, staring out of the window. Then she turns to face Connie. 'You think we might have missed the turning? Seems very empty out here. No buildings, nothing.'

Connie had been thinking the same. They are heading towards the forts and mountain ranges of Hatta. She wishes she hadn't given Marijo her phone before she knew exactly where the turn-off was. Except she *had* known, she had just been concentrating on the car behind.

'I'll turn around at the next roundabout.'

Then she will know, she thinks. Know for sure if the car is following them.

The road seems endless. She slows to a speed where anyone with an open road ahead of them would get annoyed and overtake but the car behind doesn't. Then she speeds up to 120 kilometres per hour. Marijo glances sideways at her but she nudges up to over 140. The car stays right behind them.

Then a roundabout appears ahead. Connie brakes hard, and she and Marijo are forced forward in their seats. She glances at the rear-view mirror, and her eyes widen as the white car looms up behind them, the gap between the vehicles swiftly closing. Should she keep braking and enter the roundabout safely, or accelerate to avoid the car behind crashing into them? She glances at the roundabout, sees that it's empty and, in that split second, decides to take her foot off the brake.

Her car hurtles onto the roundabout far too fast. There are only two exits, one straight ahead and the other back the way they came. She should just keep going, sail right over the roundabout, but she doesn't know when there will be another opportunity to turn, doesn't want to drive further into a bleak and empty desert. She grips the steering wheel and twists it sharply to the left.

The car lurches and Connie slams on the brakes, trying to slow enough to turn. Marijo sucks in her breath and clutches at the sides of her seat as the car skids on the roundabout. In that moment Connie knows she's heading off the road. She braces herself for the impact as the car swerves off the roundabout and ploughs into the rocky roadside desert. But the shrubs and the sandy surface absorb their speed, and they come to a halt not far from the road.

Connie grips the top of the steering wheel and rests her forehead on her hands. 'Jesus,' she breathes.

'You okay, madam?' Marijo's voice is brittle with fear.

Connie lifts her head and looks at Marijo. 'Yeah, I'm okay. You?'

Marijo nods, swallows. 'We lucky there's no railings here.'

Lucky isn't something that Connie feels, with her heart still pumping undiluted terror round her body and her palms slick with the sweat of a near miss. She looks behind her. There's no sign of the white car. Marijo follows her gaze. 'I guess it wasn't the taxi after all.'

'Either that, or he decided we weren't worth killing himself over,' says Connie, taking her foot off the brake, and letting the car crunch slowly back to the tarmac. She checks the road, then pulls back onto the E44, heading towards the women's refuge.

A minute or two later, Connie says, 'I can't stop thinking about the other girls in that apartment.'

Marijo looks down at her lap, takes a deep breath. 'I know, madam, but what can we do? If we go to the police they will just arrest them for prostitution.'

'But will they, though? If you were tricked and imprisoned maybe they were too. Did you ask what happened to them?'

Marijo shakes her head. 'They not Filipinas, madam. Indonesian, I think. Only little English.'

Connie stares ahead of her, watching the twinkling lights of Dubai come back into view in the distance. 'Even if they do arrest those girls, Marijo, it will stop the men doing the same thing to other women. That's reason enough to go to the police, don't you think?'

'But what about me? Madam Dina told the police bad things about me.'

'I've been thinking about that, Marijo. Are you sure she actually went to the police? The first thing the authorities would want to see is your documentation. Visa, sponsorship, that kind of thing. It's not just you who's breaking the law working on a visit visa, it's them too. They're risking a hefty fine so Dina would have to think carefully before she called the police, wouldn't she?'

'Maybe, madam,' says Marijo. Then she is silent, resting her head against the car window, staring out into the endless darkness of the desert.

★

When she gets back Connie speaks briefly to Rosamie, tells her that she dropped Marijo safely off at the women's refuge and that she will call them in the morning. Then she gets ready for bed with the slow, deliberate movements of an automaton made mechanical by fatigue and shock. Her children will ground her once more, she thinks, take away the numbness. When she opens the door of their room, it's not enough to see them sleeping in their beds, she has to touch their warm skin, feel their damp breath cloud her fingertips. This night has shaken her, made her mind meander into desperate places where Fate was not on her side. She climbs onto Alice's bed, and lies down beside her, slips her arm round her daughter's slender body and buries her face in the hollow between her neck and shoulder. 'I'm sorry,' she whispers, into the tangles of her hair, sweet with the scent of sleep. 'I'm here now.'

Mark breezes home the next day with airport chocolate for the kids and flowers for Connie.

'How's everything been?' he asks, once the children have been hugged, turned upside down and swung round.

'Fine,' she says, placing long-stemmed roses, one by one, into a vase.

'Did you get that maid thing sorted?'

'I tried to call you about it, actually.'

'Did you?' His voice is light as he flicks the switch of the kettle and reaches for a mug.

'Yes, a little while after you called to speak to the kids.'

'Oh,' he says vaguely, 'client dinner, very tedious.'

She looks at the flowers. They are exquisite – subtle shades of dusky pink and cream, with sprigs of pistacia – but the sight of them makes her uneasy. Perhaps she feels she doesn't deserve them, that he wouldn't have given them to her had he known she'd taken stupid risks.

She watches Mark for a moment. 'This is an unexpected treat,' she says. 'You never usually bring me flowers.'

He gives a little shrug, then tosses a teabag into the mug. 'What can I say? I missed you.'

Then Connie realizes what's bothering her. It's not that she thinks she doesn't deserve the flowers: she's wondering why Mark felt the need to give them to her.

TWENTY-EIGHT

STELLA

In April you shared a link to a newspaper article from the UAE national press. In your post you've put, *So proud to know this lady.* There is a flurry of replies asking you all about it. I had to have a look at the article, Connie, and I could hardly believe what I was reading.

> *Dubai: A man posing as a taxi driver lured a woman to an apartment then locked her up and told her she would have to work as a prostitute, a court heard yesterday.*
>
> *The 21-year-old woman from the Philippines helped expose a prostitution ring by contacting police after she managed to escape the apartment by climbing onto the car-park roof from a balcony.*
>
> *Two men were charged with human trafficking, running a brothel, confinement and forcing women into prostitution following a police raid on the property.*
>
> *The woman arrived in the country two years ago through a maids' firm. She met the taxi driver when she tried to flee the*

family she worked for who had allegedly stolen her passport and
subjected her to abuse.

There were several Indonesian women being held against
their will in the apartment, the court heard.

The hearing has been adjourned until 3 May.

I've read what you did in the comments and your replies
and I feel really proud. It made me think of that other link
you posted, and the video I saw of the woman falling from
the balcony. I'm going to tell you something strange now: it
matters to me that you were a good person. There have been
so many times that I've felt this face was a mask I was hiding
behind, but now I feel I'm getting to know you, who you
were and what you believed in. It's not a mask any more,
Connie. I feel like you've become part of me and that you're
helping me face the world again. I don't know how I would
have felt if I'd found out that you weren't kind, or had done
bad things. I mean, how would someone feel if they were
given the heart of a murderer?

The world is turning full circle and we're almost back to
where we started: your most recent posts. A few more pictures and that's it, the last thing you shared.

I'm looking carefully now. Savouring each post before
the window closes.

One of the pictures is of you sitting on a picnic blanket
with your children. It's eye-catching because behind you
there is a blaze of red trees. Not muted autumn colour, like

you might see in England, but candy apple red, the colour of a clown's smile. I've never seen anything like that before.

It's a family picnic for your birthday and it's prompted 103 likes and 87 Happy Birthdays from your friends. Your caption is, *A truly wonderful day with my family.*

CONNIE

It's May and the flame trees are out in Safa Park, a million brilliant red stars caught in their branches. Ben and Alice are playing with a ball, while their parents lie on a picnic blanket, staring at the flaming canopy above them.

Even in the shade they're sweating. Connie picks up a bottle of water lying among the containers holding the remains of their picnic lunch. 'Kids,' she calls, 'come and have a drink of water. And, Ben, put your cap back on.' She flops down on the blanket and tilts her head to look at Mark. 'We should start thinking about the summer.'

The desert is an inhospitable place in the summer. As temperatures creep above 45°C the population of Dubai shifts and alters, shedding people, like a ptarmigan changes its plumage with the seasons. The school summer holidays are long, so the wives and children, those who are able to, disappear, heading back to the countries they used to call home, leaving their husbands to carry on working alone. The men meet in air-conditioned bars as though they were twenty again, feeling both bereft and thrilled to find themselves alone.

'You and the kids could go and stay with my parents.'

A summer with Frank and Julia. Connie stays silent and stares up at the spindly red bells of the flame tree's flowers.

'Come on, Con, it would be a great chance to get things back on track, and they'd love to have you. It'll be fine, I know it will.'

'Easy for you to say. You won't be there.'

'Okay, stay here, then.' Mark is sulky, grabbing his hat and plonking it down over his eyes.

'That's not going to be much fun for the kids.'

'Then my folks are the only option. It's not as if your dad is going to have them, and we can't afford to rent somewhere all summer.'

Connie's father has remarried. She visits for Sunday lunch or a day trip once in a blue moon. It's not that they're on bad terms, just that staying with the kids for weeks at a time isn't something either of them would contemplate, and with their house in London rented out, Mark's right. It's a choking summer in Dubai, or Frank and Julia.

'Anyway,' says Mark, 'Dorset is just lovely in the summer. Imagine all those trips to Durdle Beach. The kids will have a great time.' Mark takes the hat off his face, and rolls over to face her, propping himself up on one elbow. 'What's everyone else up to?'

'Everyone else, who?'

'Oh, y'know, Liz, those kinds of people.'

He doesn't care what Liz is up to this summer, she knows that.

'No idea,' she says, sitting up and beginning to pack the Tupperware back into the cool bag.

'What about Ruby and Adrian?'

There it is, she thinks.

'Why d'you want to know?'

'So I know who'll be left in Dubai to meet up with.

Maybe I can give Adrian a call, and we can have a drink or something. It's going to be pretty lonely for us guys over the summer.'

'I'm sure,' says Connie.

'So?'

'So what?

'What are they up to?' He's trying to sound casual, but the deliberately off-hand tone just sounds self-conscious.

'They have a place in Cornwall,' she replies. 'Ruby said she was taking the kids there as soon as school breaks up.'

Mark gives a disappointed-sounding humph. 'All right for some.'

For a while they are both silent. The children have abandoned the ball and moved on to the play area a little way off. Even last year she would have followed them, shadowing Alice round the climbing frames and helping Ben up to the monkey bars, but now she just keeps an eye on them, observing their growing independence with relief and regret. They're beginning to need her in different ways. She helps them to negotiate their friendships and weather the little traumas their lives throw at them. The birthday party they weren't invited to, the team they weren't picked for. She tries to answer their tricky questions: *Why do towels get dirty? Can mermaids do cartwheels?* She promises to google the ones she can't answer.

A boy has pushed Alice off the seesaw and her face is buckling with fury and distress. Connie goes to get up, but Mark puts a hand on her arm. 'Don't worry, I'll go. You enjoy your birthday.'

Her birthday. A family picnic in the park was all she wanted. It's Friday afternoon, and over by the barbecue area she can see a group of Filipinas playing a game. It's a kind of party game, with teams. They are all laughing and shouting, passing a balloon between them. She can't remember the last time she had that much fun. When did she lose the ability to play like a child? To find such joy in simple things? She remembers something Julia had done on the last day of her visit. She'd pressed a hundred dirhams into Connie's hand and said, 'Do give that to Rosamie, won't you? They have so little, these people.'

One of the Filipinas is ticklish, and she giggles when the balloon touches her neck. It floats down to the ground, bounces away in the breeze. She chases it, squealing as it slips out of her fingertips. How wrong Julia was, thinks Connie.

Mark comes back with the children in tow. Alice is grinning. 'We have something for you, Mummy!'

Mark digs out a container from the bottom of the cool box. 'Ta-da!' he says, opening it to reveal a cake, bright pink buttercream sliding off a dome of sponge, misshapen fondant worms making the number 39 on the top.

Connie gasps.

'We made it for you,' announces Ben.

Connie puts her hand flat on her chest. She feels strangely emotional, takes a breath before she speaks. 'Kids, thank you so much. It's beautiful, really. Just amazing. I can't wait to try it!'

She pulls Alice onto her knee and Ben kneels down beside them while Mark cuts sticky, melting slices. 'Should have brought some candles,' he says, handing Connie her cake. 'That's okay,' she says, 'I have everything I need.'

TWENTY-NINE

STELLA

They're not roses, they're poppies.

When I first looked at the picture of you and your children standing on Durdle Beach I thought the flowers on your dress were roses, but I can see now that they're poppies, clustered densely at the bottom of the full skirt, becoming sparse towards a fitted bodice that's completely white. The picture's not a post, it's just a change to your profile picture, and it was Mark who changed it, not you.

It's not just the date it was changed that tells me this: it's the response from your friends, the hundreds of likes and heartfelt comments. I'm glad I didn't see all this when I first looked. I don't think I could have coped with seeing it if I'd known it was the last picture of you ever taken.

This account is just your memorial, Connie, the flowers laid at your door. If I really want to know what happened to you, I'll have to search for it again.

I go back to where I started and google your name, but

this time I add 'Durdle Beach' to it and see what comes up. I can see the results – they're screamingly clear – but I don't click on any of them. It feels too intrusive now that I know you. I don't need to see a picture of the mangled car, or the one of you that Mark will have given the press. I don't need the details of the accident, its precise time and location. The first blue hyperlink is enough: *Driver arrested after 39-year-old woman dies in car crash.*

CONNIE

It's windy up on the chalk cliffs. Seagulls float high above the glittering ocean in a sky full of slowly shifting clouds. Connie's dress is flattened against her body, her hair snapping round her face.

'Shall we walk down to the beach?' she asks Frank, lifting her sunglasses up onto her head to pin the hair away from her eyes. 'It might be less windy down there.'

'Good idea, love.'

They set off along the stony white path, Connie leading the way down the cliffside, Frank and Julia following, each holding a grandchild's hand. This part of the path is steep. Connie's plimsoll slides over the loose rocks, and she slips part of the way down. She steadies herself and looks back up the path. 'Careful on this bit, kids,' she calls, but it's not her children, trotting over the clay earth as surefooted as mountain goats, that she's worried about.

'Ooh,' says Julia, clinging hard to Ben's hand, and placing each foot carefully on the steps cut into the path. 'It's been a while since I came down here.'

'It'll be worth it in the end,' says Connie. She lets the wind carry her words back up the cliff because she has already turned and is looking at the beach below. Despite almost two years of living in the Arabian Gulf, there is something magical about a British beach. The blustery air, tangy with salt. The brilliant green of the grass carpeting the cliffs and straggling over the beginnings of the majestic limestone arching into the sea. The kiosk selling ice creams and the spinning pinwheels blurring to rainbow shades in the wind.

She walks ahead until the clay turns to beach. There are tents and windbreakers, towels and an inflatable beach ball, liberated by the wind, bouncing across the sand.

'Come on, kids!' Connie turns round and holds out her hands. Her children break free of their grandparents and scrabble down the remaining section of path, running towards their mother. Connie takes their hands and they all turn to look at Durdle Door.

It's morning and the sun is moving round the beach, warming the same bleached coast that it has for millions of years, and will do for millions more. Connie stands in its gaze, feeling like a tiny speck of humanity, humbled by a primeval landscape. Every element lays claim to her. The wind lifting her dress out behind her, poppies spilled like blood over the rippling white skirt. The sea that swells and rolls towards her. And the earth that still holds her safe.

'Don't they look lovely standing there?' says Julia.

She and Frank have reached the bottom of the path and are standing some way behind Connie.

'You should take a photo,' replies Frank. 'Send it to Mark.'

The climb back up to the car park is arduous. The kids complain that they're hungry and straggle behind in protest. Ben demands some water, but the bottle is empty. 'There's more in the car,' says Connie, sounding snappier than she wants to be. Frank marches on ahead, strong as an ox, defying his age with every step. Julia takes out a hat and puts it on, then disappears over the headland after Frank.

When she reaches the top, Connie sees Frank sitting on a bench just outside the car park. He has a hand pressed to his chest, and Julia is leaning over him, her arm round his shoulders.

'What's the matter?' says Connie, running the last few metres towards them.

'Oh, nothing, love,' says Frank, putting his palms on the top of his legs and rubbing them. 'Just had a bit of a funny turn coming up the hill. Got this new blood-pressure medication, you see.' He claps his hands onto his thighs, 'Right, let's go to the car and get home for lunch.'

Frank stands up, all gusto and purposeful movements, and strides off towards the car.

'Do you think he should drive?' Connie is walking alongside Julia, keeping her voice low.

'I'm sure he'll be fine. It's just these new meds.'

'Then he shouldn't be driving, Julia.'

Julia sighs. 'All right, then, I'll drive, but I hate these roads at this time of year. They're busy-busy-busy!'

Julia catches Frank up, and Connie sees them talking outside the driver's door. When she gets to the car she opens the back door so the children can climb in, belts them into their car seats, then slips into the middle between them. She wishes they'd hurry up: it's not exactly comfortable crushed between two bulky car seats in the back of a hatchback. The driver's door opens, but it's Frank, not Julia, who climbs into the driver's seat. He looks up into the rear-view mirror and his gaze meets hers.

'I'll be fine, love, really,' he says. 'Wouldn't take any risks with my grandchildren, now, would I?'

THIRTY

STELLA

Have you ever noticed how baddies often have scarred faces? Freddy Krueger, Darth Vader, Ernst Stavro Blofeld. A scarred face is synonymous with evil, something we're conditioned to be frightened of. A perfect, symmetrical face tells us that someone is healthy and wholesome. A scarred face tells us there is something in this person's past that means we should be wary of them. No wonder they had those blue benches outside the Tin Noses Shop.

D'you know who my favourite baddie is, Connie?

It's the Joker.

Wanna know how I got these scars?

I used to think I had to know everything I could about you, but it's the other way around. I want *you* to know everything about *me*. I told Pamela Wilson I needed to understand what had happened to you in order to accept you, but that's only half of it. I'm going to tell you something now that I've

342

never told anyone else. Not DC Bains, not Dr Clove. No one.

My mother sat on the edge of her bed staring at the suitcase with a perplexed expression. My outburst was already beginning to seem like an overreaction, a little bit ridiculous.

'I'm sorry,' I said, picking up the suitcase to take it downstairs so I could wash all the clothes, even the old ones. It hardly mattered now if they shrank or disintegrated completely.

I'd only been in the kitchen a few minutes when my mother shuffled in. 'Coat?' she said.

'It's coming,' I told her. 'I'm just giving it a wash.'

We had a cup of tea while I waited for the load to finish. I took out the bed jacket and quickly tumble-dried it on its own. Twenty minutes, enough time to fill in a few more sections of the forms to claim exemptions, reductions and allowances, while my mother hummed her relentless encouragement.

'There you go,' I said, when it was dry. I slipped her arms into it and pulled it up onto her shoulders. 'You're all ready for your nap now.'

She seemed comforted by the familiar feel of it – its fleecy material still warm and staticky from the tumble-drier – so she allowed me to take her upstairs and put her to bed. As I tucked the bedclothes round her, she looked down at my father's things, still scattered on the floor.

'Where's Patrick?'

I picked them all up. Neither of us needed any more reminding about my father. I would put them back in the suitcase, then put it away somewhere safe until I could get to the police station. That was all I intended to do when I picked up the gun case and balanced it on top of my father's bundled-up cardigan.

'Just go to sleep now, Mum,' I said. Then I closed her door.

I took my father's things downstairs and put them on the kitchen table. I went into the little utility area, built in a lean-to where the washing-machine was, to get the suitcase. When I picked it up I noticed that the pale chequered pattern was flecked with mess from the bed jacket. I would have to clean it before I could put everything back.

There was an old butler's sink in the lean-to so I took a cloth, wetted it and squirted on some cleaning product. Then I got to work wiping the inside clean. It was only then that I saw the bottom wasn't completely flat. There was something under the lining. I put down the cloth. Now that I looked carefully, I could see that along the left side of the suitcase the stitching had come away, leaving a gap. I put my hand into it and could feel all the way down to the lump under the lining. My hand closed round it and carefully pulled it out.

In my hand was a bundle of postcards, tied with string. I turned them over. *Dear Twinkle*, said the first.

I took them through to the kitchen table and sat down. I

listened for my mother, creaking across the hall, or shouting, but the house was silent. I undid the neat bow the string was tied in and pulled it off. There were almost twenty postcards, all addressed to me. They came from all over the world. The Greek islands, the Caribbean, Hawaii, and the Norwegian fjords. Pictures of wide, sweeping bays and impossibly blue oceans, huge cruise ships passing dramatic coastlines. The first had been sent not long after I turned seven. There were about five a year, until there were three, then two. In the year I turned eleven, he sent only one.

The message was almost always the same: *Dear Twinkle*, followed by greetings from whichever port the ocean liner had docked in. Then a single line about where he was, *Seals and dolphins in the sea today!* from the fjords, or *I'd better watch out, Santorini has an active volcano!* from the Greek islands. Never more than a line or two, signed off with, *Shine bright, Love Dad* and a little star with lines coming out of it as if it were twinkling.

That sin of memory I told you about, *suggestibility*, can work both ways. You can plant the seed of a memory, nurture it, and it will grow out of nothing. But you can also stamp memories out, deny them, suffocate them. A little while after my father left, I asked my mother whether anything had arrived for me from Daddy.

'Of course not. He's gone.'

'But he said he'd write to me.'

'He never said that.'

'He did. He said he'd send me postcards.'

That was when she started saying it: *You have a very vivid imagination, Stella.*

It never occurred to me that he might have wanted to leave my mother, but not wanted to leave me. Of course it didn't: my mother and I were practically the same person. I knew that, and she knew that. It was Dr Clove who used the words *narcissistic* and *co-dependent* to describe me and my mother. With her, I began to see how my need to be needed slotted in perfectly with my mother's need for control. I wasn't a person in my own right: I was simply an extension of her. She saw my attempts at independence as rejection, saw any other relationships I tried to have as a threat. I had sat in this very spot and watched Tom drive away. I had willingly crawled back under the shadow of my mother's influence, allowing myself to be reshaped by her love, whether it was given as a reward or withheld as a punishment.

I almost wished I hadn't found the postcards. It was easier to think that I had been abandoned than that I'd had a parent who wanted to love me. A father I could have contacted, according to the final postcard, c/o The Royal International Cruise Line if I wanted to stay in touch.

I felt real grief then, for the relationships I never had, and all I could think was that she had taken them from me, stolen the life I could have had. There is no rationality in exhaustion, no logic in the kind of fatigue that had become my way of life. The worst part was that I wanted to *confront* her. I wanted to be able to brandish the postcards in her face and demand to know why she had kept them from me. How she could have been so evil and selfish to have intercepted my father's attempts at love, no matter how token, or from how far away? Did you take them because if you couldn't have him, then I couldn't either? I wanted to ask her. Did you worry that he would make me leave you too? Or was it simple jealousy, because you could never bear to share his attention, even with a child? But I might just as well scream my questions at a headstone as ask my mother now.

I heard a noise from upstairs. A shout, something unintelligible that meant she had woken and found herself alone. A cry that was meant to draw me to her. It really affected me, that noise. I knew then that she still controlled me, and that her grip wouldn't slacken until one of us was gone. I opened the leather case and prised the gun out of its black suede bed. I think I wanted her to know how much she had hurt me. I couldn't explain that in words so I had to do it in actions. I wanted her to see how desperate she had made me. Then I looked at the single cartridge sitting upright in its block, like a small gold lipstick. I tugged on it and it came out so easily it was as if I was meant to push out the cylinder and slip the cartridge into one of its two-inch chambers.

I know what you're thinking: I didn't need to load the gun just to make a point.

I walked upstairs and opened the door of her room. That image of her sitting up in bed in her pink bed jacket, staring at me, is the one that has stayed with me. The memory that became like a photograph in my mind, a captured stillness before the world was blown apart.

I approached her and sat down on the edge of her bed. It was about 6 p.m. Mrs Wilson must have just thought that she'd better put the rubbish out. Maybe she was already struggling up the slope of her drive.

We've all watched too many movies. We've seen so many hammers cocked that it's almost instinctive for us. I liked the sound of it, the satisfying little click as the cylinder lines up and the trigger primes. I felt a bit like I was acting a part. You know me, Connie: *I have a very vivid imagination.*

There was only a single cartridge in the six chambers of that gun. I didn't even know which one would line up when the hammer was pulled back. In five other parallel universes, none of this ever happened. There was just a tiny click, a widening of her eyes and, perhaps, a flickering acknowledgement of what she had done.

I positioned the gun pointing upwards, wedged into the soft, fleshy groove under her chin and, for an eternal instant, I held it there.

Dementia unravels you thread by thread. It was as if my mother's awareness existed in strands, which slipped from her fingers one by one. I found out then which strand is the last to go. It's the instinct to survive. That most elementary drive for self-preservation.

I had my finger inside the trigger guard, was about to begin that graceful press down onto the trigger. Then she grabbed my hand and shoved the gun out from under her chin. As soon as I saw the gaping black eye of the barrel appearing and pointing towards me, I jerked my head back.

Her fingers were overlaid on mine. I had spent my whole life as an extension of her, not an individual, and in that moment we were still almost indistinguishable. I couldn't even tell if the pressure on the trigger was hers – or mine.

It's just as Batman said, Connie.

You either die a hero or live long enough to see yourself become the villain.

CONNIE

Frank drives fast down the roads he's driven along for almost fifty years, each bend and turn as instinctive as his golf swing or signing his name. Halfway home, Julia gasps and clutches the car seat.

'I've run out of pasta!'

Frank pulls in close to the hedgerow lining the road so another vehicle can pass. Branches drag across the window next to Alice.

'Can we stop somewhere?' Julia asks Frank. 'I don't want to have to go out again this afternoon.'

'Aw, I'm *hungry*,' says Ben. 'I don't want to go shopping.'

'But then we'll have no pasta for your dinner later!' Julia twists round to give Ben a big smile.

'Listen,' says Connie. 'Why don't you drop me off in town? I need to pick up a few things anyway and I'll get the pasta while I'm there. Then you can take the kids straight back and give them a sandwich or something.'

'That makes sense,' says Frank.

'And it'll be nice for you to have some time to yourself, I shouldn't wonder,' says Julia, still looking round at them. She gives Connie a little wink. 'You can have a coffee while you're at it. Maybe a slice of cake.'

They drop her off at the end of a crowded high street, thick with summer-holiday traffic. She takes Julia at her word and ducks into a coffee shop, pays for a latte at the counter and looks for somewhere to sit down. There are hardly any free tables, so she squeezes herself into a cramped space in the corner. I hope they all got home okay, she thinks, then decides to call Mark while she's out of the house to find out a bit more about this medication Frank's taking.

No answer. It doesn't surprise her. Their last conversation had been fraught, culminating in a childish, fractious row. Mark should have joined them in the UK by now. She was only ever meant to spend a week on her own with Frank and Julia, but he had called a few days ago and said something had come up at work and he couldn't get over there until it was finished.

She texts him: *I need to talk to you. It's important.*

The waitress comes over with her latte. Connie stirs it absently, staring out of the window at the tourists and shoppers ambling past. No point just waiting for him to respond, so she picks up her phone and starts to scroll through her social media. It's all summer-holiday pics now. Children on beaches, and glorious views from balconies. Then a post from Ruby makes her pause. It's a picture of a round garden thermometer, hanging on the side of Ruby's car port. The dial is calibrated in tens of degrees, from green, through to orange, then red. The black needle is pointing well into the red. *47°C!* writes Ruby. *Hottest I've ever known it!*

It's not the remarkable temperature that makes Connie pause: it's the fact that Ruby is still in Dubai. What happened to going to Cornwall as soon as the kids finished school?

She decides to reply to the post: *Thought you were back in Blighty already?*

She takes a sip of coffee, keeps staring at her phone. Come on, Ruby, she thinks. No one checks their phone more often than you. Then, *Ha!* appears, followed by, *Forgot to book the flights* (eye-rolling emoji), *couldn't get 3 seats till next week!*

Of course, the kids. She takes a breath, exhales it slowly, reins in her racing mind. Don't be silly, she tells herself, she's got the kids with her. What could they be doing with the kids around all day?

Oh, no! Connie types. *Finding anything to do with the kids in that heat?*

There's a tube of sugar on the saucer beside her latte. She picks it up and starts rolling it between her fingers until the paper goes soft. It starts to split, but she keeps rolling, even when brown crystals scatter over the table. Then the reply comes.

Summer camp!! And thank God for Jasmine!

Connie puts her phone down. There were so many little things that had made her wonder, so many thoughts she had quashed, or dismissed as foolish, even paranoid. But now everything begins to take on a clearer shape, a spectre resolving out of the fog, something threatening and inescapable.

The coffee turns tepid on the table as Connie's mind locks into a hamster wheel of analysis, going over and over all the times she has seen Ruby and Mark together, trying to remember how they behaved, and what they said to each other. She moves on to all the times she wasn't sure where

Mark was. What was he doing, and was she with him? Then she puts her head into her hands, scrunches her fingers into her hair. Mark's last trip to Oman. Where was Ruby then? She picks up her phone. She doesn't remember Ruby posting anything about being away over those few days, but maybe she missed it with all the Marijo drama.

Before she can look, Mark returns her call. She stares at his name for a second. She is desperate for answers, but at the same time she almost can't bring herself to speak to him, as if there is a certain peace to be found between the not knowing and the knowing.

'Hey, what's wrong?' he says, as soon as she answers.

How does he know? Has Ruby texted him already? *We need to be careful. Connie's been asking questions* . . .

'What d'you mean "What's wrong?"'

'Your message said it was urgent?'

She has completely forgotten about Frank. The thoughts and worries she was having only an hour ago have been swallowed by something so life-changing that it makes her want to crawl back in time to another moment, a split second standing on the beach when the world was a simple place of sunlight on her children's hair and pinwheels turning in the breeze.

'I need to talk to you about something.'

A woman on the next table looks round and stares at her. Connie didn't raise her voice, but it sounds taut, like a tuning fork resonating at the perfect pitch to attract attention. She doesn't want to have this conversation in a crowded coffee shop, so she gets up and grabs her bag, shuffling out round the tables.

'What is it?' Mark sounds impatient.

'Hang on.'

Outside, the high street is crowded. Connie navigates round mums pushing prams and chatting to friends, trying to talk to Mark.

'What?' he says. 'I can't even hear you. Where are you anyway?'

'I'm on the high street.'

'I'll call you back later when you're in the house.'

'No.' The force of her voice surprises her, but this is not a conversation she can have at Frank and Julia's house.

'What is it, then?'

For a moment she stands still, letting the people flow past her. Where to start? How to turn an instinct into words?

'Connie?'

'It's Ruby.'

She thinks he sighs, but she can't be sure over the beep of a car horn.

'What about her?'

'Why is she still in Dubai?'

'I don't know.' She hears this clearly, because he enunciates it so carefully. Each word a little sentence of its own.

'She said she was coming back to the UK, but she's still there. And you were meant to come back last week. You stayed to be with her, didn't you? So you could see her without me there.'

'For God's sake, Connie, you're crazy.'

'I'm not crazy,' she says, stepping round a couple of teen-agers, eyes on their phones, oblivious. 'It's not just that, it's lots of things.'

'Like what?'

'I don't know. Times I've seen you talking to her, weird things you've done recently. You—'

A lorry whooshes past and her words are lost, sucked into its noxious wake. She has reached the end of the high street, and the boutiques and coffee shops have given way to a yawning A road.

'It's the way you behave when you're around her. It's so obvious you fancy her.'

'Oh, come on! I can't go through the rest of my life never finding anyone else attractive. There must be some-one you think is quite hot. What about that tennis coach? Whatshisname – Jim?'

'Josh! And don't twist this, Mark. It's not about me.'

'No, it never is, is it? I haven't got time for this, Connie.'

'Wait!'

She can't let him hang up. On the other side of the road is a small park. A few swings and a slide, with an empty bench by some playing fields. It will be quieter there. She can sit down on the bench and have a proper conversation without being overheard or having to shout above the traffic.

'The last time you went to Oman,' she says, 'when you brought me those flowers. Was she there with you?'

She needs to hear his answer. Not just the words, but the

inflection in his voice, the pauses and when they come. Fit it all together. There's no pedestrian crossing, so she's going to have to just cross where she is.

'Mark? Answer me!'

He's saying something, but she can't hear him. She presses the phone flat against her ear, trying to drown out the rest of the world, condense it into just her and him, and what their future might be.

Then she walks out into the road. She's not concentrating, not stopping, looking or listening. Not doing all the things she would tell her children to do.

The driver of the car is just a teenager. He passed his test the day before and is thrilled to be alone behind the wheel. There's no one next to him reminding him to check his mirrors or signal. He can just drive, on this perfect sunny day, with the windows down and his music on. He scrolls through his library of songs to find his favourite track.

He looks up just at the moment of impact.

All he can see are poppies, scattered across his windscreen, blood red against pure white.

THIRTY-ONE

STELLA

There's something incredible about stepping into the light after a long period inside. Something exhilarating about the fresh air in your lungs and the warmth of the sun on your skin. The colours of the world are kaleidoscope bright, and every sound, every passing car, every chirping bird, so clear it's almost overwhelming. My life indoors muted the world. I observed it carrying on without me as though my kitchen window were a TV screen, playing an endless silent movie.

I take a deep breath, inhaling the everyday: traffic fumes and a waft of perfume from a woman walking past me, freshly baked muffins from the café ahead. They're like an infusion, a shot of normality straight through my veins.

I'm ready.

I push open the door to the café. It's quiet inside – the commuters have already rushed through, and the school mums have yet to arrive – but I still tense as I walk in, as if the world may yet stop in its tracks and stare at me. A woman with a baby in a pram is sitting by the window, but she doesn't look up as I pass. It's like I'm camouflaged, a chameleon that has morphed into the unremarkable.

I ask the barista for a coffee. He nods and smiles, more interested in getting the perfect froth to his milk than in me. I take the coffee to a table and sit down. Though it may look as if I'm doing nothing, I'm not. I'm absorbing the world, and in return it's reabsorbing me, accepting me back as a tiny moving part of its vast machine.

After a few minutes a man comes in carrying a bunch of flowers. He looks nervous. I can see the deliberate exhalation of his breath. I recognize him immediately from his photo, but he stands at the door, looking for a woman who is both his wife, and a complete stranger.

I stand up, but he knows who I am, is already staring at me. For a moment he doesn't move, and I'm left wondering who I am to him, what exactly it is that he sees. Then he seems to find himself, smiles politely and walks over to my table. It's as awkward as a first date. We don't know how we should greet each other, so we just do a jolty kind of dance – little aborted movements, giving flowers, going in for hugs that don't quite come off – until we both give up and sit down.

'Thank you for meeting me,' he says. I find it strange to be thanked, because I'm the one who's here to thank him. But now that I'm actually sitting in front of him those two words don't seem nearly enough, can't possibly express how I feel about him, and about you, so I just nod, mutely.

I ask him how he is, how your children are.

He shrugs. 'We're okay, I guess. Rosamie – the kids' nanny – she's been great. So have my parents. We've moved back to the UK now, to be closer to them.'

He orders a drink; I finish mine. We talk a little more. He asks me about myself and I try to tell him some things that make me sound interesting, but it's quite hard. The whole time I'm talking, all I can think is that I don't measure up to you. I worry that he thinks I wasn't worthy of you, that I have taken his beautiful, talented wife and made her ugly and boring.

'I'm training to be a teacher.'

It comes out suddenly, before I've really thought it through, but once it's out there I can't take it back, and nor do I want to. It's been a half-formed thought in my mind for a while, and the moment I tell Mark it crystallizes. It's like I've made a pledge: I really am going to do it.

'Well, I'm going to apply this year,' I clarify. 'I used to be a teaching assistant, but I always wanted to be a primary-school teacher. It's just that I never quite got round to starting the course.'

'Good for you,' he says. 'I think it would have made Connie very happy to know that.'

'I hope I get in,' I say. 'My grades aren't the best, but I've got loads of experience.'

'You will, Stella,' he replies. 'After what you've been through, you could do pretty much anything, don't you think?'

He's watching me intently now. I know what he's doing: he's searching for you, looking for some shadow of his wife in the face of another woman. There have been many times over the past year and a half that I've thought I was crazy – as if it was bizarre to feel so strongly that you still exist as a part of me – but I'm sure it's not just me who thinks this. Mark feels it too.

He picks up his drink to take a sip. Without his gaze on me, I feel able to say it, though it comes out as a scratchy whisper, catching on the plug of emotion wedged in my throat.

'I could never have contemplated doing it without what you gave me. What Connie gave me. Thank you so very much.' I finally manage to say the words, however inadequate they seem.

Slowly, he lowers his glass. 'It's what Connie would have wanted,' he says.

'Even so, this goes far beyond the generosity of most people'

'If I was going to be totally frank with you,' he says, 'I'd tell you that I really had to think about whether to do it. Connie's always been clear about being a donor, but I wasn't expecting them to ask me something like this. Honestly? My first reaction was *no way*. Take the organs or whatever, but please don't touch her—'

He takes a sharp breath, locks his fingers together and presses his mouth against them, staring down at the table.

'It's okay,' I tell him. 'I understand if you don't want to talk about it.'

He looks up then, rests his chin on his steepled hands. 'It's you who changed my mind. When I knew there was a real person just waiting for this chance, when I understood what they were trying to achieve with the face-transplant programme, it wasn't a question of how I could say yes, it was how could I say no? How could I possibly stop Connie having the chance to change someone's life like that? In my heart, I knew she'd have wanted to help you.'

'Can I tell you something?' I ask him.

'Anything, Stella.'

'I feel like I know her. Is that weird? I feel like Connie's my confidante. It's as if she's . . . I don't know, looking out for me.'

Mark smiles. 'Like *kababayan*,' he says. 'That's what Connie would have called you. It's a Tagalog word. It means you have an unbreakable bond with someone because you share something, have a common heritage.'

I prefer *twin flames*, but it's still a lovely thought. 'I like that,' I tell him.

He breathes deeply then, and his features seem to set in his face, pucker slightly as if they're a dam holding something back, something threatening to overwhelm him. 'You don't know what it means to me to meet you,' he says.

I don't know what to say to that, Connie. I think I'm just touched by the thought that I could give him anything, even a moment's solace, after everything he has given me.

'Could I—' His voice cracks completely then, and his eyes are filling with tears. He clears his throat, tries to speak again, but he doesn't need to. I know what he wants to do.

I nod and, slowly, he reaches out his hand. It's just the lightest stroke of his fingertips across my cheek. His tears are falling now and I'm crying too, because I've never felt more connected to you than at this moment. Mark brushes my tears away with his thumb, then says something. The words are spoken so softly, and come out so choked, that I'm not completely sure what they are, but it sounds like *I'm sorry.*

I'm still crying, but now I don't know whose tears they are, mine or yours.

The parcel is repackaged and on the little chair by the door, waiting to be collected. I think I'm going to stop ordering impractical things online that I have no use for, or any intention of keeping. It's not good for the environment and I need to start living in the real world. To that end, I've been out twice this week. Once to meet Mark, and once just to walk around the park at the end of the road. I sat on the bench that Tom and I sat on that Christmas Day, and I thought a lot about my memories. I wondered why we even have them when they're so flawed and unreliable, but I'm not sure that's the point. I read somewhere that the same parts of our brains are activated when we remember our past as when we imagine our future. It's as if they're linked: we have to make sense of the person we were in order to become the person we want to be.

The van's drawing up now. I don't feel the same excitement at the sight of it, knowing it's not Evgeni, but that other driver wasn't so bad. Perfectly polite, really.

There's a tap on the glass panel by the door, a ripple of red behind the wobbly glass.

I open the door.

'Hey, lady.'

He looks amazing. His stubble has been shaped into an elegant goatee. His red polo shirt is open at the top to reveal the smooth, tanned skin of his throat and the beginnings of the hair on his chest.

'Where have you been, Evgeni?' I hope my voice doesn't sound too breathless.

'Bulgaria,' he says. 'My father was sick, so I go home to see him.'

I knew it would be something like that. Evgeni is truly a king among men.

I pick up the parcel and hand it to him. As I watch him scan the returns label, I have this overwhelming feeling of having been given a second chance, one that I shouldn't let slip through my fingers.

'Evgeni?'

He looks up, holds my gaze.

'I just wanted to say . . . that I missed you. And that I'm glad to see you again.'

It's not the most emotional of outpourings but, nevertheless, I'm bracing myself for his response.

'I missed you too, Stella,' he says, not looking away.

Something happens then that I thought might never happen again.

I smile.

ACKNOWLEDGEMENTS

This book is dedicated to Isabelle Dinoire and the approximately 40 other people, worldwide, who have received face transplants since she was the very first in 2005. It is also dedicated to their donors, and the surgeons who have made it their life's work to successfully carry out what must be one of the most astonishing medical procedures currently possible.

Ever since the news of Isabelle Dinoire's transplant broke, I have been captivated by the thought that there could be two women – unknown to each other, yet physically similar – whose lives were destined to come together in this tragic, yet awe-inspiring way. Nevertheless, this is a book that was almost not written. I don't think I would have attempted it if it hadn't been for the early encouragement of my agent, Juliet Mushens. Thank you for believing in the idea and for championing it ever since.

I am hugely grateful to my editor, Jane Wood. Sorry about the initial shock of the subject matter and thank you for your keen editorial eye. Thanks also to the whole Quercus team; Hannah Robinson, Ella Patel, Florence Hare, my copy editor, Hazel Orme, and all the others who put so much into the publishing process. Thank you to Chris at Ghost Productions for another gorgeous book cover.

I researched and read widely on the subject of face transplants before writing this book and am indebted to all the
people who have been generous enough to share photos,
videos and anecdotes online. They were truly inspiring to
me, and invaluable in lending authenticity to Stella's story. I
was particularly struck by Andy Sandness and his surgeon,
Dr Samir Mardini. It was Dr Mardini who said that he
wanted to make Andy Sandness 'just another face in the
crowd' and, to my mind, he was spectacularly successful in
achieving this. I found the book *Someone Else's Face in the
Mirror: Identity and the New Science of Face Transplants*, by
Carla Bluhm and Nathan Clendenin very helpful in relation
to the psychological impact of having a face transplant.
Stella's near death experiences were based on information
from *What Happens When We Die: A Ground-Breaking Study
into the Nature of Life and Death*, by Sam Parnia. I used Daniel
Schacter's fascinating book *The Seven Sins of Memory: How
the mind forgets and Remembers* to frame Stella's own recollections. Any misunderstanding in relation to any of these
texts is my own.

Now to Connie's chapters. Thank you, Imie Mateo, for
your friendship and for teaching me all the Tagalog I know.
I am grateful to the many migrant domestic workers, and
the organisations providing them with assistance, who have
shared their stories, which were truly harrowing to read
or listen to. I have tried to portray the plight of migrant
domestic workers in the Middle East in a balanced way,
both acknowledging the progress that has been made in

abolishing the *kafala* system and affording greater rights and protection to these women, while also highlighting the fact that migrant domestic workers continue to face abuse and exploitation.

It goes without saying that the characters in this book are nothing like any of the parents or teachers at schools my children attend, or have attended, in England or Dubai. I am enormously grateful to all the PTAs, and even gave being a class rep a go myself this year. Special thanks to my friend, Dr Annie Middleton, for answering all my medical questions, some of which were even about this book. Any medical mistakes are entirely my own.

Finally, thank you to my mother, Sandra for fostering an early love of reading and libraries, and to my children for everything.

ABOUT THE AUTHOR

Sonia Velton took a law degree and qualified as a solicitor at an international law firm, before going on to specialise in discrimination law. Sonia relocated to the Middle East and had three children before returning to the UK. Her debut novel, *Blackberry and Wild Rose*, was published to great acclaim. *The Image of Her* is her second novel. Sonia lives in Kent.